APPRENTICE SWORDCEROR

The Blademage Saga

Volume 1

Chris Hollaway

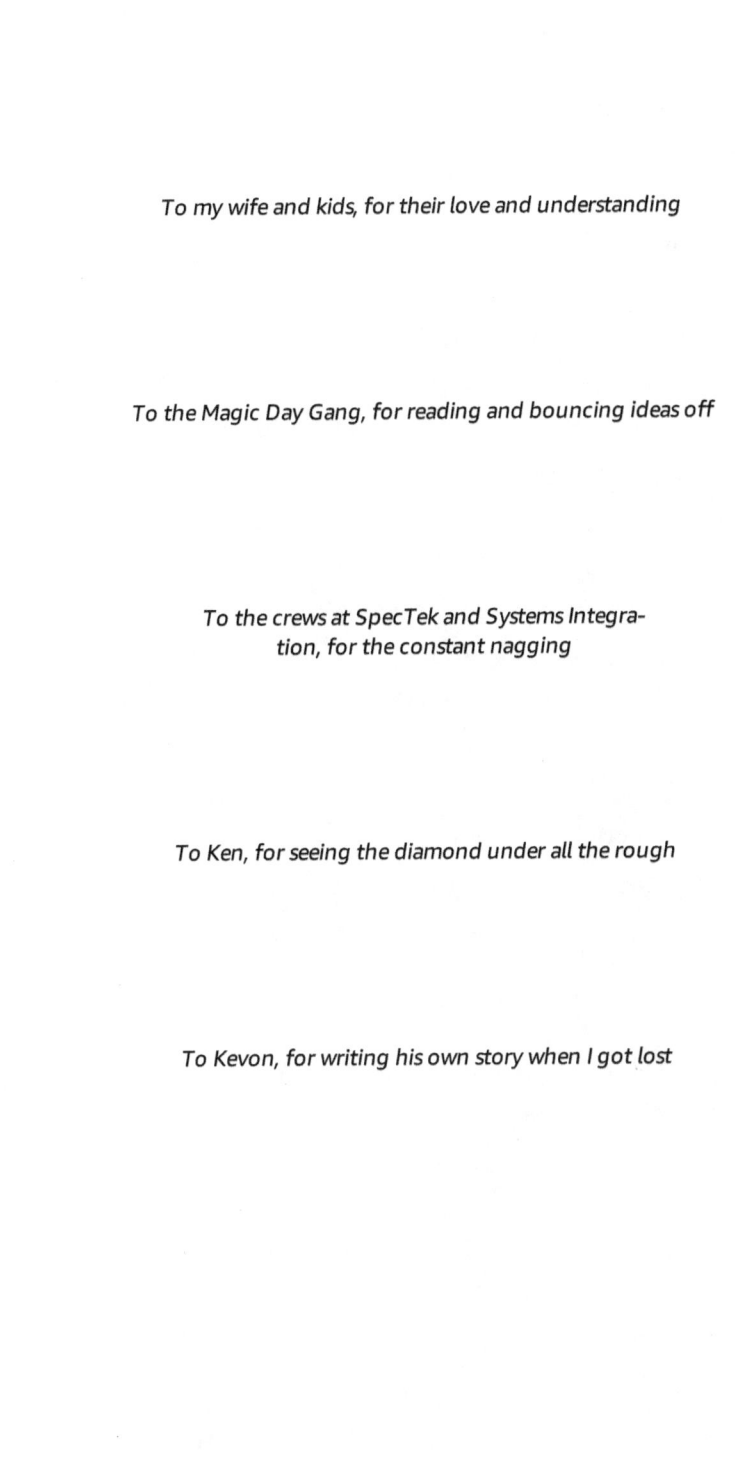

To my wife and kids, for their love and understanding

To the Magic Day Gang, for reading and bouncing ideas off

*To the crews at SpecTek and Systems Integra-
tion, for the constant nagging*

To Ken, for seeing the diamond under all the rough

To Kevon, for writing his own story when I got lost

CHAPTER 1

K evon lay back against the trunk of a tree, studying the large translucent butterfly perched on his bent knee.

"Blue." He breathed the word softly, and the wings began to change from the speckled orange they had been to a crystalline blue color. "Much better." Kevon decided.

Lowering his concentration, Kevon sighed as his illusion wisped into mage-smoke and vanished. He grinned. His Master would not be pleased to see him lounging about and trifling with illusions. Master Holten barely considered Illusion a true Art, and taught little enough of it. But armed with the basics, Kevon had pushed his skill in Illusion to heights that he had not seen Master Holten even attempt.

Making a healing potion with Alchemy, or Conjuring a flame to start a fire were satisfying, after a fashion, but they did not come as easily or inspire the joy that filled Kevon's heart when he worked illusions. He reflected upon the year he had apprenticed under Holten Magus. Just learning the Arts of Alchemy and Herbalism would have been better than the drudgery of his home life. Illusion was icing on the cake, and Kevon lived for it.

A sudden crashing in the undergrowth behind him brought Kevon clambering hurriedly to his feet. Composing himself, he listened closer and made out a loud bawling noise amidst the tumult.

Kevon began visualizing the Illusion rune he had released just moments before. The symbol sprang to mind, and Kevon forced his will into it. The symbol took on an ethereal glow and solidified in his mind. He then focused all of his attention to weaving a new illusion. Natural creatures were more susceptible to illusion thanmen, so he had little to fear if he acted quickly.

All at once, Kevon's body was wreathed in phantom flames. He pushed his Art further, and the flames burned brighter, casting light up to the treetops above him, and flickering shadows all around. Nearing the limits of his skill, he added sound to his illusion, and the crackling of the flames began to rival the crashing *something* that was headed his way.

Kevon stepped back from the tree out into the center of the small clearing. His illusion burned so brightly that he supposed that he was no longer visible through it.

A scream sounded over the oncoming din. Startled, Kevon almost dropped his illusion. Struggling to maintain his composure as well as his illusion, Kevon backed up further, wary of what might be coming.

A man burst into the clearing, clothes torn from his passage through the thorny undergrowth. Seeing Kevon, the man hesitated for a second, stumbled, and went down.

The large bear that followed on the man's heels lunged and swiped at him, knocking him several feet to the side. The man slammed against the tree that Kevon had been sitting under, the sword he carried flying wide into a nearby bush.

Screwing up his courage, Kevon advanced, raising his arms and willing the flames and crackling noises to a fevered pitch. The bear turned and fled.

Exhausted from the expenditure of will, and the sheer gravity of the moment, Kevon slumped to his knees with a grunt. He released the illusion and the symbol in his mind dimmed and faded away. He turned to see what had happened to the man.

Although it had been only moments since the attack, blood pooled around the man. As he struggled to pull himself into a sitting position against the tree, blood from a gash on his forehead dripped into his eyes so that he had to blink it away.

The man looked at Kevon, eyes fearful. "My sword..." he rasped.

Kevon cringed inwardly. He knew the man had neither the strength, nor the time to fetch the sword. But Kevon did not know if *he* had the strength, either. Since his apprenticeship had begun, he had not dared to touch iron. It was one of the strictest rules imposed on magic-users, and for good reason. The touch of iron usually meant death for a Mage.

"I need..." the man coughed, and a gout of blood spattered his tunic and oozed down toward the puddle that was now starting to soak into the ground.

In the dying man's eyes was a plea that Kevon could not ignore. He walked to the sword and picked it out of the bush. Shivers went up and down the length of his spine as he held the length of iron. Kevon rushed to the man's side and laid the sword across his knees.

The man gripped the hilt of the sword as firmly as his mangled sword-arm allowed. His other hand settled gently on the blade. "Many thanks," whispered the man, licking his lips.

The man's eyes widened, as if remembering something long forgotten. His good hand reached to the cord at his neck, and he pulled it free. "Here. Have. This." The words came between quick, raspy breaths. He pressed a cold amulet into Kevon's hand. "And take... the sword... to..."

Kevon sat there, numb, as the man went still. He had seen the dead before, but never death itself.

Long minutes later, Kevon still sat looking at the man's body. He started to stand, but staggered to the side as his knees buckled, and threw up.

Kevon rifled through his pouches and found a mint leaf to chew on, to ease the bile-taste in his mouth. He pondered the situation. The walk back to town was not a short one, and the dead man was at least half again Kevon's size. There was no way he could carry or drag him. But he did not want to leave the man for the animals.

At one end of the clearing was a game trail between two

slender pines. Kevon found a sturdy branch and began hollowing out a rut. Half an hour later, Kevon decided that it was large enough. He dragged the body as carefully as he could manage, and laid it in the improvised barrow.

Pausing to catch his breath, Kevon pulled the amulet from the pocket he had shoved it in earlier. It was a small pewter disc with a bas-relief image of a sword. Kevon regarded the body in front of him intently. This man had belonged to the Warrior's Guild. If the man's right arm had not been so mangled and covered with blood, he would have been able to see the sword-brand on it. Swordsmen were rare in these parts, as rare as swords. The nearest guild was probably over a week's travel away.

Rested, Kevon tried to remember what the proper ceremony was. Remembering a part of it, he whispered, "May your body rest, as your spirit soars." Kevon ended the blessing and pushed dirt over the body. He then began making trips from the nearby stream to the grave, carrying fair-sized stones to place over it.

A good while later, muscles aching and spirit weary, Kevon was satisfied with his work. All that remained was to clean the blood and grime from his cloak. He kneaded the cloak gently in the stream before shaking it out and hanging it on a branch to dry.

Kevon returned to the stream to wash his hands and face, cooling away the flush of hard labor. For the first time in hours, Kevon felt relaxed. He re-inspected his pouches to make sure he had all the herbs he needed. If he had been gone this long without completely filling them, his Master would not be pleased.

Kevon sighed, wishing the sun's rays would dry his cloak faster so that he could go home. He wandered back to the clearing to make sure that he had forgotten nothing.

The hair on the back of Kevon's neck stood on end as he spotted the sword still lying at the base of the tree. Kevon had thought to bury it with the man, but had forgotten in his haste and confusion. The memory of touching the blade's handle for even so short a time turned his stomach.

Kevon gasped, remembering his Art. He had not taken the time to discover if the brief contact with the forbidden iron had lessened his abilities. He focused on the Illusion symbol, and concentrated. The azure-winged butterfly from earlier materialized before him, flapping its wings lazily. Another Illusion symbol formed in his mind, and Kevon pushed even harder. The second rune flickered and lit up, glowing to match its twin in his mind. Phantom flames burst from Kevon, as bright and loud as before. Relieved, Kevon relaxed and let go of the illusions.

His cloak was still damp by the time he went to retrieve it, but it would dry before he got back. And he needed to get back.

Kevon reached the road back to Laston several minutes after emerging from the forest. He walked quietly, the weight of the day's events grating on his nerves. He walked numbly off to the side as a Merchant's wagon passed him, headed south, maybe to the Inner Cities, or beyond.

The path began to flatten out and widen as Kevon got closer to town, passing through the surrounding farms that were the main industry here. The little valley was not good for much else. Timber was just as abundant and far more accessible nearer the Inner Cities, so logging was not profitable. The town had a lumber mill, but it was small and had no trouble meeting the needs of the town. There was also a blacksmith, but he rarely fired his forge outside of the winter season. His sons were not yet old enough to tend the family farm by themselves.

And Laston was not on any trade routes. The only way in or out of the valley was the pass to the south, and not even that once it snowed.

In Kevon's experience, there were only two types of folk in Laston; those who wanted to be there, and those who were stuck there. Kevon had been stuck there all his life.

From the time Kevon could remember hearing the first stories of what lay beyond the valley, he had wanted to travel, to adventure. He longed to join one of the Guilds and make a name for himself; fighting, trading, or crafting. Much to his chagrin, he grew up too gangly, too honest, and too impatient to take up any craft.

Then Master Holten had come to live in Laston, and everything changed. Kevon no longer played at fighting with the other boys, the stick swords had been long since discarded. The Wizard had chosen *him* to be his Apprentice. His mother had been wary at first, but when she saw how focused Kevon became, she was quite pleased.

Kevon's whole life had changed. The first few months had been hard. The duties of a Novice were not much different than those he had left at home. He cooked and cleaned for Master Holten, in-between sessions of meditation, scholarly discussion, and learning to read. After a while, Kevon had been able to focus his energy to help the Wizard cast a spell. That was the first lesson every Mage learned. Master Holten called it 'Aid', one of the Lesser Arts. But it was the key to *everything* else.

As soon as Kevon had learned to Aid, Master Holten hired another local boy to do the cooking and cleaning. Kevon advanced to Apprentice. He spent more time in discussion with the Master, learning about the different Arts, and deciding which ones to pursue further.

After seeing demonstrations of the Arts that Master Holten taught, Kevon decided on Illusion. Less than pleased with his Apprentice's decision, Master Holten had assigned more lessons in Alchemy than Illusion. To Kevon's further frustration, he had to resume some of the household duties as well.

Breaking from his reverie as he rounded the last corner before ascending into the town proper, Kevon wondered what his Master would say about the events of the afternoon.

CHAPTER 2

Kevon continued into town, passing by the newer houses on the outskirts near the mouth to the main valley. He decided to avoid the long way around, the wagon path on the north side. He climbed the carved stone steps from one terrace to the next, taking more effort but saving a bit of time.

Kevon tromped into Master Holten's house after knocking his boots on the short wooden post by the front door. Most places he would not have bothered, but Holten's house had a proper wood floor, expertly joined and sanded to a smooth finish. The house, larger than most, had belonged to a retired Merchant until some years ago. Before Holten came, it had been somewhat of an informal town hall, but the extra rooms came in handy for a Master Wizard with enough books to fill two libraries and no end to potions and herbs and such.

"Apprentice!" came a shout from one of the back rooms.

"Yes, Master?" replied Kevon, dropping some of his heavier pouches on a workbench and moving toward the room.

Holten burst out of the back room with a flapping goose by the neck, and thrust it into Kevon's hands.

"Have Martin take care of this, and you had best attend to the potions. You're quite late this afternoon," the Wizard half-lectured as he returned to the room and closed the door.

Kevon sighed, and trickled energy into a hastily visualized Control symbol. The goose calmed, and Kevon made his way around to the kitchen.

"Goose again, eh?" Martin attempted to sound cheerful for a moment, but gave up mid-sentence. "Spring geese seem to be a bit scrawnier than summer ones."

"It's because they've just flown so far to get here." Kevon explained. "But Master won't call deer in after what happened the first time, more's the pity."

"My mum's still sore about that," grinned Martin. "The silly thing grazed its way through our garden, wandered in the front door, and tried to kick its way out the back wall. Didn't help she was laid up in bed and that hexed critter near climbed on top of her to get at that wall."

Kevon had heard the story several times, but it still brought a smile to his face, picturing Martin's shrew of a mother tumbled from bed into the overturned contents of her own chamber pot.

"All right. Well, I've got to stir potions and you'd better take care of this." Kevon said, handing the goose to Martin and releasing the Control symbol. Again aware of its surroundings, the goose began thrashing once more.

Before Martin grumbled, Kevon escaped back through the kitchen door and made it halfway to the laboratory. On his way back through the house, he picked up his pouches and shed his cloak. Potion making was hot work.

Opening the door, Kevon noted that four of the five sculpted marble braziers were now stocked with glowing coals, and held bubbling flasks. Kevon closed the door and began to work. Moving with a practiced efficiency, he added charcoal to each brazier to keep the coals at the optimum level. Then he turned his attention to the flasks.

The first two flasks held healing potions. Kevon crumbled pinches of thyme and mugwort into each flask. He then dropped two fresh huckleberries and a thin slice of peeled cucumber into each bubbling mixture. He thought back to his first Alchemy lesson and Holten's lecturing.

"Potions are unique in the way that they work," the Master said. "The brewing distills and captures life essence. Drinking the potion frees the energies to work in the body."

The third flask was a different story. It was a cure-all remedy that Kevon had started a week ago. The wooden phial rack in front of its brazier was filled with stoppered containers of various shapes, each with a very specific purpose. Thornleaf for poison, Blackroot to reduce fever, and so on until Kevon's head hurt from thinking about it. Kevon measured the ingredients for this more carefully, taking several minutes to finish the task.

The fourth lit brazier was new since this morning. From the looks of it, it was a sleeping potion. Powdered thistledown seeds and dried milkweed root were the only two ingredients before the brazier. Kevon mashed a small piece of root into a paste and scraped it up to drop into the flask. After finishing putting the paste and a small pinch of thistle seed powder into the simmering concoction, Kevon turned to the racked bottles behind him to begin emptying his pouches.

Some of the herbs he bottled straightaway. The rest would have to be set in drying racks over the next week or so, and chopped or powdered depending on the herb and its intended use.

Having finished the sorting, Kevon returned to the potion table, picking up the pitcher of water on the end nearest the door. He filled each flask to the line etched in the side. Then he stirred each one with a thin ivory stick, cleaning it carefully between flasks.

More than ready to escape the fragrant room, Kevon breathed a sigh of relief as he exited and closed the door behind him. A flicker of shadow from the doorway of Master Holten's study caught his eye, and he wandered over to peer inside.

"Finished?" queried his teacher, shuffling over to reshelf a book.

"Yes," Kevon replied. "They should be fine well into dusk for the next tending."

"Splendid. How is Martin doing with that goose?" Holten asked.

"I came straight here from the laboratory. I have no idea." Kevon paused. "Master?" he began.

"Yes?"

"The reason I was late today…"

"I trust this is not just excuses for your loafing and working silly illusions." Holten interjected somberly.

"Very well," Kevon continued. "One of the reasons I was late today, is, well… I was burying a man."

Master Holten almost dropped the tome he had been stretching to retrieve from an upper shelf. "You were *what?*"

"A bear killed a man right before my eyes while I was in the forest today." Kevon clutched his stomach as the images suppressed by monotonous tasks resurfaced. "I… there was nothing I…"

Holten put the book on the table by his reading chair and moved forward to steady his Apprentice, who was beginning to wobble. "Here now, come, sit." Holten guided Kevon to another chair and eased him down into it.

Kevon sat for a moment, snuffling softly.

Holten seated himself and filled his pipe with a pinch of herbs from a small pouch. He puffed a few times, lighting the mix with a magical spark. He sighed. "Did you know the man?" Holten asked. "No… Speak of it when you can." Kevon's Master sat quietly, enjoying his pipe.

Kevon shook his head. "No, he was not from the valley. I think he was a Warrior." Kevon produced the amulet from his tunic pocket. "He gave this to me, and tried to tell me who to take…"

Kevon choked on his words, grief mixing with fear from the encounter, the memory of touching the forbidden blade, and worry about his Master finding out.

Holten's eyes widened slightly at the sight of the amulet.

"There was a Merchant in town traveling with an escort. Perhaps he was with them. They are gone now, some hours ago, I think." Holten stood slowly. "I'm going for my evening walk. I'll be back to tend the potions. Get some rest. I'll have Martin bring dinner to your room."

Holten paused at the doorway and looked over his shoulder. "We'll speak more of this tomorrow."

CHAPTER 3

Morning came far too soon. By the time Kevon had finished tending the potions, he was tempted to try the cure-all to ease the aches and pains that the previous day's labor had brought upon him.

Instead, he found himself heading to the kitchen to fetch a slice of goose from the cold-box. Martin already had the bones boiling in a pot for soup, but that was far from ready. Kevon chose two of the half-dozen portions stacked in the corner of the box. He broke off an end of one of the flat loaves of bread that lined the other end.

Kevon made his way out the back door and walked to the corner of the house to catch the morning sun. He sat on a short stone stool and contemplated the stream that bubbled happily and wound its way down into the valley. Kevon ate slowly, having no pressing duties. The potions were fine until mid-afternoon, Martin had the other chores well in hand, and Master Holten was nowhere to be found.

His mouth suddenly went dry. What if Holten was with the Town Council now? Kevon had handled the matter yesterday with nothing but respect, as well as he knew how. But how might it seem to someone who was not there, who did not witness the entire affair? Although Kevon was sure he had done no wrong, he had seen the Council do things before that did not seem fitting. What if they...

"Kevon."

Kevon's hand jerked involuntarily and he dropped the end of bread he had been chewing on into the dirt.

Martin sighed loudly. "Don't eat it then. But don't waste

it. It's not as bad as last week's batch."

"Sorry. Sorry I... You just startled..." Kevon began.

"It's all right," Martin smiled. "I'll just use it for fish bait. Master's given me the afternoon, and he wants to see you straightaway. He just got back."

Martin lifted his willow-wood pole off its hanging hooks and stuffed the crust of bread into the small knapsack he was carrying. "See you later, Kevon."

As he turned to go, Martin paused. "The Master's upset," he said quietly. "I'm not sure what about, but he's trying not to show it."

Kevon stood silently as Martin hiked down along the stream into the valley, whistling a cheery tune. He straightened himself up, took a deep breath to regain his composure, and went back inside.

He found Master Holten in his study, sorting through scrolls and books, muttering to himself. Holten decided on two large volumes, and placed them carefully in his Traveling Tome. The thin leather book was magically fused with a locked chest Holten kept atop one of the other bookshelves. The enchantment was done long ago, with skill beyond what any known Mage could do now.

Holten tied the thin leather fastenings together to secure his selections in the Tome, and dropped it into the pocket of his robe.

"Ahh." Holten started as he turned and noticed Kevon standing in the doorway. "There you are. How are you feeling?"

Kevon thought for a moment. "Weary." he decided.

"Mmm." Holten nodded. "To be expected. Certainly."

"Master..." Kevon began slowly. "Did I do right yesterday? Have you spoken to the Council about...?"

"Faugh!" Holten burst out. "*That* Council has nothing to say about the well intentioned actions of a Journeyman of the Mage's Guild." Holten paused for a moment as Kevon's eyes widened and the younger man steadied himself on the threshold of the door. "Yes, I'm promoting you." Holten continued.

"I've been putting it off in hopes you would shift your studies to a more practical Art, but your skills are more than sufficient."

"Master- I..." Kevon stammered. "Thank you!"

"Well, don't put the cart before the horse. This is more sudden than I had expected as well." Holten began. "I've not acquired your new robes yet. I've no time to do it now, either. Word came yesterday that I am needed on Guild business on the other end of the Realm. I'm leaving today, and I don't know when I'll be back."

Kevon remained silent, unable to think of anything useful to say, and stood there, gaping.

"I do have a letter of introduction to another Wizard that might help further your studies." Holten continued after a brief silence. "I also have a book of his that needs returned. If you would return it to him, you would be able to study it on the way."

The fact that Kevon was going to be traveling the world, in one direction or another, in a very short time, was beginning to sink in. His eyes widened further, if possible.

"Where does he live?" Kevon fairly blurted. "Of course I'll return the book! Who is he? What Arts does he teach? What..."

"Hold on." Holten broke in. "I have everything you will need packed. The book, letter, and directions are all bundled in your spare cloak." Holten withdrew a small pouch from a pocket and handed it to Kevon. "This should more than cover the cost of your robes when you reach the Inner Cities. From West Thaddington, you should be able to head west to reach Gurlin's Tower."

Kevon held the pouch close to him for a moment before placing it in a pocket of his own. The contents were too light to feel, and made no noise. Kevon had no idea what the pouch held, but decided to wait to find out.

"And Gurlin's Arts?" Kevon asked. "What does he teach?"

"The last I knew, he taught Summoning and Enhancement." Holten replied. "The volume I am returning is an overview of Enhancement, his personal views and experiences. His

Summoning is more impressive though, as I recall. When we were younger, studying under the same Master, he once managed an Extraplanar Summoning. It was all the two of us could do to control the beast until our Master arrived and destroyed it." Holten grinned at Kevon wryly. "Not something I would like to see again, but he is the most capable Summoner I've ever seen."

"At any rate, we'd both better get going." Holten said, with an air of finality. "Martin will take care of the house and my affairs until I return. All of the potions will be done after this afternoon's tending. You're more than welcome to all of them for your journey. They'll be handy to use, and for barter."

"Thank you, Master." Kevon whispered, bowing slightly. "How will you be traveling?" he wondered aloud, quirking an eyebrow.

"There is a little known tower, leagues south in the wilderness, across the pass. Once I reach it and rest for the night, they can Send me to my destination."

"A Sending?" As if Kevon had not experienced enough surprises and new information flooding into his brain already. He shook his head. "How will you reach the tower?"

Holten's usually serious face cracked into a slight smile. "Did you eat a good breakfast this morning?"

When Kevon woke, the last thing he remembered was a vision of a small chamber with walls of stone and wood. It had contained a bed, bookshelf, and a chest and was lit with a single torch in a sconce by the door. A medium-sized tapestry had hung on the other side of the door, but the glimpse had been over far too quickly. Kevon had passed out from the exertion of aiding his Master's Sending.

Kevon's mind still reeled from the newness of the past days. Holten had spoken briefly of Sending and the other applications of the Movement aspect of Control, but had never mentioned being able to work such a powerful spell.

It had not been easy. The floor Kevon was just beginning to pull himself up off of was covered in used up chalk, charred grey by the forces it had helped channel. The circle and symbols that Kevon had barely recognized when they were solid were now scattering across the room with the slightest movements of air. He had seen the symbols during infrequent peeks at the advanced books he was not really allowed to read yet.

Another thing had been fairly surprising to Kevon. Holten, who usually disdained the use of gestures and speech during spell casting as amateurish and feeble, had been chanting *something* quite loudly. He'd also been gesturing emphatically when the spell reached its conclusion and Kevon had felt his entire magical reserve leave him, almost as if Holten had *torn* it from him.

Kevon coughed from the charred chalk smell, and the residue on the floor whorled about, further disturbing the circle. He brushed the smudges off the sleeve of his cloak, and tilted his kinked neck until it popped. Kevon rubbed at a crease on his right cheek where it had rested on a joint in the floor. He ached all over, was hungry, and sick to his stomach at the same time.

Thinking a handful of bread might settle his stomach, Kevon made his way from the library to the kitchen. He heard the sizzling sounds of the fish cooking before the wave of smell hit him. It was all at once familiar and appetizing, but far too much for his queasy stomach to handle. Kevon clapped his hand to his mouth and lurched past a bewildered Martin.

Once outside, Kevon struggled not to vomit for the second time in as many days.

◆ ◆ ◆

Sometime later, after finishing the large mug of warm cider Martin had brought out to him; Kevon ventured back inside and finished off the last two fish.

After thanking Martin and sincerely praising both his fishing and cooking skills, Kevon excused himself to finish the potions in the laboratory.

Kevon carefully transferred the contents of each flask into the wooden, resin treated flasks that were normally used for storage and transit. He filled three of the smaller containers with the two brewed healing potions, deciding they would be easier to barter with, if needed. The cure-all and sleeping potion he placed in larger containers, marking each with a different bit of colored wax in a depression near the carrying straps. Kevon thoroughly rinsed each flask and used the rinse water to quench the coals in each brazier. He then re-shelved all of the ingredients in their proper places and hung the flasks upside down on the long drying pegs on the far wall.

Kevon left the quietly hissing braziers for Martin to clean later, gathered the potions by their leather carrying straps, and went to his room.

The room seemed in order for Kevon to leave. He found his bedding was rolled and tied with leather straps, and the borrowed book was indeed wrapped in his cloak, along with directions to Gurlin's tower. A scroll case containing a sealed letter with Holten's mark was presumably the letter of introduction. These items were wrapped inside a smaller oil-treated hide to prevent damage from the elements. After inspecting them all, he noticed how hungry he was.

Kevon went to the kitchen and found Martin had already gathered a large leather wallet full of provisions; salted meat, bread, cheese, and two large skins filled with water.

"That eager to see me go?" Kevon joked as Martin handed him the supplies.

"Looking forward to having only me to clean up after for a while." replied Martin, grinning. Then his expression sobered. "You'll be missed though. Master always spoke more fondly of you when you weren't around. Who knows how he'll be when he's back and you're not."

"I'll miss both of you, as well." Kevon conceded. "You've been like family to…" He stopped abruptly.

"I've got to go see my family before I leave." Kevon dropped his supplies on the counter and made for the door. "Be back soon!" he called over his shoulder.

Kevon found his mother in her workroom, mending clothes. For the last few years, since Kevon's father died, she had supported Kevon and his sister by doing odd jobs, mending or cleaning for those too busy or lazy to do it for themselves.

"Hi, Mom!" Kevon called as he entered the room, careful not to trip over the piles of garments stacked about.

"Come to see your dear mother before you go exploring, have you?" Kevon's mother gave him a glare that could still tangle a knot in the pit of his stomach.

"Well, I uh…" Kevon stammered. "Wait, how did…"

"Alma told me before she went over to help Widow Anders with her garden." Kevon's mother's glare softened, and her eyes shimmered with a hint of wetness. "We're glad you're going, but we hate to see you leave."

Martin must have told Alma, Kevon thought. "I know," he said, placing his hand over his mother's. "I'm so excited to see the things beyond the valley, but it means leaving everything I've ever known, and everyone I love."

Kevon's mother stood, placing her work on a nearby table.

"Well," she said, "The sooner you go, the sooner you'll come back to us. Is there anything you need before you go?"

Kevon sighed. "An extra pair of arms would be nice. I've got a lot to carry with me now."

Kevon's mother shook her head slowly. "I'm afraid all I can manage are some extra legs."

Kevon blinked.

"I've been doing a lot of mending lately for the widow and her sons." she explained. "I'm sure they wouldn't mind giving you back your father's mare to settle their account." She paused, and grinned. "Especially when Alma's doing the asking."

Kevon laughed. His sister was a good girl, but she was quickly learning how to use her newly acquired feminine features to get what she wanted.

"Are you sure, Mother? That's quite a bit of trade, I don't want to..." Kevon began.

"Yes, I'm sure. I've often thought of buying her back, but we wouldn't have been able to afford to keep her." His mother sniffed and wiped her eyes. "I've always regretted having to sell that mare. It's fitting that she goes back to you now." She turned her head and wiped her eyes again. "You'd best get going; they're expecting you for supper."

Kevon thought about working up an illusion of a pot of flowers and seeing how long he could maintain it as he left. He settled for a firm hug, and a soft "Goodbye."

He returned to Master Holten's house, gathered his supplies, and set out for the widow's farm.

CHAPTER 4

Kevon rode away from the farm, relaxed and trying to absorb every sensation as his journey
finally began. The light breeze blowing from the
south down the valley brought the fresh smell of pine to min-
gle with the scents of horse and leather. He closed his eyes and
smiled as he felt the morning sun warming his cheek, and the
half-familiar motion of his father's mare's gait.

Everything he owned was tucked snugly into saddlebags
or strapped down behind him with his bedroll. The large breakfast he had just eaten would most likely last him the rest of the
day. The widow's sons had been more than happy to settle accounts with Kevon's mother for the mare, and had parted with
the saddle and some bags for one of the healing potions and the
cure-all. The sleeping potion had been brewed for the widow,
Kevon had discovered, so he left that as well.

The mare plodded unhurriedly down the track, which
suited Kevon just fine. His only responsibility now was to deliver a book that had been borrowed years ago. Kevon wondered
how much time he would really have for reading on the road.
Besides, when he began studying again he would be using Gurlin's library.

A restlessness came over Kevon and he began to rummage
through his cloak pockets. Empty herb pouches filled several of
them, but he stopped when he came to the pouch Holten had
given him. He unlaced the drawstring and poured the contents
into his cupped palm.

He almost dropped it. Kevon held in his hand a small,
but almost perfect pearl. The only flaw was a tiny dark dis-

coloration in the shape of a four-pointed star. The surface was completely smooth even where it was discolored. Trembling slightly, Kevon put the pearl back into the pouch and tucked it into a deeper cloak pocket.

Kevon had not known what to expect, but had thought at most Holten would have given him a lesser gemstone. A garnet or an opal would have been more than enough to pay for the services of all but a Master Tailor for Kevon's new robes. He would have been able to get a few garments and a new pair of shoes. But this? Kevon did not know how much things cost outside the North Valley, but he knew that this pearl was worth more than any property in Laston. He would not have any trouble getting anything he might need once he sold it.

The only unfamiliar item Kevon had in his pockets was the pewter amulet. As his fingers brushed over the raised image of the sword, a flash of memory washed over him. The Warrior had wanted his sword taken to someone. Who that someone was, Kevon realized, he might never figure out. But it was, as far as Kevon knew, the dying request of an honorable man.

Kevon turned the mare off the track and urged her into the forest.

◆ ◆ ◆

Kevon spotted the sword under the tree as soon as he entered the clearing. He dismounted, and walked past the blade to stand silently before the mound of stones.

After a moment, he knelt respectfully and spoke.

"Sir, I may never know who you were, or why you were here. Your sword may never reach who it was you intended to have it." Kevon paused. "But I will try."

Kevon stood and contemplated the mound for a minute more. Then he turned and strode over to where the blade rested under the tree. He reached down and grasped the hilt. Blackness enfolded him.

◆ ◆ ◆

Kevon woke to a warm snuffling in his ear. He had a bad taste in his mouth, and felt as wrung-out as he had when aiding Master Holten's Sending the day before. Kevon's hand lay inches from the hilt of the blade, and he jerked back reflexively.

What had happened? His mind raced as he compared the two times he had touched the blade. The first time had been only slightly uncomfortable, and this time had evidently been unbearable.

The mare nickered and began grazing on the new grass in the center of the clearing.

Kevon sat, staring at the sword. He realized that if he was going to keep his promise, he would have to figure out how to handle the blade, overcome his fear of it.

Bracing himself, he reached out again and closed his fist around the hilt...

There was a moment of queasiness, but nothing else. Kevon lifted the blade and took a few swings. From the corner of his eye, he saw the mare's ears fold back, so he stopped and held the blade close to his side.

Annoyed that he was no closer to figuring the mystery out, Kevon took a few moments to roll the sword into the center of his bedroll and cinch it back into place behind his saddle.

Kevon led the mare to the stream to drink, then sat and rested for a while before remounting and returning to the road.

Several times during the day, Kevon reached back into the end of his bedroll to touch the sword's hilt. Each time, his stomach turned slightly for a moment, and then he was fine again. Kevon found the situation fascinating.

As dusk approached, Kevon could just see the mouth of

the South Pass. Ahead, mountain walls rose to either side of the road. He turned the mare off the road and went about a hundred steps into the trees before he found a suitable area to bed down for the night.

Kevon swung down from the saddle and unloaded his mount. He tethered the mare to a nearby tree, kicked an area free of debris, and made a circle of rocks. He found some dead branches lying about, broke them into suitable lengths, and placed them in the improvised hearth.

It was not yet cold or dark enough to need the fire yet, but it was too dark to study the book with which Holten had entrusted him. Kevon picked up the sword.

He looked closely at the weapon for the first time. It was by no means a fancy weapon, but it was elegant in its own way. The front edge of the blade was slightly curved, well sharpened, and a little wavy. The thickness varied a bit from place to place. Kevon supposed it was from sharpening out nicks and chips. It came to a triangular point, which was sharp almost to the point of looking fragile.

The sharpened edge continued about a hand's-breadth down the back side before it widened into a flat surface nearly half an inch across. This too showed signs of wear as if notches had been smoothed out by a whetstone. The crosspiece was a simple narrow flare of polished iron. The hilt and joint were wrapped in well-maintained leather, up to the smooth iron sphere on the pommel.

Kevon held the sword in his hand and twisted his wrist to get a feel for it. Though he was no swordsman, the blade just felt *right* in his grasp, if a bit heavy for his untrained arm.

Kevon took a few practice jabs. He twisted, and decapitated an imaginary foe behind him. After a minute or so of disemboweling orcs and parrying strikes from enemy soldiers, Kevon reluctantly laid the sword down by the saddle and provisions near the head of his spread bedroll.

A slight breeze chilled the sweat he had raised with his childish prancing. Kevon smiled and turned his attention to the branches in the fire ring.

Nothing.

The requisite images for the spell formed as usual in his mind, but there was no rush of exhilaration as the magic flowed into them to do his will.

Kevon sat, trembling. He cursed himself inwardly for daring to think that he, little more than an Apprentice, was different. For thinking that he should be able to do things that Master Wizards dared not contemplate.

He had toyed with a forbidden blade, and his magic had left him.

Kevon drew his bedroll around him, and wept long into the night.

CHAPTER 5

Kevon woke to a light dusting of snow. It seldom rained or snowed at the north end of the valley because of the height of the surrounding mountains, but he had heard that there were often storms higher up. The narrow slice of sky he could see in the low light of approaching dawn was clear though.

He rummaged through his saddlebags for breakfast, choosing a hunk of bread and a small wedge of cheese. He ate silently, glancing at the fire ring and wishing he had some way to make a spark.

Unbidden, the symbols for the Fire spell from the night before formed in his mind. Power began to trickle through them, and Kevon pushed with all of his mental might.

The branches in the fire ring roared into flames, as did the pile beside the ring. He cried out in alarm, and the spell dissolved, the flames dying down to natural levels. Kevon kicked dirt onto the pile of wood beside the ring, and it went out quickly.

Perplexed, he crouched beside the fire and finished his breakfast. It seemed the strangeness of the last few days was showing no signs of slowing.

He tried to reason out why his Art was behaving so erratically. Before this, Kevon had been able to reliably start a fire, but had never produced flames of this magnitude. Granted, his nervousness about losing his magic, and the shock of the spell starting to work had caused him to put more effort into it.

Obviously, contact with the sword had not lessened Kevon's magical ability in the least, he decided. But his inability to use magic last night still disturbed him. He had suffered no ill effects in his first encounter with the blade, when he had taken it to its owner. He had also been able to use magic afterwards, unlike last night.

The whole affair made Kevon's head hurt. He rubbed his hands together over the fire, brushed the crumbs from his cloak, and began to re-saddle the mare. He envisioned a different set of symbols and stifled the fire with a shove of his Art.

Soon, everything was snugly affixed to the horse's back, everything but the sword and his bedroll. He stood near where the weapon lay, unconsciously clenching and unclenching his right hand.

Echoes of his promise at the Warrior's grave whispered through his mind. He braced himself, knelt down, and grabbed the sword.

The shock tore through him like a thunderclap, but he was ready for it. He struggled to keep his breakfast down, steadying himself against a nearby tree trunk. And then...

Nothing.

Kevon stared at the sword for a second, then rolled it into his bedroll and strapped it down behind the mare's saddle.

He tried to call forth his butterfly illusion, but the symbols remained dull and dark in his mind. Shrugging, he mounted and rode back to the mouth of the pass.

He reined the mare up short before entering the narrows of the pass. This was the furthest he had ever been from home. Except in stories, the world, to Kevon, was no larger than this valley. He had come to the pass once before, almost two years ago. It had been then, when the news of his father's death had been followed by one hardship after another that Kevon had contemplated running away. But by the time he had reached this point, he had begged a ride on a Merchant's wagon that had happened down at just the right time.

"Here I am again," muttered Kevon. "Older, wiser, stronger, wealthier, and better fed," He sighed. "And still just as scared."

He clucked, tapped his heels into the mare's flanks, and entered the pass.

◆ ◆ ◆

The South Pass was *long*. Kevon wondered what drove Merchants to even consider a trip to Laston. Perhaps they were being punished by their superiors.

The road wound around the side of one mountain, then peeled off around another, offering views of smaller uninhabitable valleys around each bend. At regular intervals, Kevon could look up and spot the place the road was heading, a notch in the mountain range that loomed close to the south.

As the day wore on, the wind picked up and clouds began to streak the sky. Kevon pushed the mare, stopping only once at a spring-fed stream to water the horse and refill his water skins.

Night was approaching faster than Kevon liked. He figured the open road was not a place he wanted to be during a storm at night. The terrain off the road, however, was far too vertical for his taste. He rode on.

Darkness pushed in on Kevon before he reached his goal of the high pass. Feeling too exposed to stop, Kevon formed a small, bright illusion of the sun, and pushed it out ahead of him. After a while, he had to dismount and lead the mare to keep his concentration intact.

Then it started to rain.

Half an hour later, weary, dispirited, and soaked to the bone, Kevon led his mount under the half-shelter of a large pine that grew in a wide spot off the track just inside the narrows of the high pass.

He still had the presence of mind to loosen the strap on the saddle and tip it and the rest of his gear to the ground before he slumped against the tree and passed out.

The sunrise seems all wrong. Kevon thinks to lift his head to shield his eyes from the green glow that steadily brightens, but he is too exhausted. It seems that the green glow is coming closer, but Kevon is paralyzed, unable to lift even a finger, or turn away. The glow softens and resolves into two points of light that continue their approach.

As the lights grow closer, Kevon feels more as if *he* is the one moving. His suspicion is confirmed as his approach slows and he discovers the lights are twin emeralds resting on the edge of a writing desk. As he watches, one of the emeralds teeters and falls from its place. Kevon panics, knowing he should reach out to try and catch it. He still cannot move at all.

The gem falls slowly, facets winking at him as it spins. The emerald drops onto the hard cobblestone of the street below, shattering into a fine powder and wisping away like magesmoke.

Despair and anger throb through Kevon's mind. A metallic *zing* and he holds before him a sword he does not recognize. A hand reaches out, a woman's hand, fine boned, perfect alabaster skin. She grasps the blade, grips it tightly, trembling as blood seeps between fingers that should never know a moment's pain, to drip out of sight. Kevon's shame is so great that he cannot bear to look past the hand to its owner.

Kevon's sadness manifests itself as a blue veil over his vision. The sword and grasping hand crumble into dust that swirls out of sight. Kevon's stomach lurches; he is rushing toward something.

Just as he catches a glimpse of a tall island cliff crowned by immense trees connected by a lattice of spider web-like bridges, he's propelled on by a strong breeze at his back. A wide plain of low brush and blowing grass appears, just before a wave of green crashes over everything. The world is soft and skewed by constantly shifting distortion. Kevon feels the pressure and knows he is under water, deeper than men belong. The cave he seeks comes into view. As he steps near the cave mouth, the waters drain away, the shape of the entrance twists as grass and trees spring up from the hardening earth. He takes a step and the world tilts at an impossible angle. In the blink of an eye, the cave mouth is the cauldron of a volcano, the far side out of sight through the haze and soot. Kevon struggles to regain his balance, and falls backward. He closes his eyes, waiting for the inevitable impact.

He feels nothing. He opens his eyes to nothing. He waits.

The silence is broken by a soft moan. Other voices join in, growing ever louder, shrieking, screaming, and pleading. When Kevon feels he can stand no more, the voices fade as they began, not nearly fast enough. He is left in silence again.

He feels a rustling at his back. Then comes the soft whisper, dripping with hatred.

"Die, Mage."

Pain, white-hot, lances through his lower right side.

Kevon startled awake, reaching for the pain still driving into his back. Breathing heavily, heart racing, he grimaced and tossed the sharp rock he had rolled onto across the road into a bush. Muttering softly, he curled back up tighter, and went back to sleep.

CHAPTER 6

Morning brought another clearing of the skies, and a fresh wind blowing through the pass.

Kevon woke sprawled backwards against some rocks that would not normally be his first choice for bedding. The mare was further down along the pass, grazing away at a patch of grass near a rain-filled wagon rut.

Kevon sat up, and noticed the used fire ring a few feet away from him. A stack of wood was piled against the other side of the tree his leg still rested against.

With no one else around, Kevon decided this was just a convenient stopping place, rather than a campsite that was currently in use. He tossed a few branches into the ring and ignited them with his Art.

After spreading various articles out to dry, Kevon ate a quick meal of meat and cheese, and then began to double-check his belongings.

His spare cloak had stayed almost completely dry, so he changed into it, transferring all of his pocketed supplies.

With a contented stomach, a nice fire, and a dry cloak, Kevon found himself without anything more to do until the rest of his gear dried out. Unwilling to handle the sword at the moment, he unpacked the book he was returning to Master Gurlin.

The cover was leather, careworn but well maintained. The inside was another matter.

Used to Master Holten's even, flowing script, Kevon found it difficult to read even two sentences in the cramped, uneven hand that was apparently Gurlin's. The margins of the book, instead of containing the occasional note for clarification, were instead filled almost completely with more of Gurlin's writing. This scrawling was even less coherent than the main body of text. Crude sketches crowded by random comments threatened to overflow into the paragraphs that were much saner by comparison.

Kevon closed the book. It would probably make more sense if he started from the beginning, but he did not want to try right then.

The time he had spent reading had been long enough to warm Kevon's body and spirit. The mare, satisfied for now, wandered back over to see what Kevon was doing as he put out the fire.

Kevon gathered up his belongings, now mostly dry, taking care to handle the sword with a fold of his bedroll as he rolled it up. He saddled and loaded the mare and continued on up the pass.

Just a few minutes from camp, Kevon rode over the top of the pass and reined his mount to a stop to take in the view. The mountains to his left continued on fairly straight to the south, curving slightly eastward before turning gently back to the west. The range on his right cut sharply westward before turning to the south before Kevon lost sight of it on the horizon.

And in front of him, the city of Kron lay amidst the quilted pattern of fields that stretched out as far as the eye could see.

The road veered to the right, curving down along the side of the mountain, doubling back whenever the landscape flattened. Ruts and weeds were more pronounced and unkempt on this side of the pass, from the warmer, rainier climate.

By the time Kevon was halfway down, the midday heat began to affect him. The breeze blowing up the side of the mountain was not enough to keep Kevon from sweating. He removed his cloak, folded it and wedged it between his saddle and bedroll. The more rapid pace of descent tired the mare, so Kevon rested at every other switchback, allowing her to drink from the stream that bounded the far right of the slope.

Near the bottom, the road began to widen. It rose above the landscape, and seemed more like aged, baked clay than a simple dirt track.

Well before the light began to fail, Kevon approached the first building he'd seen outside the North Valley, an inn near the crossroads before the fields began. As Kevon rode close, a young boy came out of the nearby stables.

"Staying the night?" he called out as he approached Kevon.

"Ah, yes, I think I will." Kevon decided aloud. He dismounted, loosed his bedroll and saddlebags, donned his cloak, and went inside as the stable boy led the mare away.

"Welcome to the Dancing Sheep!" cried a plump little man, bursting from the inn's kitchen into the common area to greet Kevon.

"Hello." Kevon sat his bedroll and saddlebags on a nearby chair, and tried to maintain a composure befitting his rank.

Kevon noted an older man with an icy gaze at a table in the corner, with his back to the wall. Their eyes met. The man gave what passed for a friendly nod, and turned his attention back to his mug.

The innkeeper eyed Kevon's gear. "You'll need a room then?" He ran an appraising eye over Kevon. "And a hot meal, I expect?"

"Yes." Kevon began.

"Three silver for dinner, breakfast, and the room." the innkeeper interrupted. "In advance."

Kevon's jaw dropped. He'd seen a silver piece... once. "Three?" he asked, dumbfounded.

The innkeeper grimaced. "All right. Two. But you'll be getting no ale with dinner."

Kevon's mind raced. He had the two healing potions he was planning on bartering, but who would believe that was what the flasks contained? He did not look the part of a Journeyman Mage without his robes. The only things of value he had were his horse and the pearl.

Flustered and embarrassed, he fumbled into his pocket and drew the pouch with the pearl out, and dumped it into his palm.

"All I have is this." Kevon said.

"That'll do." snapped the innkeeper as his hand darted out for the pearl.

"Wait!" Kevon shouted, echoed by another voice. He had missed the arrival of another man, dressed in simple but expensive looking clothing, and a young woman that Kevon hoped was the man's daughter.

The innkeeper jumped back as if stung.

The newcomer produced two silver coins from a pocket with a small flourish and tossed them onto the table by the innkeeper.

"Please ready this young man's room and meal. And ours as well, if you please." he said in an even tone which left no room for argument.

The innkeeper glared for a moment, snatched up the coins, and rushed off to the kitchen.

"You're right to be wary of the businessmen around Kron, young man." the man said, clapping a hand on Kevon's shoulder. "Their only chance for profit is from those passing through." The man glanced at the common room's only window and shivered slightly. "Sun's almost down. Won't you join us...?" He paused.

"Uh, Kevon, sir. And thank you. I'm not imposing, am I?" Kevon asked meekly.

"Not at all." The newcomer gestured emphatically to a table next to the man in the corner. He paused for a moment. "You don't mind if young Kevon joins us, do you Marelle?"

The young woman's eyes raised and her gaze fixed on Kevon for a moment. Her clear, bright, emerald irises contrasted with her long, raven hair, and Kevon found himself unable to move as she examined him. Kevon's throat constricted and he fought the urge to look away.

Marelle's eyes narrowed slightly and a smile curled the

edges of her mouth.

"Of course not, Father." Marelle said softly.

Her voice made the hair on Kevon's neck stand on end. Her tone and accent were all at once familiar and exotic. A lump formed in his throat, and Kevon had to swallow once before moving to the table.

Kevon had been raised with enough manners to know to wait until the lady was seated before seating himself. This earned him another smile from Marelle, a warmer one, but no more comforting.

"Forgive me, Kevon." the man began, turning in his chair to address the nervous youth. "We haven't been properly introduced. I'm Rhulcan, a trader from Eastport, and this is my daughter Marelle." He paused for a moment. "What brings you to this far end of the Realm, if you don't mind my asking?"

"It was the first decent place to rest on my way out of the North Valley." Kevon replied.

Rhulcan peered at Kevon. "We may have passed you on our way out of Laston. I thought you looked a bit familiar." The Merchant's eyes narrowed. "Tell me, what is a boy from a backwater town like Laston doing flashing a bauble like that in a run-down inn like this?"

Kevon's mind raced. Without his new robes, he dared not identify himself as a Mage. Apprentices were not allowed to travel unsupervised, in addition to being forbidden from using their Arts when not training.

"Well," Kevon began, "It's my first time out of the valley. The pearl is the only thing of value I really have, aside from my horse."

"You really must be more careful than that." Rhulcan laughed.

Someone from the kitchen brought out three mugs of ale and placed them in the center of the table, leaving without a word. Kevon could not tell if it was a man or woman, the hair was cropped short and the rough green tunic was not fitted well enough to give any hints.

Rhulcan took a mug and gestured for Kevon and Marelle to do the same. After all had taken a few drinks, Rhulcan began to speak again.

"I was just in Laston," he said, voice heavy with disappointment. "I saw no sign of wealth as you have here. Is it an heirloom, perhaps?"

"No," Kevon said, pausing to think. "It's payment. Rather, overpayment, for services rendered, and a task yet to be done. One of the reasons I left the valley."

"It must be a task of some great import," Rhulcan said quietly, "to command such a fee."

"Not really," Kevon admitted. "If I'd checked to see what the payment was before I left, I'd have probably refused it."

"A noble lad as well!" Rhulcan raised his mug quickly, sloshing a bit of ale onto the table. "What do you think of his story, Carlo?"

The man at the table beside them, silent until now, grinned in amusement. "There's more to it, likely." Carlo took another pull from his mug. "But he's not lying."

"Splendid!" Rhulcan cried, slapping the table. "Now, perhaps we can do some business."

The innkeeper and another server arrived with plates of food for the four of them. The plain earthenware dishes were filled with thick steaks slathered with gravy, a steaming ear of corn, and a large slice of freshly baked bread.

"Business?" Kevon asked as soon as the innkeeper had vanished back into the kitchen. "What kind of business?"

The innkeeper and three kitchen maids, all dressed in the same green tunics, emerged from the kitchen carrying steaming bowls of stew.

"Later." Rhulcan said with a wave of his hand, and began to eat.

Kevon watched the hurried activity of the servers with mild fascination. They moved quickly about in and out of the kitchen until there were six bowls of stew and six mugs of ale on each of the five remaining tables in the common area.

Kevon had barely touched his meal when through the front doors of the inn, a group of people in the same cut tunics as the serving maids streamed their way in to crowd around the tables and eat. Some, mostly the older ones sat, but the rest stood. The whole lot of them made less noise than a few boisterous lads Kevon knew that frequented the single inn in Laston.

The three kitchen maids came out and joined the newcomers. Kevon noticed that in addition to green tunics, some of the people wore brown ones, but those were the only two colors they wore.

Slowly, as they finished, the newcomers abandoned their tables and made their way back in groups to the sleeping quarters.

Kevon's eyes widened as the second clump of these new 'customers' filed back. "How many rooms does this place have?" he asked Rhulcan.

The Merchant chuckled under his breath. "Six. But don't worry. The farmerfolk sleep ten to a room. Three rooms are prepared for this lot, and the remaining three are ours." Rhulcan finished his ale. "Marelle and I will be outside getting some air. When you've finished, will you join us?" he asked Kevon, as if the answer were a foregone conclusion.

"Certainly." Kevon said. "As soon as I..." The smell of dirt and sweat finally registered in Kevon's mind, and the idea of eating didn't seem as appetizing as it had before. He was still very hungry though. He stood as Rhulcan and Marelle rose to leave.

As Carlo followed the pair out the front of the inn, Kevon sat and sized up the remaining food on his plate. He took a large swallow of ale and sighed. Breathing through his mouth, he continued to eat.

Kevon emerged from the inn full and lightheaded. He wasn't sure if it was from the ale or the way he'd been breathing because of the atmosphere in the common room. He was not about to complain though, now that he was outside in the freshening breeze.

Rhulcan and Marelle sat talking on a rough bench near the corner of the inn. Carlo sat near the entrance to the stables, half-watching the pair as he cleaned and cared for a longsword.

Marelle noticed Kevon first, and stopped talking to flash him one of her disconcerting smiles. Kevon started over to join the trader and his daughter when Rhulcan closed and fastened the ledger he had been studying.

"You mentioned some business earlier?" Kevon asked Rhulcan.

"Ah. Yes." the trader said, standing and handing the closed ledger to Marelle. "That pearl you showed the innkeeper earlier. Might I see it?"

Kevon nodded and pulled the pouch from his pocket. He dumped the pearl into his hand and gave it to Rhulcan.

The Merchant glanced at it quickly and rolled it around in his hand. He rubbed it against his front teeth and cleaned it gently with the hem of his tunic. He then pulled a small clear disc that hung from a leather strap from a tunic pocket and peered through it intently for a few seconds.

"It is a very nice specimen." Rhulcan concluded, handing the pearl back to Kevon and putting the disc back in its pocket. "Would you be interested in selling it?"

"Since I have nothing else of value, and no money," Kevon answered, "I think I have to sell it."

"All right then," Rhulcan paused, tilted his head in contemplation for a few moments. "Would you take twenty gold pieces for it?"

Kevon suddenly felt a bit more lightheaded. Before today, he had only seen one silver piece in his life. Now he was eating meals and staying in a room that cost two silver. And he was being offered twenty *gold* to sell something he really had no other use for!

"I, uh," Kevon began, and then noticed the glare that Marelle was directing toward her father. "I'm sorry, but is something wrong?"

"Father." Marelle stated flatly.

"Dear, it's more than he would get for it anywhere around here," Rhulcan said, not meeting her gaze. "And enough for ten lads his age to entertain themselves with!"

"Father." Marelle repeated, the intensity in her voice growing.

"Marelle." Rhulcan's gruff response made the girl flinch. "He'll get no better offer within five hundred miles of here."

"Father!" Marelle continued, scolding. "I don't know exactly how much that thing is worth, but I would guess twice what you're offering him!"

"If I had twice what I'm offering him, I would offer it." Rhulcan sighed. "But I do not." The Merchant turned to Kevon, but did not look him in the eye. "I'm sorry, lad. I can't give you the price it would fetch in Eastport."

"So, Eastport would be the best place to sell it?" asked Kevon.

"Aye. It's the largest center of commerce in Kærtis." Rhulcan looked Kevon in the eye. "Oh, you might get a better offer from a noble in the Inner Cities, but you'd more likely than not get a knife in your back before you could spend a copper of it."

"All right then. That's where I'll go." Kevon decided.

"Just like that?" Marelle asked, laughter in her eyes. "You decide to cross the Realm on a whim?"

"Sure." Kevon said. "Since I've never been anywhere, one place is as good as another, I suppose."

Rhulcan's brow furrowed. "Don't you have an important errand to run?" he asked. "The errand the pearl is payment for?"

"Yes," Kevon answered. "But there's no hurry as long as it gets done some time."

"You'll come with us, then." Marelle said. "It's perfect."

"How is that perfect?" argued Rhulcan. "We've just come from Eastport, and it'll be half the year before we return there."

"Simple. We turn back, stop in Elburg on the way and buy those wooden carvings you didn't want to load the wagon down with so early on in the circuit." Marelle explained. "We shall need to pay Kevon's expenses on the way, but if you broker the sale of the pearl once we reach Eastport..."

The Merchant's puzzled look warmed into a smile of understanding. "He could reimburse us, and with a modest commission..."

"Set by Marelle." Kevon interrupted, bringing an even larger smile to the young lady's face. Even Carlo, who had walked over to join them, grunted in amusement,

"Yes, yes, of course." Rhulcan acceded. "Just think. That's almost a year's profit in just over a season. Brilliant!"

Marelle reddened slightly. "We'd best turn in. We have an early start in the morning." She rose, and Kevon stepped aside so she and her father could return to the inn.

A few moments and an awkward silence after the pair disappeared into the inn, Kevon mumbled a hasty "Goodnight" and followed as well.

Carlo chuckled softly. "This should be interesting."

CHAPTER 7

During breakfast, Marelle explained that the territory north of the road was not good farmland and was not claimed by Kron. They could camp and hunt on that side if needed, but there were inns at regular intervals to house workers during the growing seasons. If they set a brisk pace, they would not need to camp until they left the area. After breakfast, the group set out on the eastern fork of the road.

Kevon kept his mare close to the wagon, and frequently conversed with the Merchant and his daughter. He asked many questions, eager to learn about the world that had been just outside his doorstep all along.

"What are the cities like?" Kevon asked. "Do they build houses on top of other houses? How do you remember everyone's names?"

Life in Laston was simple. You lived mostly on what you made or caught with your own hands or wits. Everything you learned was to further that end. Outside the North Valley, things were different. Marelle and her father were not surprised at the amount of things Kevon did not know, but Marelle in particular seemed to delight in seeing Kevon's reaction to things as he learned them.

"Father remembers everyone he trades with..." Marelle told Kevon as they sat talking after their evening meal. "I can't do it. I have to cheat." Marelle grinned at Kevon's shocked expression, and waved her ledger at him. "I write them down in this. I re-read my notes on a town before we get back to it."

The trip wore on, and Kevon began to understand that Laston was a place that people went to escape. Bad memories, harsh realities, and most other troubles would seem to disappear in such a secluded and sometimes harsh place to live.

As the days passed, Kevon spent more and more time listening to Marelle tell stories about the histories of the Realms. They were now at peace, but the last war had ended about two years ago.

Each human Realm now hosted representatives from each of the seven other Realms. Each Realm granted these 'Councils of Representatives' a small amount of influence in the Realm that hosted them. Merchants like Marelle and Rhulcan were prospering as never before because of the increased flow of goods between Realms.

Kevon learned that the route Rhulcan usually took led around the edges of the Realm one way or the other, nearing the Southern Frontier around the midpoint of the circuit. Rhulcan made most of his money carting arms and supplies between cities and outposts on that leg of the journey, waiting until he was well on his way back to Eastport before acquiring art or other luxury goods.

One of the things that interested Kevon the most was news of the other races. He knew that the Orcs were an ever-present threat to the south, but he had heard little more than that. The other races that were not overtly hostile to man did not seem to concern anyone in Laston, and were seldom discussed. Kevon had only recently been able to find vague mentionings of them in Master Holten's library.

Marelle told him that a good deal of the elves had settled on islands to the east, and she occasionally saw them on the streets in Eastport. Dwarves and Gnomes had migrated to the northern end of Purlon; most of them lived in caves on the other side of the Lhurridge Range that loomed close on their left. While not hostile to humans, Dwarves did not like men, and barely tolerated the Gnomes that had settled near their territories.

One of the things Kevon learned that surprised him the most was the reason his pearl would fetch such a good price in

Eastport. A few Merchants in the city represented the interests of the myrnar, the sea-folk. Though the myrnar needed nothing the seas could not provide, they enjoyed seeing treasures of the sea returned to it. And with as many ships to salvage as had been lost over the years, they could afford to pay a good price.

On the evening of their fourth day of travel, the group lodged at an inn at another crossroads. Kevon noticed that the farmed land cut sharply to the south now, and they would soon be leaving the area influenced by Kron. The road still crowded close to the foothills of the Lhurridges, almost arrow-straight to the southeast.

After dinner, Kevon and Marelle sat outside while Rhulcan haggled with the innkeeper for extra provisions, and Carlo ran through his evening routines of inspecting his equipment and practicing with his sword. Kevon was beginning to notice that the older man's movements were not flashy or grandiose, but simple, and surprisingly brief. The way Carlo executed them, however, led Kevon to believe he had been practicing and no doubt utilizing these techniques for years. The half-hour workout raised no more sweat on Carlo's brow than did the midday sun.

"So, how did the war end?" Kevon asked Marelle, as Carlo finished his sword practice and sat by the stables to clean and care for the blade.

"It's... hard to know." Marelle said, after a moment of contemplation. "There are a few differing accounts."

Kevon scratched his head. He could understand how a small thing could be seen differently by a few people, but a *war*?

"The last battle was chaotic, in any telling," Marelle continued, a frown underlining her usually cheerful features. "The armies of Kærtis had crossed the seas to take the battle back to the source of the war, to Alcron. Although our forces were divided, as always, with the defense of the Southern Frontier from the Orcs, many of our finest commanders and veteran troops were sent so that the campaign would be brought to a swift end." Marelle's voice lowered and her eyes narrowed. "Several

41

Magi accompanied the troops as well, angry that the war had taken their towers and guildhalls in its wake."

Kevon stared at her dumbly for a moment, his mouth suddenly dry. "Magi?" he croaked. "Aren't they..."

"Neutral?" Marelle countered, quirking an eyebrow. "Usually. But the battles fought here on Purlon claimed over a hundred of their number, and at least a dozen of the Great Libraries. Some say they were the focus of the war, and that the other battles were intended to hide that fact."

"At any rate," Marelle continued, "The fleet and the army performed flawlessly. With the help of the Magi they landed at night and in a surprise raid slaughtered an entire garrison to gain a foothold. They out-marched news of their arrival, dispatching any enemy patrols they came across. News reached the capital city of Alcron a mere four days before the front ranks did, leaving no time for troops to be recalled."

"So they outnumbered the soldiers in the capital?" Kevon asked.

Marelle shook her head. "Their best estimates were that forces at that point were even. The Kærtesian army had the advantage of surprise and experience, but lacked position. As much as it galled them, the commanders set up for a siege. They detached several regiments to deal with incoming reinforcements, and guided by some of the Magi, they ambushed every unit that came close before they could mass into anything resembling a threat."

Marelle paused to take a drink of ale from the mug she had brought outside. "That went on for a few weeks. Then the Magi at the siege lines grew impatient. They caused the city's water supplies to dry up. They also made all of the vermin from the surrounding countryside invade the food stores and eat as much as they could before dying. Within two days, the gates opened and the battle was joined."

Marelle stopped talking for a minute, and Kevon watched her stare into her mug, unsure what to say.

"It wasn't much of a battle, at first. Our forces had improved their positions and were rotated, fresh, well fed. Their hungry, green troops barely managed to reach the battle lines with their first charge; most who didn't fall to our arrows fell back in fear."

Marelle's eyes took on a glazed look as she recounted the battle. Unconsciously, Kevon placed his hand over hers, a gesture of comfort. She flinched slightly and looked at him.

"Are you all right?" Kevon asked. "I don't need to hear the end now if you want to stop."

Marelle smiled gently and shook her head. "I'm fine. It's just that my uncle was a sub-commander in that battle, one of the survivors. I've heard it a lot." She squeezed the fingertips that Kevon had curled under her hand, and slipped free to hold her mug with both hands.

"As the defenders fell back, several figures were seen standing on the battlements of the city, arms outstretched to the sky, instead of crouching for cover," she continued.

"Magi," Kevon breathed softly.

"Yes," nodded Marelle. "By the time our archers spotted them and took aim, the rocks were already falling. From a cloudless sky, boulders the size of a man's head tumbled into the ranks. The first volley of arrows took one of the Magi, but within moments several hundred Kærtesian soldiers were dead."

Marelle paused again to drink. "The Magi within our army responded swiftly, filling the air with lightning that struck down most of the men on the battlements, destroying trees and buildings inside and outside of the walls as well. After a minute, only one of the enemy Magi was left upon the walls." She paused again. "Kevon?"

"Yes, Marelle?" Kevon asked, peering at her.

Marelle's gaze drifted down to where Kevon's hand still rested on her leg where her hand had been.

"Oh!" exclaimed Kevon softly, quickly removing the hand and beginning to turn a rather bright shade of red. He laced his fingers and placed them firmly in his lap. "I'm sorry, I didn't mean to..." his voice trailed off, unable to put his embarrassment into words.

"It's all right." Marelle sighed and tried to remember where she was in her story. "One Mage was left on the walls. He was waving his arms wildly and shouting something at the top of his lungs. My uncle, at the back of the formation, could hear something that he thought he should understand, but couldn't. The Mage finished his flailing and thrust both arms into the air with a final shout. The sky above him began to grow a bright red, and tore apart. My uncle saw a blazing orb through the tear in the sky, like a sun gone mad. He felt the heat for a moment before a shadow passed in front of the rift. And then," she stopped.

"And then...?" Kevon asked. "What?"

"Well, this is the part that people remember differently. My uncle said that the people who tell other endings are scared of the truth, scared to the point of forgetting. He said that happened in battle sometimes. But what he claimed happened..." Marelle hesitated again. Kevon could not tell if it was fear or shame holding her tongue.

"Do you believe what he told you?" asked Kevon, looking Marelle squarely in the eye.

"Yes, of course." She answered.

"Then, I'll believe it too," decided Kevon. "You can tell me."

"The thing that blocked the light..." Marelle continued, "Was a dragon."

Kevon nodded, expecting her to continue. An awkward moment passed, and Kevon realized he had not shown the proper amount of surprise that a normal youth from a backwater town would have. He'd read of Magi from long ago being able to open doorways to other places where strange creatures, including dragons, lived. From the displays of magical prowess that Marelle had described, the gateway with the dragon had not been too shocking.

Kevon forced his eyes to widen in feigned disbelief. "You mean a *real* dragon?"

Marelle nodded vigorously. "The dragon flew through the

opening and there was a loud thunderclap. The tear in the sky disappeared and the Mage collapsed on the battlements. The beast saw the Kærtesian army first, and breathed a swath of flame through the thickest bunching of soldiers." She paused to take another drink. "There was no standing against it. The survivors broke and ran, to the last man."

"But your uncle made it back all right." Kevon said. "That was a stroke of good luck."

"Yes, luck was with them." Marelle explained. "The dragon wheeled about and saw the besieged city. It must have decided it was a better target. My uncle's luck was a mixed blessing."

"How's that?" Kevon asked. "He lived to tell the tale, and you've heard it more than a few times by the sound of it."

"Yes, he did. And I have. But..." Marelle's voice faltered slightly before she continued. "My uncle's horse carried him about half a mile before it died of its wounds. One of his cavalrymen picked him up and returned him safely to the waiting ships. One of the Magi..."

Kevon noticed the edge in her voice and the way her eyes narrowed at that.

"Gave him something to ease his pain and begin healing. But..." Marelle's eyes began tearing up in earnest. "He never saw again, and he never walked again. He was at the end of the dragon's burst of flames through the Kærtesian army. The last thing he saw was that monster killing hundreds of men he'd known for years."

"I'm sorry." Kevon's fingers twitched slightly as he fought the impulse to reach out a hand.

"The reason I know that story so well," Marelle explained, sniffing back a tear, "is that my uncle told it to me at least twice a day while I was caring for him. He was no use to the army; he couldn't see or move enough to even feed himself. He died half a season after he returned home to stay with us."

Kevon sat awhile and thought. He glanced from time to time at Marelle. She was two years younger than he, but the twists and trials life had presented her made her act far older than her seventeen years. Had she grown up in Laston, he could easily picture her running crazily through the high weeds in the meadow outside of town, raven hair trailing, laughing at some girlish nonsense. But she had not. She'd grown up hearing about what went on across the Realm, across the world, even. It had come to her doorstep. Kevon had read quite a bit in the last year, but his studies were disconnected. Lacking experience with what he'd learned, his knowledge had little bearing on much of anything.

"So that's what people in places like Laston are running from." Kevon said flatly. "I'm not so sure I blame them anymore."

Marelle sat, still snuffling over her mug. "I'd rather know," she whispered, turning to look at Kevon.

Kevon had seen men throw injured goats or calves over their shoulders and pack them like sacks of flour. He'd heard the clanging of the blacksmith's hammer for hours on end. He'd witnessed strength, to be sure. But this wisp of a girl, a full head shorter than he and scarcely more than half his weight, showed a different kind of strength. Through the sadness of remembered tragedy that was plainly evident in her eyes, Kevon could see a flame of defiance, one that dared the world to do what it would – Marelle would not fold.

A thought struck Kevon. If there was one girl in the world who did not need protecting, he was sure Marelle was it. But now, protecting her was at the forefront of his mind.

Kevon sighed inwardly. He was in no position to protect anyone. He was next to useless. The mightiest Art he wielded was best suited for a stage show, and though he currently possessed a sword, he knew nothing about using it.

"Kevon?" Marelle asked.

"Mmm?" Kevon grunted. He realized that he had been staring *through* Marelle while lamenting his inadequacies.

"Oh. Sorry. It's… late." He explained, looking away.

"I suppose it is." Marelle sighed, disappointment tingeing

her voice. "Early day tomorrow, and the last night in an inn for about a week."

Kevon rose and offered Marelle his hand.

"Thank you, but I'm going to sit a while longer." Marelle responded, clasping the offered hand for a moment. "Good night."

Kevon thought frantically for an excuse to sit back down, but nothing came to mind. "Good night, Marelle." He smiled and went inside the inn to his room.

Night was half over before Kevon's mind let him fall asleep.

CHAPTER 8

The roads outside of the Kron region were not as well maintained as those on the inside, but were still serviceable. Rhulcan told Kevon that crews came down them during lulls in the crop cycles to make sure that trade routes were not compromised.

The party left earlier than usual in the morning. Since travel would no longer be from inn to inn, time on the road mattered more. Carlo ranged ahead surveying the path more than he had been, but other than that showed no undue concern. Kevon refrained from riding with him and stayed by the wagon at all times.

At the midday pause for lunch, Marelle seemed less talkative than usual. She did ask Kevon a few questions about Laston, but for the most part ate in silence.

An hour after they would have been ready to stop the days before, Carlo returned from a scouting pass and told the others that there was a suitable campsite just ahead. Shortly they arrived at a wide, flat area that lay just off the road.

Kevon helped Rhulcan unharness and picket the horses a short distance from the wagon. Marelle gathered fallen limbs and dried grasses and piled them near a well-used fire pit. Carlo unpacked a crossbow and a short case of bolts from a trunk in the wagon and rode off in the direction they had been traveling. Rhulcan handed Kevon a fire-bow and began unpacking a large bundle of heavy canvas and several long wooden poles.

Kevon went to the fire pit, fussed about with putting the branches *just so* and layering grasses in preparation for lighting. He went through the motions, but as soon as the others were occupied with the canvas structure they were trying to erect, Kevon released a small flow of power into the Fire rune he'd been visualizing. The grass caught quickly and Kevon hovered over it like a brooding hen until it was burning steadily.

With that task completed, Kevon wandered over and helped Rhulcan and Marelle finish putting up the 'tent'.

Kevon hauled a trunk inside the tent and Marelle carried in the rest of the bags. By the time everything was situated to her satisfaction, Carlo had returned with two quail and a rather large jackrabbit slung over his saddle.

Dinner was more like what Kevon was used to at home; cold bread and cheese, fresh game, and watered down wine. Conversation was light; descriptions of the road ahead, what to expect of the countryside this time of year.

After everyone had finished eating and the talk died down, Rhulcan and Marelle retired to the tent, and Kevon went back to the spot he had chosen under the wagon. He unrolled his bedroll, tensed, and gripped the hilt of the sword so that he could move it underneath his other belongings.

"Vagabond!" Carlo's cry mixed with the metallic *zing* as his blade sang free of its sheath.

Kevon turned, looking for the danger, expecting an intruder in camp, but Carlo was advancing on *him!* Kevon dropped the sword and stood up.

Rhulcan and Marelle spilled from the tent, Rhulcan brandishing a longknife and Marelle fumbling with a small but sharp looking dagger.

Carlo's blade whipped around and Kevon jumped back, crashing into the side of the wagon. The Warrior thrust forward to rest the tip of his blade near the base of Kevon's throat. Marelle screamed.

"What are you doing?" gasped Kevon, eyes fixed on the sword that was beginning to pierce his flesh.

"I'll ask the questions!" snarled the mercenary. "Rhulcan, get that sword!"

The trader skirted around to the side of the wagon,

ducked down and grabbed the sword, keeping his longknife between himself and Kevon the whole time.

Marelle stood, blank-faced. The dagger she held dropped to the ground with a soft *thump.*

"Is that why you never told us what that bauble was payment for?" Rhulcan snapped. "Who sent you?"

"Nobody! I swear!" cried Kevon.

Carlo pressed his sword-tip harder against Kevon's breastbone and turned to look at the sword Rhulcan had retrieved as the Merchant backed around to his side. "That's quite the blade for a know-nothing North Valley bumpkin," he grunted.

"It's... not... mine..." Kevon wheezed, taking shallow breaths to spare himself the full pressure of Carlo's sword.

"So you're just a thief, not an assassin." Marelle snapped bitterly. "It's all the same to me." She shook her foot clear of the draw-strap of Carlo's crossbow and fitted a quarrel into the firing groove.

Marelle staggered slightly as she hoisted the weapon up to butt up against her shoulder and sight down it.

Carlo glanced over his shoulder and saw the bow wobbling unsteadily in Marelle's grasp as she reached for the trigger. He yelped and whirled to clear the line of fire.

Twang!

Marelle's aim was surer than Carlo had thought possible in her distressed state. The bolt whizzed past the mercenary and hammered into Kevon's arm.

Kevon shrieked in pain.

Marelle dropped the weapon and slumped to the ground, sobbing.

Kevon looked at the bolt that was sticking out of the fleshy part of his left arm, a hand's-breadth above his elbow. He tried to move his arm, but the tip of the bolt was imbedded in the wagon behind him. The pain rolled over him, turning his world a sickly shade of red. Kevon felt the blood trickling down the inside of his tunic sleeve. He watched, trembling as Carlo advanced, weapon at the ready.

A jerk against the stuck bolt proved to be too much for Kevon as the pain washed over him anew.

Darkness took him.

CHAPTER 9

Kevon woke to a throbbing pain in his arm. His tunic sleeve had been torn off and tied around his arm to staunch the bleeding. He was across the campsite from where he had been, and propped up sitting against a tree.

"Father!" Marelle shouted. "He's awake!"

Kevon stared at the trader's daughter down the sights of a reloaded crossbow.

"Don't try anything…" she warned, her eyes flashing in the firelight.

Rhulcan came from the direction of the wagon, carrying Kevon's saddlebags with him, Carlo close on his heels.

"Marelle," Rhulcan began, "Put the weapon away."

"But Father!" she protested. "He's…"

"Innocent." Rhulcan interrupted. "Naïve. Decent." The Merchant looked down at Kevon with an unusual warmth in his eyes. "And in more trouble than he knows."

Kevon tilted his head questioningly and was rewarded with a twinge from his injured arm. "What do you mean?" he asked, wincing.

"Can you read?" Rhulcan asked him, extending the letter of invitation Master Holten had given him to take to Master Gurlin. The seal was broken.

Kevon accepted the letter with his good hand and fumbled awkwardly with it, trying to open it without moving his left arm. As soon as he opened it enough, he started reading softly aloud.

Brother Gurlin,

Here is the book I borrowed those long years ago. The bearer of this letter, Kevon, undoubtedly carries with him more coin than I owe you. Unfortunately, I do not believe he can be bent to our cause. Dismiss him, kill him, or do otherwise as it suits you. It matters not.

Until we meet again,

-Holten

Kevon's arm throbbed more painfully as his heart began to pound harder. Betrayed, *by his own Master.* Tears began filling his eyes and he threw the parchment into the fire.

"I'm sorry, boy." Rhulcan offered. "Who was he?"

"A Wizard." Kevon sniffed. "One I thought I could trust." The reality of the situation was slowly filtering into Kevon's pain-wracked mind. "Rhulcan, can you hand me one of those flasks I have in my saddlebags?" Kevon asked.

Rhulcan retrieved one of the potions from a bag and handed it to Kevon with a look of mild disapproval. "This is no time for spirits, lad."

Kevon shook his head after he pulled the stopper out of the flask with his teeth. "Healing potion..." he explained.

Rhulcan started to protest as Kevon tipped the flask and began drinking.

"You trust the Wizard's brew?" the Merchant asked, concern lining his voice.

Kevon paused his drinking of the lukewarm concoction long enough to nod and respond. "He wanted me to get where I was going."

The warmth of the potion beginning its work was starting to spread throughout Kevon's body already. Before he finished, his left arm was tingling and starting to go numb. Kevon knew that if he treated his arm gently for the next few days, he would have only a small scar to show for the injury. If he drank the other potion, he would most likely be fully healed with no scarring in about two days.

"So what will you do now?" asked Marelle, finally deciding to lay the crossbow aside. "Your journey, your task, is a deathtrap."

Kevon thought for a moment. "Well," he decided, "That's the only thing that's changed. I can't return the book now." His voice grew colder, and he spoke quietly enough that his companions could barely hear. "Maybe, someday, on my terms."

The last bits of parchment crumbled to dead ash.

"I have other things to do, instead." Kevon reaffirmed, as much for himself as for the others.

"Such as?" Carlo asked, moving around the corner of the wagon into the firelight.

"I need to take the sword to someone." Kevon answered. He flexed the fingers of his left hand and gritted his teeth against the pain.

"Who?" Marelle put a folding stool down next to Kevon and sat, obviously an indication that she trusted him again.

"I don't know." Kevon confessed with a sigh.

The others gathered closer.

Kevon began telling the story of how he came to possess the blade, carefully omitting any mention of magic.

"He may have stumbled on her cub," Carlo mused. "She had no quarrel with you."

"What were you doing around there anyway?" asked Marelle.

"It's the best place to gather herbs in the whole valley. My father took me there when I was younger to gather them to stock mother's pantry." Kevon replied, thinking back. "I've been going there since I was ten. That Warrior was the first person I've ever seen there besides my father in over seven years." He scratched his head with his good hand. "And I don't think he was there to pick herbs."

"Describe his clothing..." Rhulcan suggested, leaning forward to listen more closely. "Maybe we can figure out what part of the Realm he was from."

Kevon thought hard, trying to remember. "Blue tunic, brown trousers," he finally offered, almost as a question.

"Red trim, or white?" Carlo asked, suddenly more interested.

"Red, I think." Kevon answered.

Rhulcan looked at Carlo. "East Thaddington?" he asked the mercenary.

"Most likely." Carlo nodded. "Those were the local colors the last time I was at that Guildhall."

"Now you know where to go after we take care of business in Eastport." Rhulcan grinned at Kevon. "If you'd let us know sooner, you'd have avoided that most unpleasant injury."

"I'm sorry." Kevon began. "I wasn't sure who I could trust outside the valley." After a moment he continued. "Now I'm still not sure who to trust, but I'm fairly certain of you three."

Kevon turned to look at Marelle. Tears were beginning to streak down her face. "Marelle, are you all..."

"I'm sorry I shot you!" she sobbed. "You seemed so... And then you... The sword and..." Barely discernible half sentences were punctuated by hysterical gasps for air.

Carlo and Rhulcan looked at each other. Carlo rolled his eyes. Rhulcan looked at Kevon, quirked an eyebrow, and shrugged. The Merchant and the mercenary both rose to their feet and walked off to talk about something.

Marelle ended her apologetic rant on a high note that Kevon thought might have been a question. She wiped her face and sniffed, waiting. Kevon looked her in the eyes for a moment, and shrugged his right shoulder.

"I'm so glad you're okay!" Marelle threw her arms around Kevon in a hug that he thought he would have really enjoyed if he was not recovering from a crossbow bolt through the arm.

"Ow."

"I'm sorry!" she cried, untangling herself a bit more carefully. "Are you mad at me?"

Kevon's brain hurt. The toughest, smartest, most interesting girl he had ever met had just fallen apart right before his eyes. She'd shot him with a crossbow an hour or two ago, and now she was worried that he was upset with her.

"Um, no?" Kevon guessed.

"Good." Marelle said, composing herself and flashing Kevon a half-smile. "That's very good."

"It's late." Rhulcan returned from his chat with Carlo. "We'd better get some sleep so we can get back on the road early. Will you be all right?"

Kevon removed the makeshift bandage from his arm. There was already a transparent layer of new skin covering the wound. He probed it gently, and found it was not as fragile as it looked, but was still very tender.

"I don't know if I'm going to take the other potion or not," Kevon said, grimacing. "I suppose I can wait until morning and see how it feels."

"All right. See you in the morning." Rhulcan turned to walk to the tent. "Marelle?"

Marelle, transfixed by the sight of the inner workings of Kevon's arm in the dying firelight, startled slightly.

"Coming, Father." Marelle beamed another smile at Kevon as she got up and refolded her stool. "Good night."

Kevon lay down on his side and struggled for quite some time to get comfortable before sleep finally came.

CHAPTER 10

Sunrise saw Kevon's wound nearly healed. New skin surrounded two small circular puckers that marked the entrance and exit of the bolt shaft. Kevon could use his arm in its usual range of motion, but with some difficulty and quite a bit of pain.

Not that there was much need to move it this morning.

Marelle brought him breakfast and teasingly offered to feed him. While he ate, she packed his belongings into his saddlebags and even saddled his mare before eating her own breakfast.

"What do you want to do with this?" she asked Kevon, bringing him the sword as she finished with everything else.

Kevon's bedroll was already neatly fitted behind his saddle. "I was used to carrying it rolled in the blanket. Is there somewhere you can keep it in the wagon?"

"Sure!" Marelle carried it over and tucked it safely away between some crates near the front of the wagon.

Carlo loaded half a dozen broken tree limbs into the back of the wagon, much to Rhulcan's dismay. As soon as the Merchant made sure they were secured so as to not damage his merchandise, the company set off down the road.

At the midday pause, Carlo rigged a sling to relieve the pressure on Kevon's arm while they rode.

Talk on the road was minimal, but Kevon did notice that Marelle seemed to be watching him more, and smiling when he noticed her. He found himself checking to see if she was watching more, as well.

He recalled the way his heart had sped up the first time

he saw her. Granted, there had been other factors that had influenced it right about then; an innkeeper trying to rob him, for one. But there was no denying the attraction had been there. After that, Marelle had been a *book*. She was filled with new information, and Kevon loved learning new things. He had begun to think of her as a teacher, of sorts.

Kevon frowned. Teachers, he was learning, were not always what they seemed to be. He surveyed the surrounding landscape to legitimize another glance at Marelle, who pretended not to notice.

She had worn her hair down today, instead of up in braids as she had done the last few days. She had only gathered it in back with a shiny green ribbon that matched her dress and made her eyes seem brighter than usual.

Kevon looked away. He had no business even thinking about her that way. Though he was no longer just a poor farm boy, he really had nothing to offer anyone. The small fortune he was going to collect in Eastport was from a Wizard who had sent him to his death. The same money evidently belonged to a Wizard that would kill him for it. Kevon would be safe only for as long as those two Wizards did not communicate.

Kevon tried to remember the exact words of the letter. He wished he had not thrown it into the fire. It had seemed that Holten and Gurlin were in league; with how many others, Kevon could not be sure. It also sounded like they had not been in contact for several years. But with Holten leaving town on Council business, that could change very easily.

Kevon was not about to drag anyone else into his mess. Even if he was in a position to face down two Master Wizards, he would not want anyone he cared about to be anywhere near when it happened. The best thing to do would be to run and hide. If he was careful enough, he could change his name and appearance, live out the rest of his life in relative comfort and safety.

Kevon turned his face away from the wagon to conceal the half-snarl that suddenly contorted his features. *Why should*

I have to hide? The thought came over him suddenly as his face flushed with heat. *Who does Holten think he is, sending me off to be killed on a whim?*

The longer Kevon thought about it, the angrier he became. He rode ahead to scout the road and be alone with his thoughts.

By the time they reached a suitable stopping place, it was all Kevon could do to maintain the illusion of civility. All he could think about was revenge, and none of his ideas seemed even remotely possible.

Carlo had not been able to bring down any game for dinner. Kevon sat silently, chewing his rations of smoked fish and dried apples with a glazed-over look in his eyes.

Marelle tried to start up a conversation several times, but Kevon responded with one and two word answers and averted gazes. She retired to the tent before the sun went down.

Carlo stopped carving the chunk of wood he'd been toying with for a minute to wander over and sit by Kevon. The mercenary sat for a few moments before resuming his whittling.

Kevon ignored him, wallowing in his inner turmoil.

"Feels like a knife in your gut," Carlo rumbled a few minutes later, laying the chunk of wood aside in favor of a whetstone. He started sharpening his dagger.

Carlo shifted to look Kevon in the eye as the younger man turned a questioning glance in his direction. "Doesn't it?" he asked, pausing his sharpening.

Kevon sighed as Carlo continued.

"Betrayal, I mean." Carlo spoke, seemingly more to the piece of wood he'd begun to carve once more than to Kevon. "Thinking of ways to get even, aren't you?"

"I don't know if I should run or fight." Kevon admitted with yet another sigh, glad to be able to voice his frustrations at last. "I just don't know what there is that I *could* do against two Master Wizards."

Carlo broke a small piece of wood off the larger piece he'd been working on and set the larger piece aside. "Nothing, right now," he said. "You don't know what to do, because at this moment, there is nothing you *can* do against them."

The mercenary worked the tip of his dagger at the small piece of wood he still held. "Killing Wizards is a matter of distance," he explained after another minute of carving. "At half a mile, a Wizard is worth a few units of infantry. At fifty yards, he's worth about ten men." Carlo paused to look at Kevon. "At two paces, he's something soft to stick a sword in."

Kevon's skin crawled at the Warrior's cold words, but for the first time today, he felt a spark of hope. If a determined Warrior could take down a Wizard, he might be able to hire one to do just that.

Kevon sighed again. He had no idea where Holten was. And he doubted Gurlin would allow anyone bearing arms into his tower. He could hardly travel around with swordsmen and expect them to be ready to slay a Wizard at a moment's notice. It just wasn't practical.

Carlo sheathed his dagger and gave Kevon a wry smile. "Don't get discouraged. You're a bright lad. You'll find a way to get two paces from a Wizard." The mercenary pressed the wooden object he'd been working on into Kevon's hand. "Good night, boy," he rumbled.

Kevon glanced down at the item Carlo had given to him. It was shaped like a bell, a short wooden handle flaring out into a round base. He turned it over to examine the underside that Carlo had been paying special attention to. As he turned it over, a smile came to his lips and the hope he'd felt earlier returned once again.

The bottom was a hollowed out image, the sun and three stars separated by a simple staff. It was a reproduction of the signet seal that Holten had put on the letter to Gurlin.

CHAPTER 11

T he next few days were *dull*. Kevon did not know how the Merchants could stand it year after year. He had always imagined travel was an adventure, that life on the road would be exciting. Kevon's days were filled with plotting and scheming. He tried for two days to remember the exact contents of the letter he'd burned, finally begging some writing supplies from the Merchants to write down what he remembered. He spent hours wondering what he could write to get himself close enough to Gurlin with a sword that he could take his revenge.

Then Kevon decided he wanted more. He wanted to know what Holten and Gurlin were up to, and he wanted to ruin their plans. If he was careful, Kevon might learn enough to turn the tables on Holten before he killed Gurlin.

Kevon considered several things that he thought might work, and practiced writing them in Holten's hand. Once he felt confident enough that at least one of them might work, he packed his notes away with the improvised signet stamp until he could obtain the proper parchment, ink, and wax to complete the forgery.

The next evening saw the group in to the town of Elburg. It was a comforting sight to Kevon. The small town had a feel that reminded him of home.

Rhulcan's business was with the town's mayor. This elderly gentleman lived in what served as a substitute for the town's inn. It was a large house with several guest rooms, a large kitchen, and an elongated common room with a small library at one end.

Rhulcan had explained earlier that the mayor had been selected for a life term, and the Merchant confessed he did not know the man's name. He had only ever heard the man referred to as 'mayor' and occasionally 'good sir' by some of the younger townsfolk and other visitors.

As soon as Rhulcan and the mayor concluded their trade with the carved wooden figures that were the older man's main hobby, preparations for dinner began.

Everyone pitched in. Carlo set himself to cutting the half-dozen field dressed rabbits he had killed earlier into chunks suitable for stew. A large copper pot was set on the cook-stove to boil, and Kevon and Marelle went out to the garden to gather vegetables.

The garden was the most spectacular Kevon had ever seen. Cobblestone paths curlicued throughout it, bordered by polished white stones that also divided the plots and rows from one vegetable to the next. Shade trees loomed over carved wooden benches, and the paths and plots whorled around them with a grace that even Kevon's unschooled eye could appreciate.

While he gathered vegetables, Kevon watched the mayor.

The elderly man, though slowed by his years, was extremely good at what he did. With an age-polished wooden mallet and a handful of chisels and other tools, he finished the detail on the head of an animal that he was working on. Kevon was amazed at how even the grain of the wood seemed to complement the features and markings of the horse-like 'zebra'.

In the center of the garden was the piece that Kevon found most interesting. A large misshapen rock nearly the height of a man and not quite as broad stood in a marked out circle surrounded by the cobblestone path. Chiseled out in breathtaking detail was most of a face. It appeared to be that of an elderly woman, and it looked through the mayor's house toward the center of town. Kevon was unsure if other parts of the rock had been chiseled or were the results of natural wear, it seemed as if he could catch a glimpse of an arm or a leg for a second before it seemed to vanish, perhaps a trick of the light. When Kevon asked about it, the mayor smiled and told him the statue was the 'Lady of the Mountain'.

Kevon and his companions spent the time the food was cooking taking turns bathing, a welcome change from the last few days. Kevon, the last one in a bath, spent a little extra time soaking the tension out of his newly healed arm.

By the time Kevon emerged refreshed, redressed, and somewhat lightheaded from the long soak, the others were already eating. Some of the townsfolk had brought breads and different roasted meats and vegetable dishes. Rhulcan had offered up a cask of mulled cider; it was as grand an occasion as any Feastday Kevon had ever attended. The mayor and some of the smaller children had eaten first and were now gathered on the library end of the common room, youngsters circled around the grandfatherly figure who was reading in an animated fashion. Some of the village folk had gathered to eat with Rhulcan, Carlo, and Marelle, who called out to Kevon as soon as he ventured into view.

Kevon walked over and accepted an offered chair between Carlo and Marelle. Someone passed him a steaming bowl of stew and a wooden spoon. A village girl about Kevon's age flashed him a smile and handed him a mug of warm cider.

Kevon was surprised to find that most of the older generation here were formerly farmers of Kron. The mayor himself had been in Kron for nearly twice as long as Kevon had been alive. The farmer folk had either tired of the life or decided they were wealthy enough to give it up and live elsewhere. This spot was the perfect place for that, quiet but still within easy travel of the main trade route between Kron and Eastport. The residents could acquire most of the things they needed from passing trade caravans.

The gathering wore on long past sundown. The people here had only small gardens to tend; their major endeavors were sport or hobby. Guests and entertaining were always first priority here, it seemed.

Marelle spent the latter part of the evening conversing with twin boys about her age. The pair claimed to be the town's primary hunters. They regaled the group with stories of their latest and greatest triumphs in the field.

Kevon watched as a small boy who seemed not to be interested in the story the mayor was reading pulled another book off a low shelf, lugged it over, and asked if he would read it to him. Glad of an excuse to be away from the boasting brothers, Kevon excused himself and went over to a comfier chair nearer some candles.

The book was a translated collection of Elven lore, mostly short stories suitable to read to children. Kevon read three stories before the boy fell asleep, nearly falling from his perch on the chair's cushioned arm into Kevon's lap. One of the boy's older brothers came and took him, thanking Kevon and leaving for home.

Kevon, fascinated by the book, and especially the story he had just begun reading, continued on. This story, like two of the previous tales, made mention of the Elven goddess M'lani. This one, however, instead of being a lighthearted parable, read more like a historical account. It told of how the elves had lived for what seemed an eternity in a bright land filled with many beautiful creatures. Unicorns, faeries, and spirits that were the essence of light itself moved among the elves and discord was unknown to them. They sang and danced and M'lani walked among them frequently, giving gifts and bathing in the adoration of her favorite subjects. There were times when M'lani was gone for long periods of time, but there was always great rejoicing upon her return.

Then the story told of a time when M'lani was gone for so long that the realm began to seem dimmer and for the first time the elves became worried. When the goddess finally returned, the elves were overjoyed. This time, instead of an extended celebration, M'lani told them of a new home that she and her brothers and sisters were building. She told them that there was a place much like their current home already prepared there for them, and a whole world for them to explore. The elves were terribly excited, and nearly all chose to go.

A portal was opened for them to go to their new home. The elves passed through it, taking some of their favorite creatures with them. They spent the next few years exploring the land. Then a terrible thing happened.

M'lani's dark brother L'mort introduced Death into the world. None of the others could undo this thing their brother had made. M'lani, seeing this, wrought the miracle of Birth, and gave it to all creatures, just as her brother had inflicted Death.

The other gods brought into the world similar gifts of creation and destruction. Wind and water wore down the power of Earth, and Earth joined with Fire to build back to new heights. Thus the world would be ever-changing and worth exploring.

M'lani walked once more among her beloved elves, wrapping them in her love and shielding them from Death as much as she could. Then, one day, she was gone.

Shortly thereafter, Men appeared. They were newly created, combining traits of all the peoples of the world. At the same time, rumors that all of the gods had disappeared reached the elves.

Lacking divine guidance, the peoples of Ærth began to quarrel. Men, being the shortest lived of the races besides the Orcs, but the most prolific of all, held life in the lowest regard. They swarmed across the land, and no race but the elves were safe from their savagery. The Elven people, least touched by Death, were so slow to reproduce, and so fair to look upon that Men found the gentle elves to be no threat.

Men overtook most of the world, crushing all resistance until the only remains of the Elder Races were confined or in hiding. Then, they turned on each other.

Kevon leaned in closer to read the last passage of the story.

The Wars of Men have lasted for more than a generation of elves, but the Elven people still hope for the return of their goddess, and wish for a chance to return home.

Kevon closed the book. He did not know what to make of the story. He'd occasionally heard mention of the gods, usually in the form of a frustrated curse. None of the books he'd been allowed to read in Holten's library had spoken of them. From what little he knew of elves, they were incredibly long-lived, some speculated fifteen hundred years, if not more. It stood to reason that their stories and legends would be changed the least over time, being passed down far fewer times than any others.

His head full of new ideas and questions, Kevon rose to return the book to its place on the shelf. He finally noticed Marelle watching him, a small smile on her face. The brothers were nowhere to be seen.

"Good book?" she asked, raising an eyebrow. "It sure put the little one to sleep."

"It's actually quite fascinating." Kevon replied. "If it really is a translation of Elven lore."

Marelle shrugged. "I'm going to bed. Carlo wanted to talk with you. He's out back."

Kevon started to ask what Carlo would want with him, but Marelle had already turned to go. Kevon allowed himself to watch her until she disappeared into the hallway at the far end of the room. He sighed and walked back to the kitchen.

Two of the village girls were washing dishes and cleaning up the leftover food. They both flashed Kevon sweet smiles, and the cuter one even winked at him. Kevon smiled back and continued on through to the back door.

The garden at night was different, but just as spectacular. Torches were placed in concealed sconces that Kevon had not seen during the day, and the flickering light threw dancing shadows all about the beautiful landscaping.

Seeing no sign of Carlo, Kevon continued along the lit path to a large open area where the torches seemed to end. He stood for a short while, and the ache in his arm began to bother him. He rubbed it, grimaced, and turned to go back to the house.

Thwack!

Kevon barely heard the whistle of displaced air before the wooden pole slammed into his sore arm. Pain flared up, and Kevon's hand went numb almost instantly.

Carlo whirled into view brandishing one of the whittled limbs he'd brought from the earlier campsite. Startled, Kevon reflexively visualized the symbol for Fire, but caught himself before he poured any energy into it.

"Never expose a weakness." Carlo scolded. "You never know who is watching."

"What are you doing?" gasped Kevon painfully, clutching his sore arm.

"I'll tell you what I'm going to do," Carlo snapped, giving the carved wooden sword a twirl, causing it to whistle softly. "I'm going to thump that arm again if you keep babying it."

Kevon glared and released his arm, fighting back the tears the pain was threatening to release.

Carlo nodded, and then tossed the sword to Kevon, producing another from behind his back with a flourish.

"Now," the mercenary chuckled, "Let's see what you can do."

CHAPTER 12

Kevon *hurt.*

The light beginning to stretch in the small window of his room gave his head an ache to match the pain already resounding throughout the rest of his body.

The impromptu sparring match had not gone well for Kevon. Luckily, Carlo had limited his strikes to places that were covered with clothing, or *hair.* Kevon rubbed the knot on the top of his head and frowned. This man was old enough to be his grandfather, and Kevon had not been able to land a single blow. Several times, Carlo had not blocked with his sword, but had shuffled his feet and turned slightly to avoid a lunge. Practice had ended when Kevon took a swing at Carlo's head and the mercenary stepped inside the swing, intersecting the arc of Kevon's arm with his flexed neck and sending Kevon's sword flying.

"That's enough for tonight." Carlo had told him. "We can continue this tomorrow evening if you'd like."

The mercenary had collected both wooden staves and gone back into the house, leaving Kevon to catch his breath.

Kevon sat up in bed and began collecting the willpower he would need to start moving this morning. He thought he heard faint footsteps before the knocking started.

"Kevon?" called Marelle.

Kevon pulled his tunic on over his bruises and winced. He stood and shuffled over to the door and lifted the catch so the door would open.

"Yes?" he asked, peering through the crack that he allowed the door to open.

"I brought you breakfast." Marelle said, moving the large shallow bowl into the Kevon's field of vision. "Father and Carlo have almost finished getting the wagon and horses ready to leave."

Kevon opened the door wider and Marelle averted her eyes.

"Will this be enough?" she asked. "I can go back and get more, another mug too."

Kevon peered at the bowl Marelle was holding. He recognized the leftovers from the night before, a few cuts of meat sinking into a ladle-full of stew. A slab of buttered bread balanced on the edge of the bowl and Kevon could smell the spiced cider in the mug Marelle was holding.

"Yes, this will be plenty," Kevon replied, slightly confused. "I'll be doing good to finish this off, let alone another mug, why…"

"No reason… Just thought you might be… thirsty." Marelle shoved the food in Kevon's direction and the bread tottered precariously on the edge of the bowl.

Kevon took the bowl and mug from her and as soon as she could, Marelle whirled on her heel and started back down the hallway. He called after her. "Marelle!" Without looking to see if she responded, Kevon turned to place his food and drink on the stand next to the washbasin just inside the door. He took a bite of bread and turned back to look into the hallway.

Marelle stood just outside, staring at her feet, blushing.

Kevon watched her as he chewed on his bread.

Marelle looked up and sighed.

He swallowed and raised an eyebrow. "What was that all about?" he asked firmly.

"Nothing!" Marelle snapped.

"All right. Thanks for breakfast." Kevon moved to close the door.

Marelle stopped the door from closing with her foot and poked her head inside to look around.

"Uh…" Kevon began.

"Fine." Marelle growled. "Carlo told us that from the night you had last night, you might not feel like getting up so early today."

"I do feel kind of sore and worn out, but..." Kevon stopped in mid-sentence as he saw the shock and anger flood onto Marelle's face.

"Which one was it?" she asked flatly, her suddenly watery eyes now staring past him.

"Which what?" As soon as the words escaped his lips, it hit him. More food. Two mugs. Checking his room.

"Wait. You think that I..."

"Never mind. I really don't want to know." Marelle interrupted, turning to leave.

"Wait." Kevon commanded, flickering a bit of energy into a Control rune. The last thing he wanted was a messy scene here in this peaceful place.

Marelle stopped, and turned back to face him.

"The old man beat the straw out of me with a stick last night." Kevon confessed, shaking his head.

"What?" Marelle asked, looking confused. "Why would he do that?"

"Seems like he's going to teach me how to use a sword." Kevon answered, shrugging. "He really didn't say much, just thumped me around a lot."

"Oh." Marelle blinked a few times and the corners of her mouth twitched as if trying to hold back a smile.

"So," Kevon grinned. "What did you think I was doing last night?"

Marelle stared at the floor and waited a few breaths before she answered. "The way those girls were whispering about you last night, and with what Carlo said this morning, I..." she sniffed. "I didn't know."

Kevon reached out and gently lifted Marelle's chin so he could look her in the eyes. "No one who lives here interests me," he whispered. "In the slightest."

An awkward silence followed.

"Okay." he said finally. "Thanks again for breakfast, I'd... uh, better eat it so we can get back on the road?"

"Yes!" Marelle said quickly, snapping out of the stillness and backing away a few steps into the hall. "And I need to finish getting ready."

Kevon ate bites of food and took swigs of cider in moments between the gathering of his belongings. As soon as everything was packed snugly and piled by the door to the room, he finished his meal and carried the dirty dishes to the kitchen. The two girls who had been cleaning last night were there again, and bumped shoulders trying to get his plate and mug. As Kevon turned to leave, he wondered if these two had been the ones whispering about him.

Kevon had retrieved his belongings and was about to exit through the front door of the house when the Mayor entered and stopped him. Kevon started to thank the man for his hospitality, but the man waved it off and ushered him down toward the library end of the room.

"Rhulcan has passed through this town at least twenty times in the last ten years," the Mayor began. "He, and recently, his daughter, has brought nothing but kindness and good will since we've known them.

"Yes, I can believe that," Kevon agreed, somewhat confused.

"Rhulcan told me of your situation," the mayor continued. "And as much as I would like to be able to offer you sanctuary here, I cannot put my people at risk."

"Nor would I ask you to, Good Sir." Kevon responded. "I'd not bring my troubles down on a place so pleasant."

"I suspected as much," the old man chuckled, clapping Kevon on the shoulder. "So I brought you this." The mayor produced a small carved wooden box from a pocket and handed it to Kevon. "Open it." he suggested.

Kevon eyed the latch and pried the inlaid wooden catch open. Inside were six small depressions, each filled with a different type of seed.

"Seeds?" Kevon asked, obviously confused. "I don't under..."

The old man winked. "That's because I haven't explained it... I have several friends that after years of farming have decided to try their hands in other pursuits. One of my dearest friends works in the iron mines near the Southern Frontier. He cooks for the miners, and grows the herbs he uses in a small garden there. I send him seeds now and again because the climate there is less than ideal for some plants. He occasionally sends me new woodworking tools."

"You want me to take seeds to an iron miner?" Kevon asked, still not sure what to make of the request.

"Where better to go now than where Magi cannot follow?" the Mayor explained. "Bearing this box, my friend will know you have my trust, and he can find you a place there. Until you decide otherwise, I think hiding would be wisest."

Kevon nodded somberly. "I agree. The iron mines would be a perfect place to get my wits together and decide what to do."

The Mayor nodded. "Ask for Normic the gardener. Give him the box and tell him whatever truth you feel he needs to know. And give him my regards."

Kevon closed and latched the box, withdrew the pouch from his inner pocket, and slid the delicate looking case in to rest against the pearl. Returning the pouch to its place, he thanked the Mayor again and took up the bags he'd set down while he was speaking with the old man.

When Kevon emerged from the house, he found the wagon ready, the horses harnessed, and Marelle holding his saddled mare, stroking her muzzle and feeding her a carrot. He clucked his tongue in greeting as he approached the mare and patted her flanks a few times before beginning to affix his gear to the saddle.

"Carlo's already headed up the road," Rhulcan said, double-checking the wagon harnesses. "As soon as we've taken care of everything here, we can follow." The Merchant eyed

Kevon. "You've spoken with the Mayor?"

"Yes, thank you." Kevon answered, patting the box in his pocket.

Kevon tightened the last leather tie, accepted the reins that Marelle offered, and swung up into the saddle. "I'm ready," he announced.

Rhulcan gave Marelle a hand up into the wagon and flicked the reins. The wagon rumbled through the center of town. Several families had gathered to see them off, and half a dozen children were roughhousing in and around the street.

Half an hour from Elburg, Kevon grew bored with the pace that Rhulcan had set, barely half as fast as previous days.

Rhulcan explained that though this was a well-traveled road, the stretch ahead was known for more than its share of bandits. It was a small swath of land between the influences of Kron, Eastport, and the Dwarven Hold to the north. Once Carlo returned from scouting ahead, they would go faster, but not until then.

Kevon lasted another five minutes. "I'm going on to see what Carlo's about now," he declared. He urged the mare up to a lope, easily outdistancing the wagon. His mount tried to go faster; but Kevon shortened the reins, keeping her to a smoother gait.

Another half hour passed. Kevon now rode in somewhat different terrain. The land started to bunch together. Outcroppings of rocks jutted like something more suited to the mountain passes. Though the road continued on its eastward course, it snaked around the protruding rock formations and some of the larger trees.

Kevon slowed the mare to a walk, taking a few moments to study the road ahead as he crested a larger hill. The next hour's journey would be the most likely place to be attacked by bandits. Boulders and trees crowded the road, some large enough to conceal a handful of men.

Kevon drew back on the reins and started to turn back. He did not want to go into this stretch of road alone, nor did he want Marelle and her father to have to either.

As the mare started to turn, she pricked her ears up and tossed her head against the pull of the reins to get a better look at something.

About a quarter of a mile down the road, what appeared to be Carlo's horse was half-obscured by a tree growing near one of the large rock outcroppings. Kevon steadied the mare and drew breath to shout at Carlo.

Then Kevon noticed the movement on the other side of the rock formation. Kevon squinted and could just make out two figures dragging a third.

Carlo had to be the third.

Kevon dropped to the ground and formed the Illusion rune in his mind. He focused on the area between himself and the others, throwing waves of distortion up. If they happened to look his way, they would see only the heat-haze of early after-noon.

Kevon quietly led the mare back over the ridge and dropped the illusion. He tied her to a nearby tree and returned to where he could see what was happening.

Carlo was still being dragged by one of the figures. The other bandit had gone back for Carlo's horse, but the stallion was not being cooperative.

It seemed to Kevon that the two men were headed for a dense grouping of rock some distance from the road. Boulders and up-thrust slabs surrounded two large trees; it was possible that there was a small area in the middle of the formation that could not be seen from any direction.

Kevon figured the best time to head down would be now, when both were busy trying to drag their respective loads into hiding. He started down the hill, trying to keep behind rocks or trees to shield himself from view. He threw up a haze whenever he needed to move from one concealing obstacle to the next, surprised at the lack of effort the improvised spell was costing him. He could feel his magical reserves slowly depleting, but there was no physical strain at all.

As Kevon drew closer to his destination, he added another focus to his spell. He muffled his already quiet footsteps down to silence, and continued his advance. Kevon reached the last bit of cover shortly after both of the bandits reached their destination. Worried that the two might start keeping watch, Kevon leaned against the rock he was hiding behind to rest and collect his wits.

The bandits did not look like much from what Kevon had seen. To have subdued Carlo must have taken a good deal of either skill or luck, though. Kevon hoped it had been luck, and that it would not hold.

Kevon considered several things. The bandits were now armed with at least one sword, and possibly a crossbow. There were at least two of them. Kevon doubted there were any more; they would have come out to help the others if there were. They were now where they were headed, and if Carlo were still alive, Kevon figured it would not be for long.

He wasn't sure what to do. His Art would be useless in a direct assault on someone wielding a sword. He did not think he could pull off an illusion that would be convincing enough to scare off two men. He also did not want to risk exposing his magic to Carlo, or anyone else, for that matter.

Carlo's Horse!

Kevon formed a Control rune and visualized the stallion, willing the animal to move away, and then flooded the symbol with power.

Carlo's horse fairly screamed in anger, and two voices rose in anxious shouts. There was a sickening *crunch* and one of the shouting voices turned to a scream and trailed off.

Good, Kevon thought. He hadn't expected that, but he'd take it. The sound of hoof-beats trailing into the distance was Kevon's cue to drop his concentration. He stood and stalked over to one of the entrances to the hideout.

As he peeked around the corner, the first thing he saw was Carlo, hands and feet tied, slumped against one of the trees. Kevon's heart skipped a beat. They wouldn't have tied him up if he was dead.

Then Kevon noticed the two bandits, one leaning over the other. *Seeing how badly his partner is hurt,* Kevon thought. *And his back's to me!*

Kevon quickly scanned the area for weapons. Carlo's sword was lying sheathed an arm's length away from the bandits on the ground. That was no good. Leaned against a boulder a short distance away was a club, and next to it a stubby, strange looking crossbow.

Kevon wrapped himself in improvised magical silence, and dashed over to snatch up the club. He grabbed the end of the weapon and sprinted toward the kneeling bandit, trying to reach his target before his concentration or magical reserves gave out. Less than ten feet away from his target, Kevon felt the runes go dim in his mind. Pebbles skittered unhushed beneath his feet. He was already swinging the club upward from its lowered position as the bandit turned, looking for the danger.

The blow meant for the back of his head caught Carlo's assailant squarely on the bridge of the nose. He went down without even a whimper.

Kevon threw the club aside and swept Carlo's longsword up from the ground and out of its sheath into a defensive stance, keeping both of Carlo's attackers in view to make sure neither was a threat.

The man that was already down would never threaten anyone again. His chest was caved in a grotesque fashion, and blood seeped through his layers of threadbare garments. His breath came in shallow, ragged rattles, and his open eyes stared at nothing.

Kevon rushed over to where Carlo was bound, and cut his legs free. The mercenary was breathing evenly, so Kevon took the longest length of rope from the cut bonds and pounced on the bandit he had just clobbered. Maintaining pressure in the upper part of the man's back, Kevon wrenched his captive's arms behind him and bound them as best he could.

Feeling no resistance at all and halfway sure the ties

would hold, Kevon returned to finish cutting Carlo free.

The mercenary was just starting to wake as Kevon started cleaning the gash on the older man's forehead. "Ah." Carlo winced and spit dirt and blood. He shut his eyes hard for a moment before opening them to focus on the two fallen bandits. "Boy," he began, "Sometimes I wonder about you."

"Say..." Kevon retorted, "Isn't this the kind of stuff you're supposed to be protecting us from?"

"Mmm. Saw one of the little bastards hiding watching the road the other direction. Thought I'd sneak in close enough to draw down on him with the crossbow." Carlo poked at his head experimentally. "By the time I heard the other one, he let fly with that prodd over there." The mercenary tossed his head to indicate the odd crossbow that was still leaning where Kevon had taken the club. "That's the last thing I remember."

"Well, you'll live." Kevon declared, handing Carlo the dampened rag. He moved the mercenary's sheathed sword to where Carlo could reach it. "What'll we do with them?"

"Bring me the live one." Carlo answered.

Kevon had not even noticed the other man's shallow, labored breathing had stopped. He shuddered at the thought of it and went over to the other still form. He grabbed a double handful of the back of the bandit's tunic, lifted his upper body off the ground, and with a moderate amount of effort dragged the limp form over to where Carlo was sitting. Once there, he let the body slump back down.

"Lift him up a little, pull his head back." Carlo ordered, drawing his dagger.

Kevon felt a sudden chill. He had not even noticed when Carlo recovered the knife. "Are you sure about..."

"Just do it!" Carlo snarled.

Kevon grabbed his captive by the back of the tunic with one hand, and seized a handful of hair with the other. He lifted until Carlo spoke.

"That's good." Carlo made two swift cuts across the unconscious man's forehead, and then pressed the bloodied rag against it. "You can put him down now."

Relieved that the mercenary had not cut the bandit's throat, Kevon lowered him back down to the ground, propping him so that his forehead stayed pressed to the rag.

"Your horse ran off," Kevon offered, not knowing what to say next.

"He'll probably head back down the road to the wagon to be with the others." Carlo grunted. "Likely out of earshot already." He stuck two fingers in his mouth and blew a few short, piercing notes.

"So, what *are* we going to do with him?" Kevon asked again, gesturing at the limp form still lying bound at his feet.

"Nothing. He's marked now. Anyone will be able to see he's a thief on sight." Carlo explained. "Decent folk won't trust him, and no other thief will want to work with a marked man." Carlo stood stiffly, pickling up his longsword as he did. "Grab that prodd if you want it. Might come in handy sometime."

"We'd better get up to the road before Rhulcan catches up to us." Carlo said, seeming to retake control of the situation.

Kevon collected the prodd and found a pouch of lead shot tethered to the odd weapon.

Carlo bared his sword to inspect it quickly before slamming it back into the scabbard. He double-checked the contents of his pockets and nodded.

The two headed out of the hideout and back to the road.

Kevon and Carlo had barely reached the road when they saw the wagon coming over the hill, trailing both of their horses. Rhulcan urged the team forward while Marelle sat, watchful, drawn crossbow at the ready.

"Whoa!" cried Rhulcan, hauling back on the reins as the wagon reached and threatened to pass Kevon and Carlo. "Wouldn't riding be...?"

Marelle's gasp cut Rhulcan's jibe short as she saw the gash and swelling bruise on Carlo's forehead.

"By the gods, man! What happened to you?" asked Rhulcan, jumping down to get a closer look.

"Ambush," Carlo growled. "Saw half of it. Didn't see the other half." The scowling mercenary jerked a thumb in Kevon's direction. "Ask him. I missed all the action." Carlo untied his horse from the wagon and mounted a bit slower than usual. "But ask him later. We need to get down the road, *now.*"

Kevon followed suit and was shortly astride the mare and ready to go. Rhulcan and Marelle seemed concerned, but understood the need for haste.

The four made their way swiftly through the broken landscape, stopping only once to dole out strips of salted meat and fresh water skins. By late afternoon, the road wound up the side of another ridge and onto a wide open grassy plain.

Kevon stopped at the top and looked to both sides. The sharp contrast between the rolling steppe and the broken scrublands zigzagged away for as far as he could see.

Just before dusk, Rhulcan pulled the wagon off the side of the road near the corner of a wooden fence. It was the first they had encountered since Elburg. The fence followed the road off into the distance. Kevon wasn't positive, but he thought he saw a house off in the distance.

The night was clear and warm. Rhulcan and Marelle chose not to put up the tent and instead laid bedrolls across the upper and lower bench boards of the wagon.

Still troubled, the three men worked out a watch rotation and mulled over the day's events around the campfire.

"I couldn't really say where they were from," Carlo said, pausing the whetstone for a few moments to test the edge he'd been working on. "Looked like several layers of homespun. No regional markings or color schemes."

"Local runaways?" Rhulcan asked.

Carlo shrugged. "They'd been at it awhile, I think."

"They were my age," Kevon stated flatly, staring into the flames. "What would make them think they needed to do that?"

"How would you be getting along if you'd not met us that night at the inn?" Carlo turned to ask Kevon.

"Okay, I guess." Kevon answered, and tried to think about

how he would have handled himself if the others had not shown up.

Carlo shook his head. "Maybe," he answered finally. "But sometimes people think that doing the *right* thing is not always an option."

None of them spoke for a while after that. Rhulcan had chosen the last watch, so he and Marelle excused themselves to get some sleep.

Kevon lingered a while longer, thinking about everything that had happened.

Carlo picked a comfortable spot for his watch not far from the embers of the fire. "Better get some sleep," the mercenary suggested to Kevon.

Kevon rose and walked over to sit by Carlo. "I've never had the option, let alone the need, to do evil to protect myself or someone else," he began.

Carlo nodded slightly.

"But," he continued, "Unless I run and hide for the rest of my life..."

"You'll have to make some hard choices." Carlo offered. "You've had a taste of that today. But you could refuse to change, stay an innocent... and live in fear, waiting for death." The mercenary spat on the ground. "I've known some that would call that a victory."

"Doesn't sound like it to me." Kevon said soberly.

"Nor me." Carlo agreed. "The world is always changing," he continued, "and to refuse to change along with it is to give up. That's no virtue in my reckoning."

"Indeed." Kevon fidgeted a moment. "But to change enough to deal with men who would have me killed..."

"Afraid to become a killer yourself?" Carlo asked.

"Almost as afraid of that as dying." Kevon admitted.

"Good answer." Carlo tossed another branch on the fire. "But I figured as much already. Get some sleep, boy. Your watch is next."

Oddly comforted, Kevon returned to his place and within

minutes was fast asleep.

CHAPTER 13

The group was on the road before the sun lifted off the eastern horizon. Kevon's watch, as the rest of the night, was uneventful. Without the tent to tear down and put away, there was much less to do in the morning. Rhulcan had used most of his watch to quietly pack away any loose articles and prepare what he could for breakfast.

Carlo and Rhulcan had agreed that they wanted to be well into the rangelands before making camp that night. The fenced fields beyond the broken scrub they had passed through were used by the locals to pasture various animals.

Carlo showed no signs of being bothered by the wounds he'd gained the previous day. Kevon had offered the mercenary his last healing potion to speed recovery, but it had been refused. Carlo had instead mixed and powdered some leaves from a pouch in a saddlebag, adding water until it became a sticky paste. After applying the mixture to his forehead and covering it with a thin strip of cloth, Carlo had cinched a rather ornately sewn strap of leather about his head. Helping to keep his hair out of his eyes, the strap looked practical or fashionable rather than something to bind a wound. Kevon was impressed.

Several times in the morning the group came across herds of sheep, goats, and cows behind the sturdy stone and wood fences. All were accompanied by at least half a dozen armed keepers. Most of the groups knew Rhulcan's wagon by sight, but whenever they actually spoke to the herders, Carlo handled everything. The mercenary knew at least half the herders' names and bantered briefly with all who approached.

When the group stopped for lunch, Carlo reported that

he'd heard no news of recent attacks in the west. The only news of note was that a local farm owner had died recently, and several herders had been released from service by his heirs. They had tired of the family business and had decided to turn their overly small tract of land into a sale yard with an inn and various shops.

Marelle's face brightened at the mention of an inn. The others were not against the idea, either.

The turnoff to their destination was not too distant. The road was newly worked, not as packed as the main path. Dust swirled around and got into everything. The beginnings of rock fencepost piles lined both sides of the road. This road, Carlo explained, was through what used to be the main pasture of this farm less than three weeks ago.

After an hour of travel down the dusty path, they reached the inn. The remodeled farmhouse had almost the same home-like feel as the inn in Elburg. The owners, four brothers and their wives, were thrilled to have customers this quickly. They stopped the work they had been doing on various projects around the compound and took turns conversing with, entertaining, and preparing dinner and rooms for Kevon and his companions.

By the time dinner was finished, Rhulcan was deep in conversation with the two elder brothers about the specifics of their new business, giving advice on which types of shops and recommending specific Merchants that might be interested in such a venture.

Kevon pushed his chair back from the table and handed his plate to one of the smiling wives that swept toward him.

"Wait." Carlo told him as he started to rise from his chair.

"Hmm?" asked Kevon.

"Give me a minute to finish eating," the mercenary told him, "and then we'll go outside and... talk."

Just thinking about the last 'talk' Carlo had given him made Kevon hurt, but he nodded and waited patiently.

Carlo finished eating, complimented the hosts on all aspects of their hospitality, and then he and Kevon excused themselves to go outside. The two of them walked across the compound to the outbuilding where the wagon was parked. Carlo rummaged through a corner of the wagon and retrieved the two wooden practice swords. He handed one to Kevon and gestured toward a large flat open spot nearby.

"Defense." Carlo said, swinging the wooden sword to get a feel for it. "One on one, defense is usually what wins a fight. Defend well enough and there will be an opportunity to win."

"All right," Kevon said, stretching his arms and imitating Carlo's warm-up swings.

"Offense." Carlo continued. "Especially when you're facing more opponents than you feel comfortable with, take a few out quickly; it will give you a chance to size the rest of them up."

"Um... okay..." Kevon said, not sure what to say to that.

"Observation." Carlo said, staring icily at Kevon. "Always. You can get clues about how someone will act in a fight from how they walk. How they eat. How they treat their women. You just need to know what to look for, and how to use what you see."

"Wow." Kevon stared blankly at Carlo for a moment. "I thought all there was to fighting was knowing where and how to stab people."

"Most people think that," Carlo agreed, "including some of the *best* fighters you'll ever hear about. But knowing all the fighting techniques in the world won't help you if you don't know when to use them."

Kevon nodded. Holten had told him much the same thing about magic when he began his apprenticeship.

"Balance." Carlo resumed his lecture. "Learn to keep it whenever possible, and when it's better to give it up."

"Why would you want to lose your balance?" Kevon asked.

"You wouldn't *want* to." Carlo replied sternly. "But if you had three swords coming at you at once and thought you could fall backwards and get in under the defenses of the guy behind you... it's worth a try."

Kevon sensed a story behind that particular lesson, but kept silent.

"And conditioning." Carlo concluded. "Being strong helps, surely enough. But there are different types of strength you really need to handle a blade. I've seen miners with arms as thick as my legs drop a sword the first time they're parried. Ankles and wrists need more work than most see fit to put into them."

"Sounds like balance and conditioning could be applied to a lot more than swordplay." Kevon observed.

Carlo grinned. "That's the reason I'm even considering training someone again. It's been ten years since I met someone who sees things that way, and he wouldn't let me teach him. Didn't want to get good at killing. Must be something in the water up there."

Before Kevon could ask what the mercenary meant, Carlo began taking rocks from a nearby fencepost pile and tossing them to the ground. Carlo continued this until the rocks made a roughly circular pattern around the remains of the pile.

"All right. Watch closely." Carlo ordered. He began swinging his practice sword in a fairly simple pattern, the tip describing a figure-eight that wrapped around the front of his body. Every so often, he would change hands in mid-swing and use his left hand to go a revolution before transferring the length of wood smoothly back into his right hand. "Got it?" he asked Kevon after a minute.

"I think so," Kevon answered, beginning to swing his own wooden blade in clumsier figure-eights.

Carlo watched for a minute before nodding. "Now, keep it up while stepping from stone to stone."

Kevon stepped onto the nearest stone. Both he and his pattern wobbled somewhat before he got it back under control.

"Pile the rocks back up when you're done." Carlo said, and turned to leave.

"Wait..." Kevon stumbled off the rock he was standing on

and almost dropped the length of wood. "How long should I do this?"

"As long as you think you need to," the mercenary called over his shoulder.

Kevon resumed the exercise and stepped to another stone. After a few minutes of exertion, he did not know how much longer he could continue. He slowed his motions, concentrating on accuracy and angles rather than speed. He adjusted the tension in his wrists so that it felt more natural when he rolled through the pattern.

Before Kevon felt completely exhausted, an idea occurred to him. He visualized the symbols for Control and Movement. Feeding the runes power, he focused on tightening the pattern the blade wove and stabilizing the movements his feet made.

His magical reserves drained steadily as the power behind the runes pushed his body faster around the circle of stones, sometimes jumping over a rock, or twisting his upper body to swing the pattern to and fro. Nearing his limits, Kevon leapt down and relaxed his concentration. The magical support the improvised spell had been providing left him, and he leaned on the wooden sword to keep from falling.

"Wow." Kevon whispered to himself. He had no idea that such things were even possible. All of his efforts with Movement thus far had been on objects that were across a room, and he'd moved them by magic alone. It had never been suggested that Movement or Control could be used as a supplement to physical exertion.

Kevon contemplated the possibilities while he labored to replace all of the stones to their place in the fence pile. He returned his practice sword to its corner of the wagon and walked slowly from the outbuilding towards the inn. The evening breeze felt good after the workout, and he was in no particular hurry.

"Good evening."

Kevon turned abruptly and saw Rhulcan standing in the

shadow of a tree's trunk. "Oh, hello," he answered. "It is nice out."

"Yes, I had to get out of there for a while." Rhulcan rubbed his temples slowly. "The brothers are not, by any stretch of the imagination, Merchants. Finance does not come easily to them, I'm afraid."

"Ah." Kevon nodded.

"At least not as naturally as some things seem to come to others." Rhulcan said, eyeing Kevon.

Kevon stared at his feet, unsure what to say.

"I'm not concerned about your intentions," Rhulcan continued. "You've proven those beyond a reasonable doubt. Your friendship is quite welcome, and your recently proven loyalty surpasses reason, quite frankly."

"I've enjoyed traveling with all of you, as well." Kevon agreed.

"There are, however, other things that concern me." Rhulcan said sternly. "The more I know of you, the more questions arise without answers. That unsettles me."

"Some things I can't explain," Kevon said, "but I haven't lied to you."

"I believe you." Rhulcan nodded. "But my life and livelihood are based on what I know of the people I deal with. How to use what I know for long-term gain. Though I've grown fond of you, you remain an unknown element. For that reason alone, I am eager to conclude our dealings."

"I understand. I..." Kevon struggled to find the right words. "I don't wish to bring my troubles on people I care about."

"When I was your age," Rhulcan explained, "I was half tempted to join my brother in the army. I felt he needed to be watched over, being the younger of us. But he was more suited to that life, and I to this one. In the end, nothing I could have done would have helped him."

Kevon nodded, recalling the account Marelle had given him.

"I feel much the same now, but I have many more obligations." The Merchant sighed. "And I've become far too cynical."

Kevon wondered what to say for a moment, and the front door of the inn opened and Marelle appeared briefly in silhouette before spotting the two of them.

"Father," she called softly, hurrying over. "There appear to be some differences of opinion that require your judgment inside." She huffed slightly. "They wouldn't listen to me."

Rhulcan rolled his eyes and Marelle giggled quietly. "I'll go sort them out as quickly as I can," he grumbled. "You'd best turn in. Early start tomorrow."

"I'll be in shortly, Father." Marelle countered. "I need some air."

Rhulcan grimaced and turned to go back inside.

Kevon pretended to stifle a half-fake yawn. "I'm done for the night. See you in the morn..."

Marelle touched Kevon's arm gently and interrupted him as he walked by. "I'd feel better if someone were out here with me."

"Oh. Well, I..." Kevon looked to Rhulcan for any reaction, but the Merchant was already entering the inn. "...suppose I could stay."

"Sit with me awhile?" Marelle asked, sitting before Kevon had a chance to answer. The bench they'd been standing by was wide enough for two to sit comfortably, but narrow enough to make Kevon feel self-conscious.

"We haven't had much of a chance to talk these last few days," Marelle began. "I've missed our conversations."

Kevon wrenched his gaze from Marelle's moonlit face and stared blankly across the compound. "Circumstances being... and such..." he mumbled.

"You know," Marelle continued, "boys in Eastport always treated me differently because of who my father is. They were either very nice because our family was wealthier than theirs, or very rude if they were better off."

"There was some of that in Laston," Kevon offered. "Not

much, because most folk were poor anyhow."

"There were other reasons boys were nice to me, too." Marelle smiled at Kevon.

"I've heard a lot of that went on in Laston too," chuckled Kevon. "Not much else to do in a small town."

Marelle smiled at Kevon nervously, and fidgeted with the end of her braided hair. "So… why are you so nice to me?"

Kevon sat in silence for a few moments, trying to formulate a safe answer.

"Kevon?" Marelle asked again, voice taut.

"You've never given me any reason to treat you otherwise, I suppose." Kevon answered.

Marelle poked him in the arm. "I shot you with a crossbow. That's not reason enough?"

"No," Kevon said, catching her finger and holding it firmly. "Your intent was good. Misguided, but good."

"What?" she asked, bewildered.

"You were protecting yourself, and your family, as far as you knew." Kevon explained. "You wouldn't have done it if you'd known the whole story, right?"

"Of course not." Marelle extracted her finger from Kevon's grasp and pouted. "How can you ask that?"

"Because I already knew the answer. You're not the kind of person that could do that without a good reason. But you'll act if you think you need to." Kevon paused. "I'd like to think I'm that kind of person myself."

"Charging unarmed into a bandit hideout to save someone you barely know…" Marelle feigned intense concentration for a moment. "I think that qualifies."

"Does it?" Kevon asked. "I'm not so sure. If they had more time they might have robbed or killed all of us. From what I saw, when I saw it… what I did seemed like the only thing to do."

"No," Marelle said. "You could have run. People run from trouble all the time."

Kevon's jaw clenched involuntarily. "I'll be doing my share of that soon enough," he muttered.

"That's different," Marelle scolded. "Just like yesterday, you have to fight the battles you can win. You had some understanding of what those bandits were capable of. You're going to run from the Magi because you can't know everything they could do." She thought for a moment. "And once you do make up your mind what to do about them, I don't think they'll be any better off than those bandits."

Kevon laughed. "I guess anything's possible. A month ago I never would have contemplated some of the things I've resigned myself to doing now."

They sat quietly on the bench for a while longer. A few times, Marelle opened her mouth as if to say something.

Feeling more and more uncomfortable, Kevon visualized the symbol for Wind and with the small amount of magic he'd built since his workout, caused a cool breeze to blow around them.

"We'd better get inside." Kevon rose and offered Marelle his hand.

"Yes, that would be best." Marelle accepted the offered hand and stood, looking Kevon in the eye for a bit longer than he felt comfortable with. "We will talk more, time permitting," she stated matter-of-factly as she walked past Kevon to the door of the inn, leaving him to deal with the lump in his throat.

Kevon swallowed twice and released the Wind magic he'd been working. He drew his cloak tighter about his shoulders and shivered a moment before following Marelle into the inn.

CHAPTER 14

Summer was bringing its full force to bear on the plains across which Kevon and his companions traveled. Though the days were longer, the journey was trickier. The party would leave early and travel until noon, then rest the horses until late afternoon before continuing. They would usually stop with plenty of time to set up camp before dark, for the bulk of the traveling was better done in the morning.

Afternoons were spent relaxing in whatever shade could be found, reading, talking, and planning. Evenings were devoted mainly to training.

Carlo was an odd teacher. Some of the lessons were as simple and torturous as holding a practice sword out at arm's length for as long as possible. Others were quite humiliating, practicing sword strokes in time with a silly lullaby that Carlo made Kevon sing. And most days, when the initial lesson was over, sparring began.

Kevon counted himself lucky to be able to parry a third of Carlo's strikes, or land a tenth of the blows that he took from the older man. Nearly every time that Kevon connected with his practice sword, it was a glancing blow, at best. In addition, the mercenary's length of wood always slammed into Kevon a fraction of a second later.

Kevon even tried to use his Art to speed his movements to defend himself against the flurry of Carlo's attacks, but he was unable to hold the symbols in his mind. The uncertainty of where Carlo would attack from next, and the pain, was preventing Kevon from even attempting to focus on his Art.

Travel and training drew the days together into a mish-mash of memories. Kevon could no longer remember exactly how long he had been with the Merchant and his entourage. It did seem that each night, though his training exercises became more demanding, Kevon hurt a little less.

Then one night after Kevon had spent about an hour packing an annoyingly heavy rock in a wide circle around camp, something unusual happened.

Tired beyond what he was accustomed to, Kevon had essentially given up any hope of blocking or dodging any of Carlo's attacks during sparring. Kevon knew the strike was coming, and that it would hurt. For a moment, he felt a detached amusement, knowing exactly how much the blow would hurt, and how long it would take the bruise to heal. That sure knowledge gave him a strange sense of comfort, a moment of clarity. In that instant, the symbols for Control and Movement solidified in Kevon's mind. He let the magic flow into the runes and unconcernedly swept his wooden sword up in a swift arc to intersect with Carlo's.

Amused at the barest furrowing of Carlo's brow, Kevon leaned into the next two parries and smiled. Seeing an opening, he slid the rounded point of the practice sword into Carlo's gut just below his ribcage. He got the satisfaction of a soft 'oof' of surprise right before Carlo's sword thwacked into the side of his head.

The runes faded and crumbled in Kevon's mind as his vision blurred.

"Ha!" Kevon chortled briefly as he tried to prop himself up on the side he had fallen on. "Heh heh... Ow." He pulled himself into a sitting position and smiled at Carlo, who had sat down as well.

"Now where did that come from?" Carlo asked.

"I stopped caring about getting hit," Kevon answered bluntly. "Kind of calmed me down."

"It's about time you realized that," Carlo sighed. "I was running out of stupid things for you to do to wear you down."

"What?" Kevon asked, still trying to focus his eyes clearly.

"You're going to get hurt when you're training. It'll be worse when it's for real. Accepting that fact is the first lesson you must learn, but it can't just be explained... It has to be embraced. Now, it's a part of you, and everything will be easier."

◆ ◆ ◆

Easier, as Kevon soon found, was a relative term. Although the mandatory exercise sessions were cut from his training, and sparring became less frequent, the lessons became far more difficult. Carlo always seemed to expect twice as much from Kevon as Kevon thought he was capable.

Instruction now consisted of becoming familiar with different attack and defense postures, learning their uses and weaknesses. Kevon learned many specific thrusts and slashes, differing for a variety of reasons; an opponent's armoring, positioning, size, or weaponry. Each new attack was tried over and over until it was done perfectly half a dozen times in a row before Carlo would move on to something else.

During practice, Kevon struggled to maintain his concentration on a variety of the runes he was familiar with. He decided not to use magic as a crutch while fighting anymore; using real weapons would eliminate that possibility in a genuine confrontation. Kevon did not want to come to rely on something that would be useless when he needed it most. Nevertheless, Kevon found the mental state required for using magic seemed to lend itself to the Warrior's arts as well, and the focus seemed to make a difference in practice.

Marelle began watching the evening sessions with more interest, and insisted on treating any wounds by either participant afterwards. Kevon found himself taking more interest in afternoon walks and talks with Marelle. He often took along the practice sword and swung it idly to work his wrists while walking, or twisted it back and forth, as it lay across his knees while sitting and talking. He also rocked back and forth from his heels to the balls of his feet while standing in place for any length of time to strengthen his ankles.

As the trip wore on and Eastport grew ever closer, Kevon began dreading their arrival. He'd grown far too accustomed to the way things were in the company he was with. They had seen few people since their stay at the inn some two weeks ago. The occasional passing of a full wagon drawn by a four-horse team headed to Eastport, or an empty one returning to Kron was the only exception.

Kevon noted the taint of sadness in Marelle's voice when she told him of the things he would encounter in Eastport. More and more she asked about his family and seemed eager to hear stories of things that happened in Laston when Kevon was younger. It made Kevon a little homesick, and more than a little worried about how his mother and sister were doing. Or how they would be doing when Holten returned.

That was not the only thing that disturbed Kevon. Over the last few days, Marelle had seemed to use nearly any excuse to brush against him, or touch his hand or arm. A few days before, Kevon had been feeling uncomfortable about the way his clothes were fitting, and had mentioned it to her. She had been very amused. Not one to pay any particular attention to clothes unless they were torn or otherwise damaged, Kevon had missed noticing he'd grown about an inch in the last month. In addition, though he'd never been a lazy child, the last few weeks had been the most brutal exercise he'd ever experienced. Soon his old clothes would not fit because of the increasing width of his neck and arms.

Kevon managed to talk Rhulcan into parting with one of his less fashionable sets of extra clothing. They were far from the Merchant's finest, but much nicer than anything Kevon had ever worn. The trousers were a bit long, and the tunic hung loosely, but at the rate Kevon was growing, they would fit soon.

Since he had decided to avoid involvement with Marelle,

anything that resembled an advance on her part became increasingly frustrating. He realized that his attraction to her was growing, but he was trying to keep it to himself. Sometimes he thought about the future. If his troubles could be resolved, who knew? If Kevon ever felt he was truly safe, he promised himself he would come looking for her. But for now, he dared not hope, or do anything that would raise false hopes for Marelle.

"What was your father like?" asked Marelle one afternoon while the two of them sat eating lunch in the shade of a large oak.

"I really don't remember all that much about him," Kevon admitted. "He was recalled to the Inner Cities when I was twelve. He'd only been back home with us for three years."

"Where was he before that?" she asked.

"He was a city guard in Navlia." Kevon answered. "He would send enough money that we could live in Laston fairly comfortably, but he was saving enough to build fences and buy goats we could raise when he came home."

Kevon wiped the crumbs from his hands and picked up the practice sword that was leaned against the tree. He gave it a few twists before continuing. "He came home with a herd of goats. Not all of them made the trip. We built a house in a decent spot, but the herd wasn't as profitable as my parents had hoped. We were working hard and barely getting by, but it was better having Dad around."

Marelle nodded, but kept silent.

Keeping half of his life secret was wearing on Kevon. He took the opportunity to share more than usual. "One thing I do remember about him. I don't know that he ever told me that he loved me. I don't think I ever heard him tell my mom or sister either. But we all knew he did. The way that he acted, how hard he worked for the things we needed. It was almost as if it would have cheapened the work he did by saying the words." Kevon sighed. "If my children know they're loved half as much as I did, think even half as well of me as I did my father, I'll count myself a success."

Under a nearby tree, Carlo stopped the mending he was doing on some of his gear. He put his work aside and stood. "Do you know what precinct your father was assigned to?" the mercenary asked.

"No, he didn't like to talk about it." Kevon answered.

"While I was in the Guard, I met a man who wanted to give it up and move back up north," Carlo recounted. "The first time I saw him was at a protest over conscription for the war. The protest broke out into a riot. Guards from three precincts showed up to handle it. He'd fixed his shield, but hadn't drawn steel. He waded through the crowd, and anyone that swung a club at him got a face full of reinforced leather and their club taken away. The rest of his unit poured in behind him. They split the crowd in half and broke the mob's momentum. Saved a lot of lives."

Carlo walked over closer so that he could talk more easily with Kevon and Marelle. "I wanted to thank him, so I asked around to find out who he was. Turned out he was an unranked city guard. I put in the paperwork to get him a commendation, and sent him a letter to ask him if he was interested in Guild membership. He'd already collected his last wages and left for home."

"You saw him again, though?" Marelle asked. "You said that was the first time you saw him."

"Yeah," Carlo nodded. "It must have been four years later when I saw him again. The conscripts from the cities were getting stretched pretty thin on the battle lines. They started pulling Guardsmen from duty and tracking down everyone they had records on to replace them. One night, we'd tracked a murderer into another precinct. The man we were chasing turned out to be a prominent member of the Thieves' Guild, and was holed up in a safehouse. The local patrol came through and saw us, offered to help. Kohan was the subcaptain..."

"Kohan?" Kevon exclaimed. "My father's name was Kohan!"

"As soon as I heard you talking about him just now, I could see the resemblance. I figured it was him," Carlo agreed. "Your father was a good man. I wish I'd known him better. I was saddened to hear of his death at the siege of Alcron."

"Your father was at the siege of Alcron?" Marelle's eyes widened.

"No," Kevon said, shaking his head. "My father died while on guard duty in Navlia."

"You were misinformed." Carlo sighed. "I tried to get Kohan into the Guild after the raid on the safehouse. He told me he'd consider it, but would rather not live the rest of his life tied to a sword. Next thing I hear, he'd volunteered for the attack on Alcron and had already shipped out. His name's carved in the monument at the palace in Navlia. I've touched it." Carlo grasped Kevon's shoulder. "I'm sorry, boy. But I thought you should know."

"Your father... My uncle..." Marelle whispered.

"Were killed by the same man," Kevon rasped, clutching at the sword in his lap so tightly that his knuckles appeared completely drained of blood.

"The same *Mage*," Marelle added, an unusual hardness edging her normally soothing voice.

When Marelle first told Kevon the tale of the siege, and her uncle's demise, Kevon felt quite a bit of sympathy. Silently, Kevon vowed to find and kill the Mage responsible for his father's death. He was even more resolved to deal with Gurlin, and put an end to Holten's treachery so that he could focus his attention on finding his father's killer.

Kevon let the wooden sword fall from his grasp, and as it clattered to the ground realized that he was standing. The world wobbled as Kevon's vision blurred red.

"Are you all right?" Marelle asked, draping an arm around Kevon's neck, gently drawing him closer to give a degree of comfort.

Forgetting himself, Kevon allowed the embrace and was instantly all too aware of his mistake. Now both of Marelle's arms, like slender silken cords, held him firmly to her. His face rested in the curve of her neck where her braided hair wrapped around to dangle across her shoulder. The scents of lilac and honeysuckle mixed with another smell Kevon could not identify. The effect was intoxicating. His head spun, and Kevon put a hand on her waist to steady himself.

Half a dozen breaths later Kevon was silently questioning his decision to avoid Marelle. If they were careful, they could make it work out.

I could take another name, Kevon thought to himself. *My appearance is already changing. We could still head south and live for a time among the iron miners. We could...*

"Time to start getting back on the road," Rhulcan called from the other side of the wagon. "Marelle, would you help me with the horses?"

Marelle released Kevon slowly, her fingers trailing lightly across the back of his neck and halfway down his arm. Despite the warm afternoon sun, Kevon fought the urge to shiver. Marelle started toward the wagon, keeping her gaze fixed on Kevon until she was nearly halfway there. "Coming, father," she called, and hurried around to start helping.

Kevon took a step and stumbled slightly, still dizzy.

"Boy, I remember what that was like," Carlo chuckled. "Hate to be in your boots right now, though."

"Hmm?" Kevon asked, struggling to regain his composure. "What? Why?"

Carlo shook his head, grinning, and started gathering his things.

Kevon stowed his practice sword in the back of the wagon and saddled the mare. When he finished, he approached the wagon to help finish harnessing the horses.

Rhulcan moved to intercept him. "We're almost done. Don't worry. Maybe you should re-check your gear." The Merchant's suggestion was gruff at best.

Kevon noted the stern set of Rhulcan's jaw, the broad, square stance he had stepped into. He recognized it from the inn of the four brothers. Nodding, Kevon retreated to his mount and went through the motions of checking his gear over once more.

Kevon realized what Carlo had been saying. Given enough time to think, Kevon would make the right choice and leave. What had happened just minutes ago would not change his mind. It *would* make the choice that much more painful.

Soon, everyone was mounted up and ready to depart. Wanting to be alone with his thoughts, Kevon motioned to Carlo in the code that the mercenary had been teaching him. The brief hand signal that meant 'I'll take point' was answered with a slight nod and a knowing smile. Both men urged their mounts into motion to take their places as the wagon clambered back onto the road.

Kevon dug his heels into the mare's flanks and began to distance himself from the wagon. He rode hard for a few minutes, then stopped until he could just hear the wagon approaching. He gave the mare some rein and she dropped into the familiar traveling pace without further instruction.

They traveled until late in the evening. Every time Kevon saw a suitable campsite, he would slow after passing it to see if the wagon was going to stop. When it continued, he would distance himself again.

Finally, just before twilight, Kevon rode over a hill and spotted an inn not half a mile away. Beyond that, small farmhouses dotted the countryside, and in the distance Kevon saw half a dozen reddish-white triangles catching the last rays of the evening sun. Squinting, he looked closer and saw that they were sails, all lined angling in the same direction. Following the line they drew toward shore, he spotted it.

Eastport.

CHAPTER 15

"Very well, then. I shall pay for it myself." Marelle said to the innkeeper. "I do have money of my own." She shot a glare at Rhulcan.

Kevon plopped his bedroll and saddlebags down on an empty table in the common room and edged closer to the fireplace.

"You will do no such thing," Rhulcan argued. "I won't hear of it."

The innkeeper stood silently.

"Father," Marelle's voice dropped into her practiced lecturing tone. "I enjoy making the trade routes with you. I'm fascinated by the business, and enjoy the scenery and people. But I'm tired of not having any privacy!"

"We'll be home tomorrow. You'll have all the privacy you want then." Rhulcan countered. "It's just one more night. I don't see the sense of it. Next time will be different. We'll bring another tent, you can have your own room at every inn. All right?"

"Father, it's late. These good people don't want to have to move beds to accommodate us when I'm willing to pay extra for another room that's already prepared."

The prospect of more money for less effort prompted the innkeeper to speak up. "I've got a leg of lamb in the larder. If you're all staying in separate rooms, I'll have time to get it cooking and served up to you instead of the..." he lowered his voice. "...swill these other folks are eating."

Marelle's face lit up and she began talking excitedly with the innkeeper, taking his arm and steering him toward the kitchen. She asked him a few quick questions about food preparation and thanked him, smiling as she propelled him from the common room.

Rhulcan shook his head and sighed in defeat as Marelle turned to flash him a victorious smirk. He slid into a nearby chair and signaled a serving girl to bring him something to drink.

Kevon pulled up a chair across the table from Rhulcan and sat down. He sat in silence, tracing his fingertip along the grain in the wooden table's edge. He thanked the waitress as she delivered his mug of ale, grateful for something else to occupy his hands. Kevon lifted his mug toward his lips, but paused as he met Rhulcan's icy gaze.

Rhulcan bobbed his mug in a friendly gesture. "To women."

"Sir?" Kevon asked, a little confused.

"Love them while you can," he toasted, "For you never know when they'll leave you."

"Leaving?" Kevon asked, glancing over at Marelle, who was gossiping with one of the barmaids.

"Not all at once," Rhulcan grumbled, staring into his mug. "Doesn't hurt any less, though." Seeing Kevon's blank stare, he snickered softly. "Someday, if you're lucky, you'll understand."

Rhulcan caught the arm of another serving girl and pressed a silver piece into her hand. "We're going to need a lot more ale."

Kevon was all for that, after the extended afternoon of riding, not to mention the last few weeks of travel and training. Nothing sounded better than drinking until everything was kind of fuzzy and then getting a good night's sleep.

"Carlo!" Rhulcan called as soon as he spotted the mercenary entering the inn. "Sit, grab a mug!"

Carlo glanced about the room, and pointed to another table.

Rhulcan laughed and got up to move. He stood aside as Carlo circled the table to place his back to the corner.

Once the three men were situated, Carlo seemed to

lighten up, and began drinking in earnest. An hour or so later, with half a dozen mugs emptied, he began to sing.

The first song was a cheerful one about the joys of youth and a particularly fortunate lad's experiences with them. When it was finished, the few other patrons broke into scattered applause and asked for another. Carlo nodded as he finished the mug of ale he'd been drinking between verses. The next song began quietly, and the interested listeners leaned forward or carefully moved closer to be able to hear better. The song, far more solemn sounding than the last, was called 'The Ballad of Bartok Brokenblade'. Though Kevon had never heard it before, the understated force in Carlo's gravelly voice was so powerful that he found himself mouthing the words by the third chorus.

When the song was over, there were murmurs of appreciation, but no one cried out for more. The serving girls brought everyone more ale, and all drank in silence for a time.

Marelle, not usually one to drink more than one mug at any given time, was halfway through her third. She seemed disinterested in any of the conversation around the table. She stifled a yawn and shook her head slowly. "That's it for me," she announced, speaking slowly to keep the slurring to a minimum. "Good night. I'm going to *my* room now."

Rhulcan, having emptied nearly as many mugs as Carlo, snorted and waved her off. He shoved another mug of ale in front of Kevon.

Kevon was slightly beyond the point where everything was pleasantly fuzzy. His second trip to the outhouse had taken him a while because shrubs and rocks kept jumping into his way. He was reluctant to drink any faster because he knew he'd have to make the trip again soon. "I really shouldn't," he protested. "I'm really tired too. I'd better just go to…"

"No!" Rhulcan slammed his mug down on the table. He looked toward the door Marelle was exiting through and then glared at Kevon. "You're drinking until someone has to carry you to your room," he hissed.

"Aww," groaned Carlo. "Do you really think that's nesesh… neshesh…" the mercenary licked his lips. "Needed?"

Rhulcan glared at Kevon for a while, until he lost his focus and his eyes began to glaze over. "I don't know," he whispered. "I just feel like I'm losing…"

Kevon stood up shakily. "Nature…" he grumbled, motioning toward the exit, and headed outside.

Carlo furrowed his brow and pressed a palm to his forehead for a moment, attempting to clear his mind a bit. "I've spoken to the boy about it," he told Rhulcan. "He'll do the right thing." He swished his nearly empty mug around thoughtfully. "If I were his age you'd have good cause to worry. As things stand now…" Carlo drained his mug and pushed his chair away from the table. "We've all got more reason to fear the hangovers we'll have come morning."

The Merchant sat a while longer, staring into his half empty mug. A barmaid, noticing he was alone, breezed by to ask him if he needed anything.

"The drink's not helping," he lamented, as he stood and poured a small pile of coins onto the table. "Let's hope time does the trick."

The barmaid flashed him a quizzical smile, and then began to clear the table as Rhulcan exited the common room to go to bed.

CHAPTER 16

Kevon would have *preferred* being beaten with a stick. A few times during his preparations for departure, he'd actually opened his eyes wider and looked around to make *sure* no one was beating him with a stick now.

He was not quite sure what had happened after he'd left to use the privy the last time. He hoped no one had actually needed to carry him to his room. He decided that he would not be drinking that much anytime soon.

Kevon opened the door to his room and peered out, squinting against the late morning sunshine that shone down the hallway from the commons. There was activity in that part of the inn, but he could not pick out familiar voices or see well enough to recognize anyone. Groaning softly, he shouldered his gear and trudged out.

The rest of the group was up and gathered around a table. Kevon noted that for once, Carlo seemed to be in the best mood of any of them. Rhulcan was in about the same shape as Kevon, and Marelle just seemed bored and annoyed.

Carlo pushed his cleaned plate away from him and leaned back in his chair with a smile. Rhulcan and Marelle's meals had barely been touched, and Kevon did not know if he would fare any better.

"So…" Carlo began, clearly amused at being the most chipper individual at the table. "When do you think we'll be on our way?"

"In a great hurry now, are you?" asked Rhulcan. "The trip you signed on for was more than twice as long as it's turned out."

"And if you wish to leave immediately, I'll stay on and agree to an extension, as well," Carlo countered. "If not, I'll take a fair percent and be on my way. I've no need of more than I earn."

Rhulcan nodded, still frowning. "As soon as we're all done with breakfast, then."

Marelle stopped the halfhearted picking at her plate she'd been doing and pushed it forward by Carlo's. "I'm done," she said, yawning. "I'll go have the team harnessed."

Carlo stood and followed her out, humming a tune Kevon half-remembered from the night before.

A kitchen maid brought out a plate of food for Kevon and a large pitcher of water. Kevon sat and tried to eat quickly, knowing that he was the one the others were waiting for. The food looked good, but Kevon's mouth was so dry that he had to drink several mouthfuls of water in between each tasteless bite.

"We'll be in town well before nightfall," Rhulcan explained, abandoning his breakfast. "I'll arrange a room at an inn near my home for the week. It shouldn't take that long to settle affairs, but you never know."

Kevon could no longer expend the effort required to eat, and stood to collect his gear. "Might as well just get on with it," he said.

Rhulcan nodded and stood to follow Kevon out to the courtyard. The horses were saddled and ready to go. Marelle was tightening harness straps on the team, and Kevon strapped his gear into place behind the mare's saddle.

As soon as everyone was ready, they mounted up and departed with scarcely half a dozen words said between the four of them.

The pace was unhurried, and they did not split up to scout ahead as they had done the previous days. They were in range of regular patrols from Eastport, so there was little chance of encountering the kind of ambush Carlo had fallen into. Conversation was even scarcer than it had been in the last few strained days of travel. Twice Kevon thought he saw Marelle's head bob as if she were falling asleep in her seat on the wagon.

As they neared Eastport houses became more frequent along the roadway. The larger farmhouses gave way to smaller dwellings that Kevon had not seen the like of outside a town.

Most of the folk around the roadside houses paid the group little or no mind, but Kevon did have to slow several times to stay clear of excited but unattended youngsters who ran too close to the mare.

Twice the group passed local patrols. Each time, two of the four men in a patrol touched their left hands to their right shoulders as they rode by, and Carlo did the same. Kevon decided he would ask the mercenary what it meant later.

Evening approached as they crossed the bridge into Eastport. The small river that meandered over the plain from the northwest was channeled into cut stone canals that ran around and into the city. The wagon was stopped, and one of the officers from the guard post watched carefully as two guards inspected the cargo.

"Ahem. Rhulcan?" one of the guards asked, pulling the sword that Kevon had nearly forgotten about from the wagon. "Have you any weapons to declare?"

"It's the boy's," Carlo rumbled, flipping a silver to the officer, who caught it with a smile. "That should cover the tax?"

"Certainly." The officer motioned to the guard, who replaced the blade.

Carlo edged his stallion closer to Kevon and the mare as they passed through the checkpoint and the guards waved the wagon on behind them. "Most blades are taxed when you carry them from one district to the next," he told Kevon. "We'll have to see what we can do about yours."

Kevon nodded slightly, but the full force of the largest port city in the Realm had stolen most of his attention. The salt breeze pushed against his face as they pressed inward, his eyes watering and nose wrinkling at the unfamiliar sensory assault.

The scenery was unlike anything he'd seen before. The buildings were taller, packed more closely together, and crowded with so many people that Kevon was unsure how they all lived here. Most of the first and second stories of the structures were mortared brick or stone, but as far as he could see down the narrow plaza, the tops of all of the buildings were wooden.

The main street was just wide enough for two wagons to pass each other, allowing space for pedestrians if they were careful. The cramped side alleys were barely wide enough to admit one wagon.

As they passed further into the city, shadows lengthened and the streets darkened. Structures here seemed sturdier; most were completely made of stone, brick, or wood, rather than the mismatched buildings they had passed earlier.

Just about the time a patrol rode through to light torches that hung ensconced over the street, the wagon stopped in front of a rather nice looking inn.

"The Maiden of the Bay," remarked Rhulcan, pointing to the plaque hanging out over the street from above the door. It featured a creature that was part woman, part fish, which Kevon recognized as a mermaid. Rhulcan tossed Kevon a pouch full of coins. "A week's lodging. We'll contact you sometime tomorrow." He flicked the reins and the wagon started to move again. "Sleep well!" the Merchant called as he turned the team to round the corner.

Kevon opened his mouth to say something, but there was hardly time. Marelle's eyes locked him in her gaze for a long moment as the wagon slid out of sight. With the wagon's wheels clattering against the street's cobblestones fading, Kevon became aware of the other noises the city offered. Hawkers, fewer in number and better dressed than their counterparts in the outlying areas, called out occasionally. They were less concerned about making sales than they were about gathering up their wares and bantering with nearby associates. Mothers peered out from doorways and summoned their children from the mischievous looking packs that rambled around the streets.

He dismounted and handed the mare's reins to a waiting groom. He unfastened his gear and was about to sling it across his shoulder when another youth in identical dress reached across to take it for him. Kevon was about to protest when the young man started for the inn's entrance, but turned and waited for him to follow.

Kevon thought that the stonework on the outside of the inn was nice, but was totally unprepared for the interior of the building. Intricately carved pillars depicting merfolk engaged in various activities flowed upward into stone archways. The ceiling, barely visible in the torchlight, seemed made from the same material as the floor, which Kevon examined more carefully. At first glance it looked wet, but Kevon decided that the seasoned planks must have been coated with a hardened waxy substance.

The young man carrying Kevon's things waited patiently at a counter to the side of the entrance. An older man behind the counter cleared his throat.

As Kevon approached the counter, the young man spoke. "A friend of Trader Rhulcan, Mister..."

"Kevon." Kevon supplied.

"Kevon...?" The older man asked slowly, perhaps waiting for a title.

"Just Kevon."

"Very well. Mister Kevon, how long will you be staying with us?" the innkeeper asked.

"A week." Kevon answered. When the innkeeper calculated the bill, Kevon dug through the coin pouch and paid the amount without comment. A season ago, Kevon would not have thought he'd ever see that much coin in his lifetime. Now, it was enough for a week's lodging and a little extra for fun.

Kevon thanked the innkeeper and followed his gear up to the third floor.

"Would you like anything from the kitchen?" the youth asked Kevon after depositing his things on a bench in his room.

Kevon thought for a moment. It was late, but he hadn't

eaten since noon, and not much then. "Sure. Just grab anything that looks good." Kevon handed the young man three of his remaining silvers.

"Meals are included…" the youth said, staring at the coins in his open hand.

"Oh." Kevon said, realizing that was probably part of the reason a week's lodging was so expensive. "Well, that's for you, then, for having to pack my gear all this way… what was your name?"

"Bertus." The young man grinned and pocketed one of the coins. He dropped the other two on the small table near the bed and added, "You're going to be here a whole week. I'll get those two soon enough, and feel better about it when I do."

Kevon smiled and patted Bertus on the back as he exited the room. While he waited, he took time to examine the room in the glow of the tallow candle Bertus had left lit on the bedside stand. The room was larger than any he had stayed in yet, and was the only one so far to have a window. Since it was the only room he'd ever stayed in above ground floor, he supposed it made sense. The single portal was circular, framed by a round of wood, the glass far thicker than any Kevon had ever seen. What little he could see in the deepening evening was distorted by the sturdy pane. The east-facing window looked out over many of the surrounding buildings, but the bay was not visible now even in the light of the nearly full moon.

Kevon removed his outer cloak and rinsed his hands and face in the washbasin near the door. He pulled Gurlin's book from a saddlebag and had just sat down on the edge of the bed to read when Bertus knocked on the door with his food.

Bertus walked carefully into the room balancing a large wooden tray laden with food. He set it carefully on the small table by the bed, and then knelt down to reach underneath the bed. He pulled a strange looking item from its hiding place, and with a few practiced movements that Kevon did not quite follow, surprised Kevon with another small table that was just the right height for eating. The tabletop was slightly larger than the tray, and looked as if it would seat two comfortably.

Bertus wiped down the tabletop with a damp cloth from the tray he'd brought, and swiftly transferred the food to the table. There was half a leg of lamb in a light looking gravy. Two medium sized potatoes roasted in corn husks and a small loaf of bread steamed next to a dish of butter. A mug of cider, a mug of ale, and a large pitcher of water were the last items moved to the table.

Bertus scooped up the tray to carry it under one arm, and as he was halfway out the door asked if Kevon would need anything else. When Kevon shook his head, the young servant nodded curtly, closed the door, and was gone.

Kevon was not sure if he imagined the flash of a grin on Bertus' face as the door closed. He thought about it for a moment and dismissed it as absurd. He had just pulled his chair up to the folding table and sat down when there was another knock at the door. Mildly annoyed, he rose to answer it. "What do you need Bert..."

Kevon stopped the door in mid-swing as well as mid-sentence.

"May I come in?" Marelle asked quietly.

"Of... course." Kevon was unable to mask his surprise at seeing her. He opened the door the rest of the way and gestured for her to enter. "Have you eaten?" he asked, indicating the set table with more than enough food for two.

"I haven't, thank you," she answered, moving over to the table and lifting the top plate off to put on the other side of the table.

Marelle quickly made herself at home, scooting another chair over, seating herself, and moving the mug of ale closer to her side of the table. "Are you joining me?" she asked, taking one of the baked potatoes.

"Yes, I..." Kevon took his seat, confused by Marelle's sudden appearance and nearly wanton familiarity at this late hour. "Why are you here? Not... that I mind, really, but it doesn't..."

"Seem proper?" Marelle smiled at Kevon over her mug and

then drank deeply.

"I was going to say 'make sense', but yes, 'seem proper' works just as nicely." Kevon sighed and took the other potato. "Your father said you would be contacting me sometime tomorrow."

"Oh, that," Marelle said dismissively. "We chanced upon the Myrnar liaison between here and the house. Our meeting with them is at lunchtime tomorrow. I'll send a messenger over tomorrow morning to tell you that, and I'll be over mid-morning to pick you up for the meeting."

"Messenger?" Kevon asked, puzzled. "But you already told…"

Kevon's mouth went suddenly dry and he took a swig of cider. "Your father didn't send you to tell me about the meeting, did he?"

Marelle's eyes widened in an expression of feigned innocence. "I'm at home, sound asleep." Her eyes narrowed and she began to smile. The muted glow of the candle made the green in her eyes seem to dance. Kevon felt the blood drain from his face.

"Well," Kevon said weakly, "I'm glad you came to have dinner with me. I've grown used to taking meals with you… It'll be disappointing when it ends."

"I'm not particularly hungry," Marelle commented, and took another drink of her ale.

"Is there something I need to know about the meeting tomorrow? How I should act or anything?" Kevon asked hopefully.

"Nothing we can't discuss on the ride from here to there," Marelle answered, clearly amused.

"All right." Kevon put his fork down and looked Marelle square in the eyes. "Just so we're clear, why *are* you here?"

A hurt look began spreading across Marelle's face. "If you need to ask…" She turned away.

"I don't need to ask. I have to *know*!" Kevon responded, his voice cracking.

Marelle turned back and leaned slightly over the table,

reaching out and taking Kevon's hand. "But you do know."

Kevon looked down at their hands, unable to face Marelle. "I... don't want you to get hurt."

"Then don't hurt me," Marelle laughed.

"No, that's not what I..." Kevon looked up to see Marelle grinning mischievously at him. "There are at *least* two Mages I have to see dead before I feel safe. I have to live with that." He pulled his hand free from Marelle's grasp. "You don't."

Marelle's grin faded and her gaze lowered to her empty hand lying on the table. She sighed deeply and Kevon could see her eyes glistening with as-yet unformed tears.

Unwilling to watch, Kevon looked down and away, covering his eyes and resting his head on his hand, struggling to remain in control of himself. He saw bits of movement, heard Marelle rise and walk around the table and toward the door. Kevon forced himself to remain still. He was afraid that if he stood out of courtesy, he would be unable to keep himself from asking her to stay.

Kevon jumped slightly as he felt Marelle's arms circle around beneath his from behind. He shivered a bit when her unbound hair trailed across the back of his neck as she leaned in close to his ear.

"Tell me to leave," Marelle whispered softly, her lips brushing against Kevon's earlobe as she spoke. "And I will."

Kevon remained immobilized as Marelle's hands clasped together on his chest and she drew herself tighter to him. Three large, warm tears fell onto his neck and his resolve shattered. With one hand, he covered hers on his chest. With the other, he reached up to cradle the side of her face as she nestled into his.

"I may have to run," he said, easing his head back to catch a glimpse of her, "But I could *never* send you away."

Marelle began disentangling her arms and drew Kevon up and around into her embrace.

CHAPTER 17

Kevon woke late the next morning to a loud knock on the door. Panicked, he reached for Marelle, but she was not there. A folded sheet of paper lay on the bedside table. Kevon ignored it for the moment and threw on his trousers and under-tunic before rushing to the door.

"Bertus?" he asked as he opened the door a crack.

"Unhappily, yes, it is I." The attendant winked at Kevon. "I do have food, though."

Kevon opened the door and Bertus whisked in with breakfast. Kevon was more than slightly disappointed to see there was only enough for one.

Bertus swiftly exchanged the dishes from the tray with the used ones on the table, humming a merry tune under his breath. When he turned to go, Kevon handed him two of the silvers from the bedside table. Bertus grinned, nodded, and exited quietly.

Kevon sat to eat. He took a few bites of everything, but it was all still very hot. He rested his chin on his upturned palms and started waiting for the food to cool.

Images, flashes of memory and ghostly sensations began intruding on his silent meditation. The night had been full of softness and warmth, exploration and enthusiasm. Kevon remembered one thing more clearly than any of the delightfully hazy others. Several times, he had felt the same kind of calm, clear assurance that he had only ever felt before when completing a spell.

Kevon sighed loudly, and picked the paper up from the table. He unfolded the note and smiled as he read it.

Until you secure my hand
Be content with my heart

Marelle

Kevon traced a few letters with the tip of his finger. Marelle's handwriting was small and neat, well-practiced from writing in business ledgers and such, no doubt. He rubbed his eyes self-consciously for a few moments before folding the note and slipping it into a pocket. He sniffed, still smiling, and started eating again. Pushing all thought of Marelle aside for a moment, he started planning. If things went well today, the next few days would be full of frantic activity. He would have to get re-provisioned for the trip to the Inner Cities. Kevon could think of at least half a dozen things he would need immediately, and there were probably more that he would need eventually.

Kevon turned his thoughts to the upcoming trade negotiation. Rhulcan would undoubtedly be there. He wondered if he would have any chances to spend even a moment alone with Marelle. The prospect of holding her hand or stealing a kiss was far more exciting than the fortune that would soon be his. Kevon shook himself out of his all-too-pleasant daydreams and finished his breakfast.

After using the washbasin to clean himself up a bit, he finished dressing and stowed his extra belongings in the chest at the foot of the bed. He took only his spare coins, the pouch with the pearl, and as an afterthought fastened the pewter amulet around his neck as a reminder of his quest.

Kevon left the room and wandered downstairs to wait.

By the time he reached the front desk, the messenger from Marelle was already arriving. Kevon identified himself, received the message he already knew, and tipped the runner a silver.

The meeting was two hours away. Figuring time for the ride and a little more to be safe, Kevon supposed he had about an hour to explore. He opened the door and followed the messenger out into the bustling streets of Eastport.

The streets were considerably louder than when they had arrived last evening. Most of the street vendors had younger assistants extolling the virtues of their wares for all to hear.

Kevon walked up the street until the inn's sign was almost out of sight, and then ducked into the nearest shop to get away from the crowds.

The counter that separated him from the rest of the shop was two paces from the front wall, chest high, and ran the entire width of the room. Behind it were racks of displayed weapons, tools, and accessories. Kevon could not help but smile.

A grim looking man with a scar that puckered its way across his nose and halfway down his cheek strode up to the counter across from Kevon. "What do you want?" the man asked, eyeing Kevon critically.

"Well, I might need a sword later, but I suppose I could use a good knife in the meantime," Kevon answered.

The man turned to gesture at a display of assorted knives, and Kevon noticed that half of the man's right ear was missing. "These over here are about all I can sell you that won't be taxed," he said. "Anything bigger, you'll pay about what it cost you every year if you travel much. That is, unless you're a Guildsman..." the man turned to look more closely at Kevon. "Which I'm sure you ain't."

"You're right, I'm not," Kevon nodded. "I will be traveling quite a bit very soon though. I could use something for dressing out game, and if it would come in handy in a fight as well... all the better."

The man smiled, and took the knife Kevon had been glancing at off its hanging pegs. It was similar to the sword that Kevon had taken from the fallen Warrior. The blade was nearly eight inches long, and it was wider than most of the other knives in the display. The back edge was unusually thick, and the hilt was wrapped in the same fashion.

"Do you know where this came from?" Kevon asked.

"It's a sturdy blade, if that's what you're asking," the man grumbled.

"No, but it looks very familiar... May I?"

The man nodded and held the knife out, hilt first.

Kevon braced himself and accepted it, making sure to brush the crosspiece with his fingertips first thing so that he could relax while holding the knife afterward. The now familiar shock tore through him, but he barely flinched. He tested the edge with his thumb, and sighted along several angles. He gripped the knife by its handle and twisted his wrist around a few times to get a feel for it. It seemed heavier than a simple knife, but he got the same feeling he had when first handling the Warrior's sword. A feeling of *rightness*.

"Yes, I want this knife. Do you know anything about where this came from?" Kevon asked again.

"No, but it's got to be a southern blade. There's enough steel in that for three good knives."

Kevon gave the man a questioning look.

"Smiths near the mines in the south have more iron to work with," the man explained. "Seems wasteful to me."

"How much for the knife?" Kevon asked, eager to own the already familiar-feeling blade.

The man grunted in amusement. "Twelve silver. Twice, at least, what any of the others over there would cost."

Kevon placed the knife on the counter. The man moved to pick it up to replace it on its display pegs, but Kevon reached for his money pouch.

"Nine," Kevon muttered dejectedly.

"For nine you'd get no belt or sheath," the man said sternly.

"Nine is all I have until later today, maybe tomorrow," Kevon thought aloud. "I might need one or two for other expenses." He stared hard at the coins in his hand.

"Sheath, no belt," the man countered.

Finally aware he was in a negotiation, Kevon smiled. "Throw in the belt and in the next day or two we'll talk about swords."

The man behind the counter looked closely at Kevon trying to decide if he was telling the truth. "Done," he said, finally. He rummaged behind the counter briefly and produced the sheath and a serviceable leather belt. "You buy a sword and I just might remember who I bought the knife from." He turned back to the saddle he was repairing.

Kevon opened his mouth to say something, but decided against it. He could not help but grin as he strapped his belt and knife on and drew his cloak tight to conceal them. He would be back.

He edged back out into the crowd and worked his way back to the inn. He did not feel comfortable exploring further with an empty purse, and decided to wait for the meeting in the *Maiden*'s common room.

Kevon had no more than sat down when Bertus happened by and asked if he wanted an early lunch. When Kevon told him he was just waiting around, Bertus nodded and strode off. He returned shortly with two mugs of ale and a small plate of cut fruit.

Kevon thanked him, and Bertus nodded politely before disappearing back into the kitchen. He picked up a piece of a sweet-smelling, stringy fruit, and was about to taste it when he felt a hand on his shoulder.

"You're not watching the entrance," Carlo rumbled, thumping Kevon upside the head.

"Good morning, Carlo," Kevon said, rubbing the sore spot and checking for lumps. "Have a seat, and a drink."

Carlo picked up the full mug and took a swallow. He pointed to a corner table.

After the two had seated themselves, Kevon spoke.

"So, what are you going to do now?" he asked.

"I've collected my pay from Rhulcan. That gives me enough to live on for a while." Carlo looked at Kevon. "Are you still headed to East Thaddington on this journey of yours?"

"Yes," Kevon answered. "As soon as I get the money from the sale, I'll spend a day or two gearing up, then head for the Inner Cities."

Carlo nodded. "I suspected as much. I have some things to take care of, myself." The mercenary paused, and then looked directly at Kevon. "If you'd like, meet me here later and I'll show you something that might make your trip easier."

The Mercenary ignored the puzzled look on Kevon's face. He stood, finished off his ale, and thanked Kevon for the drink. As quickly as he had appeared, Carlo stalked out of the common room and was gone.

Kevon sat, nibbling at the different fruits on the plate. He was almost done with his ale when Marelle arrived to look for him, but it took a few moments for him to recognize her.

She was wearing a soft blue dress that swept along just above the floor, and a shimmering green shawl that matched her eyes. Her normally straight hair now fell about her in soft waves. She noticed Kevon as he stood to walk over to her, and smiled so perfectly that Kevon could feel his heart beating in his throat.

The background chatter of the room faded. All Kevon wanted to do was make it across the room to her as quickly as possible, without looking like he was rushing. He threaded his way through the tables, feeling more lightheaded than one ale merited.

"Shall we go?" Marelle asked, her picturesque smile transformed to an impish grin. "Do you have the item?"

Kevon patted his tunic pocket and nodded.

Marelle turned and walked back down the L-shaped hallway that led from the common room to the lobby, Kevon in tow. As soon as they rounded the turn, Marelle swept around and trapped Kevon in a light embrace against the wall. After a few moments of playful kissing, she backed away, put her finger to her lips, and continued out.

Rhulcan was waiting outside the inn, fretting. He was just finishing reprimanding some passerby who had come too close to the carriage he was standing by. The driver atop the delicate looking wagon sat, looking rather bored.

"Ah, very good," Rhulcan said, edging closer to Kevon and

Marelle, tugging slightly on the reins of the horse he was holding. "I trust everything is in order?"

"Yes, father." Marelle replied with a sigh. "We're all here, in plenty of time, and everything is ready to proceed."

"Very well, very well," Rhulcan trailed off, looking somewhat distracted. "What do you say we meet back here this evening for dinner?" he asked, looking at Kevon.

"That's fine," Kevon replied, looking confused.

Marelle steered Kevon by the arm to the carriage, and Rhulcan climbed onto his horse. Kevon helped Marelle into the coach first, and shot a questioning look at Rhulcan.

"Good luck," Rhulcan called, and turned his mount into the flow of street traffic.

Kevon pulled himself up into the carriage and closed the door. "Wow," he said, eyeing the craftsmanship of the conveyance. "This is nice."

"We keep it for special occasions, when appearances are important," Marelle said, rolling her eyes. "I don't know if it will ever earn back what it cost." She seemed lost in thought for a moment. "Father won't sell it because it was Mother's idea to buy it," she added quietly.

Kevon remembered from earlier talks with Marelle that her mother had died when she was about a year old. He leaned across the space between the facing seats to clasp one of Marelle's hands between his. The carriage lurched into motion and Kevon nearly fell from his seat, bringing a faint smile to Marelle's suddenly darkened face.

After the carriage had been moving for a while and the pace had evened out, Marelle gave Kevon's hand a squeeze and withdrew hers.

"All right," she began. "Father has decided to allow me to act in his stead, on your behalf, for these negotiations."

"That's great!" Kevon exclaimed. "This is really a big step for you, isn't it?"

Marelle nodded. "I'll get half the commission, plus the experience and recognition with a major economic power."

"So, why is your father not here doing this himself, or at least here supervising?" Kevon asked.

"He's taking care of the other trade goods from this trip, and reprovisioning for the next one," Marelle said, frowning. "He can get everything else done today if he lets me do this."

"Oh." Kevon's smile turned down to match Marelle's sour look. "So you're..."

"Leaving tomorrow," Marelle finished.

Kevon sat, stunned for a moment until a bump of the carriage snapped him out of it. "I thought there would be more time..."

"For us?" Marelle asked, staring blankly out the coach's window. "So did I, but... Maybe it's better this way. I won't be here to keep you from your responsibilities. And you won't have to worry about endangering me..." She wiped her eyes. "It's for the best."

Kevon knew it was practical, knew it was safe. Even though every logical argument pointed to this solution, Kevon could not help but feel that it was *wrong*.

"So... where are you going this time?" he asked.

"South, along the coast," Marelle answered. "It's earlier than we normally take this route, but it's the most profitable." Marelle smiled at Kevon slightly. "If I invest my own money wisely this trip, I'll have enough to buy my own shop here in town when we return."

"And give up the life of a traveling Merchant?" Kevon asked, teasingly.

"I get to sleep in my own bed roughly four weeks a year," Marelle answered, turning her gaze back inside to Kevon. "Having a reason to stay here would give me back my home."

Kevon nodded, his thoughts turning back to his own home. He almost wished everything were as it was before he left. He hoped that his mother and sister were all right, that Holten had not decided to mistreat them because of him.

Kevon looked up to see Marelle staring expectantly at him. He furrowed his brow, thinking. "So... two seasons from now, you'll likely be here permanently?"

Marelle smiled and nodded slowly.

"Oh," Kevon replied, scratching his chin in contemplation. "That's good to know."

"How about you?" Marelle asked. "Where do you think you'll be by that time?"

"At this point, I'm more concerned about *how* I'll be," Kevon answered with a shrug. "Hopefully alive."

"Have you thought any more about just running away?"

"No," Kevon answered flatly. "He's far too powerful. I've seen him travel long distances in an instant with very little help. I've also seen him control animals from far away, luring them to him for food." Kevon paused. "Who's to say he couldn't do the same to me?"

"Oh," Marelle said, disappointment tingeing her voice.

A moment later, Marelle gasped in surprise and flushed in embarrassment. "We're almost there!"

"And?" Kevon asked.

"There are a few things you need to know about dealing with the myrnar," Marelle groaned. "And now there's no time to tell you."

"I can follow your lead, that's why you're here, right?" Kevon asked. "Are there any extremely important things I should know?"

"Don't stare!" Marelle blurted. "Whatever you do!"

"What?" Kevon asked.

"There are mermaids at every negotiation. They think it helps to have them as spokespersons," Marelle explained. "They're probably right. They're very attractive, and don't wear much to cover up. They like being looked at," she added.

"So, why shouldn't I stare?" Kevon teased.

"The mermen get very jealous," Marelle answered. "Many deals have fallen through because someone couldn't tear his eyes away from a mermaid."

"All right, I'll do my best." Kevon said. "Anything else?"

"Your price," Marelle continued. "Father checked around,

the prices for this size and quality of pearl have dropped. You'll probably only get about thirty gold for it now."

"Why is that?" Kevon asked.

"Fewer shipwrecks recently? Myrnar treasuries drying up?" Marelle offered. "It's hard to say."

"Whoa!" The driver called out to the horses, and the carriage rolled to a halt.

Kevon got out first so he could help Marelle out of the coach. When they were both clear and the driver pulled away, Kevon turned to take in the view.

The sea stretched all the way to the horizon ahead of them. The circular cove's shape was visible from here, the fingers of land reaching out on both sides. The bay itself was sprinkled with high-masted sailing ships, most still with their sails furled, rocking in the warm afternoon breeze. On some of the nearer vessels, Kevon could see deckhands, bare from the waist up, scurrying about, and moving cargo around.

If Kevon had not been impressed by the normal goings on of the busy port, the building he and Marelle approached was awe-inspiring. The doorway of the building, as well as some of the structure around it, reminded Kevon of the *Maiden*'s construction. Kevon understood now from seeing some of the ships up close that the *Maiden* was built to resemble a ship, probably from materials salvaged from them. But this building was quite different.

The wood, marble, and brick gave way to a different cut of brick the further away from the entry you looked. It seemed a creamy, off-white color, more porous than the red brick. Near the edge of the building, the material made up the structure entirely. The sections were larger, and billowed like frozen clouds. The strange material also extended into the water to form the foundation.

"Impressive, isn't it?" Marelle asked. "I've never been inside before. Neither has father."

The doors creaked open and a portly gentleman squinted at them before speaking.

"Mistress Marelle?" he called.

"Yes," she answered, quickening her pace down the cobbled pathway to the building, Kevon directly behind.

The man at the door huffed and wiped the sweat from his brow before shaking both Kevon and Marelle's hands. "I'm Alnam, Chief Liaison to the Myrnar," he asserted. "You must be Kevon," he continued, stepping back a pace to look Kevon over.

Kevon did not like the way the pudgy little man was smirking as he sized him up, and was just about to say something when Marelle stepped ahead of him.

"Gentle Alnam," she said politely, curtseying slightly. "We are eager to meet with the trade representatives so that we can determine if we can do business."

"*If you*?" Alnam sputtered, then regained his composure and mopped his brow again. "Very well. I shall see if the envoys have arrived." He motioned for the two to go into a room just off the entrance lobby.

Kevon followed Marelle into the room. His murmur of appreciation echoed Marelle's sharp intake of breath at the sights the room offered.

"The coral on the outside is beautiful," she said, "But nothing like this."

As Kevon's eyes adjusted to the change of lighting, he began to see more and more of the true artistry worked into the building. Some of the white coral that made up the exterior of the building was present here, where it flowed into ornate benches that were part of the walls.

Kevon was not sure if the rest of the coral were dyed, or if the color were natural. Either way, the effect was breathtaking. Scenes of underwater life in raised contours and vivid hues melted into each other all around the room's walls.

"Now would be a good time to practice not staring," Marelle jibed as Kevon's gaze locked on a scene of a mermaid.

Kevon flushed and looked away before realizing that Marelle was studying the scene intently as well. "They really don't cover up very much, do they?" he asked.

"Lucky those ferns were there," Marelle answered, giggling.

"Ahem." Alnam cleared his throat in the hallway behind Kevon and Marelle. "The trade representatives have arrived, and await negotiations in the Tidal Room."

"Thank you, Alnam." Marelle turned and smiled. "Lead on."

The liaison led the pair down a long hallway toward the back of the building. At the end of the corridor, two large, thick wooden doors stood open to the room beyond.

The room was circular, and Kevon thought that half of the chamber must have been able to seat well over a hundred people. The other half was water. Some of the room's lighting came from the half-circle of sea that was the far end of the room. Light reflected off the brilliant white sand that lay beneath the surface. Other shafts of light streamed through vents in the domelike ceiling, striking large crystal formations that refracted back up, resulting in a soft glow that cast few, if any, shadows.

The path down to the water was a straight, gentle stairway, wide enough for the three to walk abreast. Every fourth stair, carved coral benches followed the half-circle curve of the room to the railing that bordered the middle of the chamber, overlooking the ocean. The focal point was the table in the very center. It was not large, perhaps eight feet across, but it was the only place in the room that the railing did not separate the two halves.

Alnam continued down the stairs to the bottom and led Kevon and Marelle to the table. "Please, be seated," he said, gesturing to the chairs arranged around the near side of the table.

Kevon helped Marelle with her chair, and then seated himself.

Alnam took a seat next to the railing. He smiled at Kevon and Marelle, and fidgeted for a few moments.

There was a sudden swirling of water, and the myrnar surfaced. Marelle had been right. There was a mermaid in the trade delegation.

Kevon tried to get a good look at them quickly without staring. As the two myrnar approached the table, they rose further above the waterline, and the sinuous motion they used for swimming became more pronounced.

The merman swam in the lead. He looked twice Kevon's age, bare-chested, and physically intimidating. Muscles rippled visibly from below his thick neck down to the point where the brownish-pink of his skin gave way to the sleek grey of his lower body.

As the two neared the table, the merman stopped and held position in the water while the mermaid circled around and grasped the table's edge. She slid sideways a bit and sat down. The merman approached and did the same to sit directly across from Kevon.

Up close, Kevon could see differences that he had not noticed immediately. The myrnar's heads were narrower than those of a human, making their bodies look broader than they really were. Their noses started further up their foreheads, and sat higher above their mouths. Their mouths were wider, and their lips were the same grey as their lower torsos.

Kevon felt a mix of disappointment and fascination. The myrnar were certainly not the half-man, half-fish creatures from stories. However, seeing the similarities and the exotic differences was very exciting. As the merfolk sat, Kevon found himself wondering what they had to use for chairs on their side of the table. He decided against peeking underneath to investigate.

"Shall we begin?" Alnam asked, sweeping a glace around the table.

The myrnar nodded stiffly, grinning as they had since they reached the table.

"May we see the item in question?" the mermaid asked, her melodious voice rising clearly above the lapping noises of the surf below.

Marelle nodded to Kevon, and he took out the pouch with

the pearl and undid the drawstring. He poured the pearl out into his hand, looked at it a moment, and stood to lean out over the table to hand it to the mermaid.

The touch of the mermaid's fingers as she took the pearl was surprising. Rather than feeling like skin, even wet skin, her fingertips felt... The best description Kevon could imagine was damp, spongy leather.

The mermaid examined the pearl. She held it up and turned it to examine the whole surface, taking special note of the flawed discoloration. She trilled a sharp note, and showed it to the merman. He looked, thrummed a gruff response, and nodded, grinning all the while. Kevon began to wonder if they smiled to keep their mouths open to breathe.

"We are prepared to offer fifty gold for this pearl," the mermaid said softly.

Kevon's eyes widened in shock, and he felt Marelle's hand squeezing his leg.

"We will consider your offer," Marelle responded. "The Elven envoy I spoke with earlier expressed some interest in purchasing the pearl as well."

In an instant, the mermaid's exotic beauty was transformed into a vision of horror. Flaps of skin on her neck as large as an outstretched hand flared forward; the red-rimmed appendages made it look as if her face had doubled in size. Her lips pulled back as she hissed, displaying at least two rows of formidable looking teeth. She lunged forward, planting her arms palm down near the center of the table, aimed straight at Marelle.

"*The elves will NOT have it!*" she rasped loudly, all attempts at humanlike diplomacy apparently abandoned. Alnam whimpered and fainted, slumping to the side into the chair between himself and Marelle.

Marelle's grip tightened on Kevon's leg, but she jumped no more than he had. "Compose yourself," she growled angrily at the mermaid.

The myrnar hissed once more for good measure. She then

took a deep breath and folded her neck flaps back, craning her neck back and forth to settle them back into their places. As soon as they disappeared from sight, she closed her mouth and eyes, and slid back into her seat. After a moment, she opened her eyes, and the ever-present mer-smile returned to her face. She made as if to speak, but the merman touched her arm and she shrank back.

"Forgive my mate. She has a... personal interest in this matter." The merman sat forward and looked toward Alnam's seat. "Shall we wait for the liaison to recover?"

"Do you suppose he'll stay once he does?" asked Marelle.

"Your mate is wise for someone so young," the merman said, looking at Kevon.

"She's n..." Kevon started. He peered down at Alnam, who was drooling on the chair, snoring softly. "Yes. Yes she is."

"You have not spoken with the elves, have you?" the merman asked Marelle.

"No." Marelle blushed at the revelation of her bluff nearly as much as that of being Kevon's mate. "The offer was so much more than we were expecting that I thought I could get you to pay more."

The merman made a strained gurgling noise that could only be laughter. "Know now that we will not return the pearl to you. It was undoubtedly stolen; its owner would not have given it freely."

Kevon buried his head in his hands. "Of course. It would have to be stolen."

"Does this surprise you?" the merman asked, as Kevon sat back upright.

"Nothing about the man that gave me this pearl will surprise me from now on." Kevon sighed. "I have incurred expenses in bringing the pearl here. Marelle can detail these to you. They are all I ask. I'm sorry." Kevon stood and walked up the stairway and down the hall to the front of the building.

As he was just about to leave, Kevon realized that he didn't know the way back to the inn, and didn't have a copper to his name. He turned aside to the waiting room and sat on a bench to wait for Marelle.

Another crime Holten must pay for, Kevon thought angrily, drawing the dagger from under his cloak to test the edge with his thumb. The shock of touching the blade was numbed by his fury.

Marelle poked her head inside the room, grinning. "Are you all right?" she asked.

Kevon sighed. "I should have known better. There's no way I can ever..."

The pouch plunked down in front of him.

"What is...?" he began.

"Your reward," Marelle laughed. "And they paid even more because you're *nice.*"

He picked up the pouch. It felt heavy. "How much is this?"

"Eighty." Marelle smiled. "I already took twenty out for our fee." She walked in and sat down next to Kevon. "Father decided weeks ago that he would waive expenses because of what you did for Carlo... and because I shot you with a crossbow."

"Um. I don't know what to say."

"Well, you could start by going back in there," she said. "The myrnar asked if you would speak with them a bit more, alone."

Kevon pocketed the pouch of gold. "They've paid well for my time, I suppose I should."

"They made it clear you weren't obligated..." Marelle offered.

"But I am. Because of Holten."

Marelle nodded. "I'll wait here."

Kevon walked back down the long corridor. Near the entrance to the Tidal Room, a frightened-looking Alnam hurried past him, avoiding his gaze. Kevon did not see the myrnar at the table, but by the time he reached the bottom of the stairs they had resurfaced and taken their seats again.

"You wanted to see me?"

The merman spoke. "We would like to know all you can

tell us about where you acquired the Sea Star."

"It was given to me by a man, a Magi, who I thought was a friend." Kevon pounded his fist on the table. "I've since learned otherwise. He tried to have me killed. If he's wronged you as well…"

"My sister…" the mermaid whispered. "Princess of the Sea Realm."

"She's been missing for three years," the merman explained. "With the return of the Sea Star in this manner, we must assume the worst. And although this is a sad truth, it will restore some order to our lives. My mate will ascend and assume control of the Realm. But this Magi…"

"I will deal with him. I have to…" Kevon's fist clenched and turned white in spots. "It's the only way I can be safe. Your revenge is already my duty."

The mermaid removed one of the shell necklaces that hung around her neck and slid it across the table to Kevon. "Call on us if you have need. Your fortune is joined with ours now."

Kevon rose and bowed, sliding the necklace over his head. "Thank you, your highness."

There was a soft splashing noise, and when Kevon looked back up, the myrnar were gone. He tucked the necklace inside his tunic by the Warrior's amulet and walked back up the stairs.

Marelle was still in the waiting room, convincing Alnam that he had passed out from the heat and had a bad dream. She smiled at Kevon as he entered the room. "All done?"

Kevon nodded and waited for Marelle to finish with Alnam.

The coach was waiting out front when they exited the building. Once securely inside, Kevon asked Marelle about her plans. She launched half-heartedly into descriptions of trades and purchases she was likely to make at a few stops on the coastal route, but she seemed distracted.

"Oh, if you are leaving tomorrow…" Kevon interrupted, "I'll need the sword I was carrying that you were holding for me."

Marelle nodded. "It's behind your seat cushion."

Kevon reached back and pulled on the cushion to reveal a hidden compartment. He decided to leave it until he was ready to go, and replaced the cushion with a firm shove.

"I'll probably leave tomorrow, too," Kevon told Marelle. "Nothing for me here once you leave."

Marelle nodded glumly.

"Hopefully, in a year or two this will all be over. I just need to figure out how to deal with Gurlin and Holten…"

Kevon stopped as he heard Marelle sniff back a tear. "What's wrong?"

"I'm just worried about what might happen to you when you find those Magi. I've seen what can happen…"

"They don't know I'm coming," Kevon said soothingly. "I won't fight them unless I know I can win. I've already got some ideas…"

The carriage rumbled to a halt. Outside the window, Kevon could see the front of the *Maiden of the Bay*. He reached behind the seat cushion and winced as his magic left him when he grabbed the hilt. He drew out the sword and closed the compartment.

"Well," Kevon said, "Good luck with your trading and everything…"

Marelle leaned forward, wrapped her arms around his neck, and drew him forward into a tight embrace. "Just come back to me," she whispered in his ear.

"As soon as I can." Kevon squeezed her in return and they disentangled just as the driver opened the door. Kevon climbed down, careful of the bared blade, and turned back to Marelle.

The driver moved to close the door, but Marelle held it open.

"I'm sure my father will be pleased with this transaction," she said, gazing at Kevon. "I know I…"

Marelle stopped speaking, and frowned. "Appearances be damned," she announced, hopping out of the carriage, leaning on Kevon for support. "You already know how pleased *I am* about this," she murmured. She wrapped her arms around Kevon and rested her cheek on his chest. Still holding the sword, Kevon returned the embrace carefully with one arm. He closed his eyes and focused on the moment; the feel of Marelle's breathing, the floral scent of her hair against the faint salt tang of the city, the dainty curve of her ear.

The driver cleared his throat, and Kevon released Marelle. She drew back slowly, moistened eyes locked on Kevon.

"I wish…" he began.

"Don't." Marelle whispered. "Don't wish. Find a way."

The driver helped Marelle back into the coach and closed the door. He gave Kevon a disapproving look before climbing onto the front of the carriage and urging the team back into the street.

Kevon stood, watching silently as the coach rolled out of sight. He thought a moment, and tucked the blade underneath his cloak. Holding the sword close to his side, he headed for the weapon shop.

"Back already?" The scarred shopkeeper put down the bandolier he was working on and walked over to the counter across from Kevon. "Ready to talk about swords now?"

"Yes." Kevon pulled the Warrior's blade from behind his cloak. "And a scabbard for this one." He gripped the blade and held it out for the shopkeeper to inspect.

"Mmm. Much like the knife. I don't have anything that would fit this right now. I could make something in a day or two…"

"I'm in a hurry," Kevon interrupted. "I'll just buy another sword and have a scabbard made for this later."

"Now, now…" the shopkeeper motioned for Kevon to calm down. "A good customer might get moved to the top of the list… I could have it done by morning?"

"That's acceptable," Kevon agreed. "What kind of sword would you recommend I get?"

After a short discussion Kevon settled on one of the nicer sabers. It was light, sturdy, and longer than the Warrior's sword.

"Three gold for the sword and the extra scabbard," the shopkeeper began, looking at Kevon, expecting a counter-offer.

"Done." Kevon plunked three coins down on the counter. "Tell me what you know about my sword."

The man did not know as much about the blade as Kevon had hoped. The knife he'd bought earlier had been sold to him by a young Warrior who had needed some extra money for traveling. The shopkeeper did not remember seeing the sword with the Warrior, or what he looked like. He did remember the man said he'd traveled up the coastal road from the Southern Frontier.

Kevon strapped his saber on and thanked the shopkeeper as he left. He went back to his room at the *Maiden* and left both swords and the knife with his gathered belongings before heading down to the common room.

Bertus met him on the stairway, and hurried ahead to the kitchen to get something for Kevon to eat.

Well after Kevon had finished his meal and was on his second mug of ale, he spotted Carlo. The mercenary had made it almost to his table unnoticed, possibly by using the kitchen entrance.

"Better," Carlo admitted. "I'd been waiting in the kitchen for five minutes for a chance to get this close. Much better."

Kevon laughed and shook his head. "All right. So what is this about?"

"Best if I showed you. Come along."

Kevon took another drink and left the rest to follow Carlo out the front of the inn.

Carlo strode purposefully down the streets, the crowd parting just ahead of him. He sidestepped occasionally to avoid those who were not watchful. Kevon followed closely in the older man's wake, trying to match stride and demeanor, earning smiles from some and a wide berth from others.

They wove their way through the streets and narrow alleys toward the harbor. One neighborhood they passed through was larger than Laston, and Kevon guessed housed more than ten times the people his hometown did. The buildings here seemed to be older and not as well kept as those nearer the main road. Carlo headed for a large blocky building that seemed to be in much better shape than any other in the area.

Carlo pounded on the sturdy-looking door. A sliding panel in the door opened, and he pulled something from inside his tunic to show to the man inside. The slide closed and Kevon could hear the door being unbarred.

The door opened and a burly man wearing a large sword strapped to his back gestured for Carlo to enter. "Who's he?" he asked Carlo as he walked in.

"He's with me."

The man nodded and barred the door after Kevon entered.

Tapestries and wall hangings crowded the brick and wood hallway, scenes of knights and castles, some more fanciful than Kevon could believe.

After passing several closed doors, the hallway opened into an area that resembled an inn's common room. Mismatched tables and chairs were grouped together, men sat around eating, drinking, and carousing. Servants hovered around, refilling mugs and carrying away empty plates.

Where a stage or a central fireplace would be in a typical inn, was another space that took up nearly half of the large room. Racks of weapons, real and wooden, lined the back and side walls of the room. The floor was wooden except for the brick-lined square of sand that took up perhaps two-thirds of that side of the room.

Where...? Kevon looked around at the men. Most wore silver medallions, and Kevon saw one or two with gold ones. They bore the raised sword symbol of the Warrior's Guild.

Carlo turned, and seeing Kevon's expression, laughed softly. "Figured it out, eh?" The mercenary sat at an empty table in the middle of the room, not making any effort to monitor entrances.

Kevon sat across the table from him, and was about to ask

what they were doing when he saw Carlo's medallion bared over his tunic. It was gold.

"You boys hungry?" one of the serving maids asked, playfully ruffling Carlo's hair.

"The boy must be. Spending a lot of time with his mouth open lately," Carlo rumbled in amusement, slapping the table.

Kevon closed his mouth. "I'm fine," he mumbled. "I could use something to drink."

"I'm for that!" Carlo agreed loudly.

The serving girl winked and disappeared into a side room.

"Back so soon, Carlo?" Another man, far younger than Carlo, wearing a gold medallion, sat down at their table.

"Yep. Change of plans. You know how flighty Merchants can be."

The man nodded. "Who's your friend?"

"Student," Carlo corrected. "Kevon. He's here for Trial."

The newcomer tsk'd softly. "No Novices here today. There's a few on watch, but they won't be here until late, if then."

Carlo sighed. "Kind of in a hurry."

The man tilted his head toward a younger man who was chatting with a serving maid. "There's Waine."

At the mention of his name, the young man stood, whispered something to the maid, and strolled over to the table.

"Anything I can help with, Blademaster...s?" Waine asked, tripping over his tongue as he saw Carlo also wore the gold medallion.

"Waine, this is Kevon. He's here for Trial," the Blademaster smirked slightly.

"Hey, good luck to you then," Waine smiled at Kevon and raised his mug. "Who's he facing?" he asked, looking around the room.

"How about you?" the Blademaster asked.

"I'm a Seeker, not a Novice," Waine laughed. "Lem will be here in a few hours, it can wait 'til then."

"They're in a hurry, Waine," the Blademaster corrected.

"You can go easy on him."

"No, Marco." Carlo rumbled.

"Too rough for your boy, eh?" Marco said mockingly, smiling at Kevon.

"No." Carlo leaned forward. "Don't go easy on him."

Whoops of excitement and cries of approval thundered from the surrounding tables. Carlo and Marco stood, and Kevon followed suit. They wound their way through the crowd to the other side of the room.

Waine removed his boots, socks, and the light leather jacket he was wearing. He walked to the far wall and picked out a practice sword. He sat down at the far corner of the sandy pit and began wiggling his toes in the sand.

Kevon removed his boots, socks, and cloak. He folded the cloak neatly, sat it on a bench, and reached for one of the practice swords on a nearby rack.

"What is the meaning of this?" cried Marco. More angry shouts rang out and Kevon turned to see what was the matter.

He turned to see all of the hall's occupants glaring or shouting at *him.*

Carlo walked quickly over to Kevon and cuffed him upside the head. "What were you *thinking*?" he roared, snatching the Warrior's amulet from Kevon's chest. The leather strap broke, but not before cutting into Kevon's neck. "You have not earned the right!"

The crowd quieted somewhat, but dark murmurs still ran through the ranks.

"We will deal with this later," Carlo hissed loudly. "Get a sword!"

Kevon retrieved the sword he'd reached for earlier and padded back to Carlo's side near the sand pit.

"You're going to bleed," Carlo said softly. "Make sure he does too. He's more experienced than a Novice, but overconfident, and angry. Use that." Carlo shoved Kevon roughly into the pit.

Laughs, jeers, and assorted yells of 'Hurt him, Waine!',

'Pound his head in!', and other such inspirational cheers built into a dull roar.

Waine stood, grasped both ends of his sword, and stretched out a bit. He let one end go, whipped it around himself rapidly a few times, and stepped forward into a guarding stance.

Kevon took a few swings to get a feel for the weight and balance of the unfamiliar weapon. He calmed himself, evened out his breathing, and advanced.

Once Kevon closed within two sword lengths, Waine was upon him. The Seeker, having the advantages of reach, experience, and strength, pressed Kevon viciously. Kevon blocked the first two probing strikes with relative ease, but the third came faster than expected, rapping him on the knuckles. Kevon swore and shifted his grip an instant too slow to block a kick to the gut.

Waine whirled out and away as Kevon doubled over. He took a quick bow for the crowd, which whooped even louder. Grinning, he turned back to face Kevon, who was just starting to straighten back up. Waine launched into a series of attacks that used quick, short, sword swings and parries at close range to make openings that would admit the fist of his off-hand, or a maliciously thrown elbow.

Within the first three minutes, Kevon had more bruises than all of Carlo's lessons combined. He looked over to the side of the ring and saw Carlo drinking unconcernedly from a mug. The aside glance cost him an elbow to the mouth. He tasted blood, and his lip seared and throbbed all at once.

Waine stood back, sword forward but lowered, and contemplated his opponent.

Kevon pressed his fingers to his cut lower lip, inciting an uproar of insults from the rambunctious crowd. He wiped his fingers on his tunic, spat blood off to the side, and gripped his wooden sword again in both hands.

Waine raised his sword in an exaggerated salute, winked, and pressed forward once more.

Kevon smiled and shifted his own sword with the help

of the Movement rune he'd just formed. He quickly parried the three sword strokes from Waine's rush, and brought the wooden hilt down with blinding speed to knock down the elbow that was intended for his ribs. Reversing with the rebound force from the counterstrike, Kevon shifted back on his left foot and lashed out with his right fist, which still held the sword's hilt. He twisted his hand at the last second to smash into the side of Waine's head while parrying the follow-up stroke of the Seeker's attack.

The crowd quieted as Kevon shifted back on his left foot again to let Waine's momentum carry him stumbling past.

The Seeker spun around, wobbling slightly. He put a hand to the left side of his face and examined it quickly for traces of blood. Seeing none, he glared at Kevon, who had dropped back into his two-handed stance. Waine waited, thinking.

Remembering the wink that had been intended to throw his concentration, Kevon mimed a kiss in Waine's direction.

Snarling, the Seeker charged again.

Shutting out everything but his Art and his opponent, Kevon did not even hear Carlo's gruff bark of laughter at his taunt. The calm that Kevon felt deepened as he widened the focus of his Movement spell from his hands and sword to his whole body. With his mind, he made every part of his body move exactly as he wanted it to. He met the Seeker's charge with a sweeping block that stole the momentum from the next intended strike. Flicking his opponent's sword wide with the tip of his own, Kevon stepped inside and chopped downward near Waine's hand, knocking the practice sword to the ground.

The Seeker sidestepped in behind Kevon and shoved him forward. He ducked to avoid Kevon's one-handed backswing and recovered his sword. Waine backed away to a safe distance to rethink the situation.

Not knowing how long he could keep his Movement spell active, Kevon decided to attack. He advanced in a posture he had seen Carlo use when he practiced alone, body turned sideways and sword slanted across his body, ready for attack or defense at a moment's notice.

Waine tried to circle to one side, then the other, but Kevon adjusted accordingly as he approached. Waine made a few quick jabbing thrusts to try and pierce Kevon's guard, but Kevon deftly parried each attempt. Waine made another jab, toward the outside, and Kevon parried again. The motion of the parry overextended the younger man, and as he wobbled to recover, Waine struck at his weapon, disarming him.

Kevon moved toward to fallen weapon, but Waine stepped over it and kicked it backwards, shifting himself in between the challenger and his sword.

The crowd roared with laughter. Waine raised his sword in celebration, and began to take a bow.

Kevon was not done. Screaming defiantly, he lurched forward.

The Seeker moved to end it with a slash across Kevon's upper body. The already raised weapon flashed downward.

Kevon had counted on it. He checked his forward movement for an instant, and the tip of Waine's sword whistled past his face. Regaining speed with the help of his dwindling magical reserves, Kevon stepped inside Waine's sword reach and grabbed the hilt above where the Seeker gripped it. With all the strength he could muster, Kevon lifted and swung the downward pointed tip from right to left in front of him. As the end moved enough to allow it, Kevon stepped further in and past Waine, shifting his upper body even more to the left to either break the Seeker's hold on the weapon or unbalance him.

Waine's grip failed. The force of the improvised technique caused him to shuffle away a few steps. His sword arm twinged from the awkward angle of the sudden wrenching motion by Kevon. By the time he realized what was happening, it was too late.

Kevon pivoted once more, swinging the wrested weapon around full circle, heading straight for Waine's face.

The Seeker flinched back, turning away from the strike. The end of the sword grazed near his temple, where the previous blow had struck. Though not as painful or jarring as the first, Waine could feel the telltale burn of an open wound as soon as it hit. After he verified it by touch, he nodded to Kevon, who was leaning on the wooden sword, breathing hard. He then picked up Kevon's fallen practice blade, and walked over to exchange them.

"Well done." The Seeker grinned widely despite the blood flowing freely down the side of his face. He raised his voice and turned to the main body of the crowd, who murmured in confusion amongst themselves. "Let me be the first to welcome our new brother!"

Half a moment passed before enthusiastic shouts of welcome and encouragement erupted from all those assembled. The crowd spilled into the arena, jostling to be next in line to shake Kevon's hand in greeting. Passersby carried off the wooden swords and Kevon found himself being steered toward a table on the common side of the room.

Waine offered Kevon a chair, which he took gladly. Ale was poured, and everyone encouraged him to drink. Exhausted, sore, and dizzied by the previous few minutes, Kevon was glad of somewhere to sit and something to wet his throat. As he lowered his mug to take a breath, he saw Carlo in front of him, smiling.

"Bite down on this," the Blademaster suggested, handing him a loosely rolled leather tube.

"Mmm?" Kevon grunted, quirking an eyebrow at Carlo.

Laughter rang out around him as several strong arms grabbed him at once.

He panicked, and dropped his mug. Ale spilled across the table. The stained leather roll that Carlo had offered was shoved into his mouth, and it tasted worse than it looked. His right tunic sleeve was pushed up and over his shoulder. He turned to look, but Carlo grasped the top of his head with one huge hand and turned Kevon back to face him.

"It's better not to look," the mercenary said, smiling.

Kevon felt the heat a split second before the brand

touched his skin. The pain of the burn, coupled with the out-flow of what little magic he had left was more than he could bear.

CHAPTER 18

K evon woke in strange surroundings. A strong smell of liniment accompanied the half-wet sensations that lingered where he'd been cut and scraped, and a bandage rode high on his right arm.

It was so dark Kevon could only see the outlines of shapes in the room. A soft snoring noise seemed to come from somewhere above him. He threw off the rough blanket that covered him and dropped his legs over the side of the bed to sit up. He cracked his head on the bunk above him. Swearing softly, he called up a globe of Light without thinking. He got a quick glance at the room before thinking better of the magical light, which he promptly dismissed.

What he'd seen in the split-second was enough. His cloak hung on a peg near the door. Two of the other walls each had another two bunks like the one he was sitting on. A single table was the only other furnishing.

Kevon was done playing at being a Warrior. All he wanted to do was get out.

As his eyes readjusted to the small amount of light coming from under the door, his head stopped throbbing. Kevon stood carefully and crept across the room to retrieve his cloak and pull on his boots. He slipped quietly out into the muted light of the hallway, easing the door open and closed under a magically induced hush. He stalked down the hallway past two closed doors that were probably rooms like the one he'd been in. The next door was open; low voices and flickers of light came from inside. It sounded like the kitchen.

Peering around the threshold, Kevon saw a very large man

with a meat cleaver talking with three serving maids. A quick pulse of energy through a Movement rune caused a broom in the far corner of the kitchen to clatter to the ground, and Kevon slipped past the door as heads turned away.

Kevon pushed through the door at the end of the hall. Beyond it lay the common room, and as he entered, it went from virtual silence to near chaos. Every head turned, cheers, whoops, and random obscenities spewed forth from those still gathered.

A hand touched his arm and Kevon jerked reflexively. He turned to see the serving maid attached to the hand lean in close.

"Is there *anything* I can get you, Novice?"

"W-water would be nice." Kevon blushed so fiercely that the maid leaned in closer.

"*Are you certain?*" she whispered huskily.

"Yes, just the water!" Kevon called over his shoulder, nearly leaping over a chair to distance himself.

"Have a seat!" Waine called out to Kevon as he passed by the Seeker's table.

Kevon paused and tilted his head to glare at Waine.

"Relax..." Waine said consolingly. "The rough part is over. Although... Nilda would probably get rough if you let her."

"Probably," Nilda agreed from directly behind Kevon, causing him to jump once more.

Kevon turned, still red-faced, and accepted the mug of water from Nilda, who winked and resumed her other duties.

Kevon pulled up a chair and sat down. He rubbed the bandage on his shoulder experimentally. "So... That's all it takes to become a Warrior, huh?"

A smattering of laughter from nearby tables answered his question.

"No." Waine set his mug down. "That's more than it usually takes. No one here expected you to make it."

"Then why did he bring me here?" Kevon wondered aloud.

"Oh, Blademaster Carlo thought you had a chance. He

wouldn't have brought you here if he didn't. But to match with a Seeker instead of a Novice…" Waine trailed off for a moment. "You surely surprised him as much as the rest of us."

"He'll have to do better." Carlo sat down at the table. "Real weapons, he'd have lost in the first few seconds."

You don't know the half of it… Kevon thought as he nodded in agreement.

"Well, he's stronger than he looks, and some of those techniques I've never even seen before," Waine offered.

Carlo grunted. "That's because no one has."

"What use is having techniques that people can recognize and react to?" Kevon asked.

"You're not always going to have the luxury of knowing your life's not in danger," Carlo explained. "If you practice the basics you can act quickly, without thought when needed. You'd be hard pressed to improvise like that with more than one opponent."

Kevon nodded, frowning.

"Which is not to say I have any idea how you did as well as you did. Must have trained some with your father," Carlo mused.

Kevon remained silent.

"He could teach you a thing or two, Waine!" came a taunt from a nearby table.

Waine shrugged affably. "We all learn from each other. That was the most interesting match I've had in a long while. I'm looking forward to training with our newest Novice."

"I'm not staying around," Kevon said. "Leaving in a day or so."

"Not joining the City guard?" Waine asked, a little surprised.

"No, I have business elsewhere." Kevon answered. "Why?"

"Most Novices hire on to local guard forces until they advance to Seeker. Easy way to make a living and get extra training time," Carlo answered. "You'll face your Seeker trial when we get to the Inner Cities."

"Eight weeks as a Novice?!" Waine laughed. "I'd like to see that!"

"We're not in that much of a hurry," Carlo said, shaking his head. "More like ten weeks."

"You're serious, aren't you?" Waine asked Carlo setting down his mug and leaning forward.

Carlo nodded, and Kevon gave a half-shrug.

Waine laughed loudly. "So, when do we leave? There's no way this old bag of bones – no disrespect intended, Blademaster – can train you that quickly by himself. Besides, this town is getting stale."

Carlo looked at Kevon.

Kevon's eyes widened. "I don't know!"

"It's your mission. I'm just along for the ride." The Blademaster chuckled.

"I'll need a day to finish gearing up," Kevon said, "And that's all I need to do. Day after tomorrow, in the morning?"

"I don't have any gearing up to do, but it'll take a day and a night to say my goodbyes." Waine winked at Nilda, who rolled her eyes dramatically before she couldn't stop herself from smiling. "So, that's perfect for me."

Carlo nodded in agreement. "WestBridge an hour or so after sunrise, then." The Blademaster pushed away from the table. "I'm going to bunk down for the night. Well, at least what's left of it. I suggest you do the same. You wouldn't want to go out unarmed around here this time of night."

Kevon sat for a while and drank his water while he listened to Waine tell Nilda about the time he went hunting boars in the Parzoth Wastes. The Seeker was very animated and enthusiastic about the recounting, rising from his chair and stalking around tables to enhance the tale.

Kevon said goodnight and excused himself back to the room he had crept out of. He removed his boots, hung his cloak, and returned to the bunk he had left.

Lists of things he needed to do and buy the coming day echoed through Kevon's mind until he drifted off to sleep.

CHAPTER 19

Neither Carlo nor Waine were anywhere to be found when Kevon woke and prepared to leave. The kitchen crew was completely different from the night before. They stopped him on his way out to feed him a large breakfast of bacon, eggs, biscuits, and gravy. Two of the three serving maids took turns fussing over him as there was only one other Warrior still around. When Kevon finished, they bid him a good day and disappeared back into the kitchen with the dishes.

Kevon exited the guildhall and strode purposefully through the sparse morning foot traffic back to the Maiden of the Bay.

Bertus's eyes widened in shock as Kevon entered the front of the inn still bruised and scraped from the night before. "Are you all right?" he asked, rushing over to Kevon. "What happened?"

Kevon laughed. "I'm fine. My shoulder hurts worse than the rest of me." He slid his tunic sleeve up to show the brand that was white around the edges and still puffy to the touch.

"Congratulations, Novice. You never mentioned you were here for Trial," Bertus said, awe showing in his eyes.

"I wasn't..." Kevon admitted. "But now that things have turned out this way, I could use some advice."

"What is it?" Bertus asked, still staring at Kevon's now recovered shoulder.

"I need a guide for the day, one who knows the area, where the best deals are. I have one day to get ready to leave again."

"Wait here." Bertus hurried into the common area and

disappeared around the corner. A few minutes later he returned with a different tunic and overcloak. "Let's go."

Bertus directed Kevon to a nearby stable that sold decent horses at a fair price. After some haggling, Kevon bought a young stallion that seemed healthy and even-tempered. He paid extra for a packsaddle and extra saddlebags. After arranging to pick them up first thing in the morning, they moved on.

The next place was a tailor. Kevon was measured for two new sets of clothes, one heavier cut for winter, and one of lighter cloth for the coming summer. These he did not haggle for, but paid extra to have then done by morning.

Bertus led Kevon through the streets of Eastport from one Merchant stall to another, to shops large and small. With his help, negotiations were quick and fair. Small purchases were carried back to the inn to be readied for the trip, and larger ones arranged to be delivered.

By mid-afternoon, Kevon was exhausted. They had been going nonstop for the greater part of the day, and Kevon thought he'd surely prepared everything he could. All that remained was for him to return and organize his belongings at the inn so that he could leave first thing in the morning.

"Thank you for all your help today, Bertus," Kevon said, handing him some skewered meat and vegetables he'd just bought after seeing the boy eyeing them. "What do you think would be a fair wage for what we've done today?"

"Take me with you," Bertus said without hesitation.

"What?" Kevon asked. "You don't even know where I'm going."

"Doesn't matter," Bertus countered. "I just want to leave. If I'm bothering you, just leave me at the next town you go through."

"I don't know..." Kevon began. "What about your parents? What will they..."

"Never knew them," Bertus cut in. "I was sold to the owner of the Maiden when I was ten. He pays me, but between food and clothes, I still couldn't afford to pay him back until yesterday. Your tips got me out of debt."

"Oh. Well…" Kevon thought for a moment. "It's not safe to travel with me, to go where I'm headed. I can't let just anyone tag along."

"It would be more dangerous for me to leave by myself, wouldn't it?" Bertus asked. "One way or another, I'm leaving Eastport."

Kevon looked at Bertus and saw the look that he had likely worn when trying to leave home after his father had died. Bertus would be in more danger if he got as far as Kevon had; there was no isolating valley to protect him. Kevon sighed. He dug through his money pouch and pressed three coins into Bertus's hand. "You'd better hurry if you want to be ready tonight. We're leaving early."

Bertus opened his hand enough to see the color of the money, then clamped his fist tightly about it and shoved it quickly into a pocket. His eyes glazed over for a moment and Kevon could almost see the frantic planning that was crowding the boy's head. "I'll wake you up before dawn, and we can finish getting ready!" Bertus slipped into the crowd and was gone.

Kevon made his own way back to the Maiden easily enough. He found it amusing that when he was finally getting the feel of where things were here, he had to leave. He packed his things as snugly and securely in the new saddlebags as he could. He went downstairs and found someone to bring him a late supper, and after he finished, Kevon went back upstairs and double-checked everything he'd already packed.

Sore, tired, and mentally exhausted, he climbed into bed and drifted off, Marelle crowding his fitful dreams.

CHAPTER 20

Bertus pounded on Kevon's door well before sunup. Kevon grumbled a bit, but dragged himself to the door.

"Let's go!" Bertus urged, a little too cheerfully for Kevon's taste at this early hour.

Kevon scrunched his face and blinked the sleep from his eyes as Bertus waited, fidgeting. "All right," Kevon said, finally. "First thing we need to do is go get my horse from the other..."

"Both of your horses are in the Maiden's stable, saddled," Bertus interrupted. "Mine is, too," he added with a smile. "All the supplies have been delivered, and are stowed properly. Your new clothes are packed in one of my saddlebags for now, we can move them around later."

Kevon scrunched and blinked again. "Did you sleep at all?" he asked Bertus.

"A little. It should be enough," the youth replied.

"All right, then. I'll get washed up and pack this down to the stable. Then I'm buying us breakfast."

As Kevon readied himself for the day, he wondered where Marelle and Rhulcan were in their journey down the coastal route. He could not help but imagine how her sudden bid for more independence from her father would change her by the time they met next. If the last few days were any indication, Kevon had no idea what to expect.

Bertus returned and insisted on carrying some of Kevon's belongings to the stable so that they would only need to make one trip. Kevon was unable to buy breakfast, since Bertus had rented his own room, and was already entitled to his morning meal.

They ate, chatting quietly about the road ahead. Kevon told Bertus about Carlo, Waine, and the general happenings during his Trial at the guild.

"Not worried about him trying something because you embarrassed him?" Bertus asked through a mouthful of bacon.

Kevon shook his head. "I get the feeling he wouldn't waste his time on something like that."

Bertus nodded and swallowed. "Sounds like a decent fellow. I can't wait to meet him."

Kevon pushed his plate away and slid his chair out a bit from the table. "I'm not sure how they'll take the news that you're coming with us. As Carlo said when Waine joined our little group, it's my journey... but Waine is better prepared to handle the danger. Carlo might be a bit more concerned about you."

"I won't be any trouble," Bertus assured Kevon.

Kevon smiled and eyed the light beginning to come in the front window of the inn. 'We'd better get started. They'll be waiting for us at the West Bridge soon."

Bertus nodded absently, watching one of the kitchen maids cleaning tables off. As she moved to take the dishes from their table, Bertus dumped his money pouch into his open hand. A small handful of silver and copper was all that remained. He took the girl's hand and poured the money into it.

The vacant stare that had occupied her face a moment before turned to a look of panic and confusion for a few breaths. As her trembling hand clenched around the coins, tears filled her eyes. She sat down the dishes she held in her other hand and stepped around the table to wrap an arm around Bertus, leaning over to kiss him on the top of his head. She dropped the towel that was draped over her arm in the center of the table and left through the kitchen door.

Kevon raised an eyebrow at Bertus.

"That was enough to pay off her debt," he explained. "And a little extra."

Kevon laughed and stood up to get ready to leave. He was sure that Bertus would not be any trouble to travel with. Seeing the boy's selfless act made him worry even more about the danger Bertus was putting himself in by choosing to come along.

Kevon followed Bertus out of the inn, around the corner and down the side-street that led to the stable used by patrons of the Maiden. His spirits continued to lift; excitement for the next leg of his journey was building. The spring in his young friend's step and the cheery tune Bertus whistled was infectious.

Bertus called ahead loudly as they neared the stable, their horses were out front waiting as they arrived. Kevon's mare was loaded with the packsaddle and the majority of the supplies. She was tethered to Bertus's mare, which in turn carried a larger load than Kevon's stallion.

Kevon inspected the arrangement for a moment before deciding that it was quite acceptable. He strapped his swords in place on the stallion's saddle, like he had seen Carlo do on occasion, checked the fastenings, and mounted up.

Kevon and Bertus turned onto the main street heading toward WestBridge and foot traffic parted before them as their horses' shod feet clacked against the cobbles. The stallion strained to push ahead faster, but Kevon reined him back.

As they reached the bridge a good half-an-hour early, Kevon spotted Carlo's stallion tethered by another horse near the guard shack. Carlo and Waine stood idly chatting with the officer keeping watch as traffic entered and left the city. Waine waved to Kevon as soon as he spotted them. Carlo quirked an eyebrow at the stallion, his gaze drifted to the mare following Bertus.

Kevon dismounted and walked the last twenty yards to where the other Warriors were talking. Bertus, having had a little difficulty climbing into his saddle earlier, opted to remain seated.

Carlo peered around the side of Kevon's stallion opposite Bertus. "Is this all of us?" he asked half-expectantly, grimacing.

Waine picked up on Carlo's surprise at Bertus's arrival. "Is it to be 'Sir Kevon' then? Is this your squire?"

The post officer and two of his subordinates who were not busy inspecting cargo laughed loudly.

"He's headed in the same direction," Kevon answered. "Thought it might be safer if he traveled with us."

Carlo nodded absently as he walked around to inspect Kevon's horse. "Where did you get these?" he asked after a quick look at the stallion's teeth and two of the hooves.

"Lubber's Landing," Bertus piped up. "I help out in the stables there when I have some free time."

"So, you've already checked them over, several times, I'd imagine," Carlo said, more than asked, and backed away, stopping his inspection.

Bertus nodded and smiled at the implied compliment.

"We're ready to go whenever you are," Carlo added, turning to address Kevon.

"All right, let's go." Kevon shortened the reins he'd been leading the stallion by, and scratched him behind the ear for a moment. He patted his mount reassuringly on the nose and climbed back into the saddle.

Carlo and Waine swung easily into their saddles and Waine called out goodbyes to several of the guardsmen scattered about.

As they crossed the bridge headed out of town, Kevon could feel his heart pounding in his chest, the anticipation of the new leg of his journey bubbling to the surface. Bertus resumed his cheerful whistling, and the horses seemed to pick up on the youth's enthusiasm, heads held higher and ears pricked to listen more carefully.

A mile or so from Eastport, Carlo turned onto a smaller road that headed in a more southwesterly direction. The group maintained a lively, yet unhurried pace for the rest of the morning, and by the time the noon hour had come; they were in sight of the wooded hills that lay between Eastport and the capital, Navlia.

While they stretched their legs and ate a quick meal, each from their own provisions, Carlo estimated that they could be making camp near the forest by early evening.

Kevon helped Bertus back into his saddle and they resumed their journey.

They reached the edge of the forest as the sun stretched to touch the western horizon. Waine dismounted and pulled his unstrung bow and full quiver of arrows from behind his saddle. Handing his reins to Bertus, the Seeker laughed and ran into the trees.

Carlo dismounted and removed the saddle from his stallion. Kevon helped Bertus remove the gear from the remaining four horses and picket them all between two outlying trees. Bertus began fussing over the horses with an assortment of brushes, and Kevon led them one at a time to drink from a nearby stream.

Kevon left Bertus to finish caring for the mounts and returned to see what Carlo was doing. The Blademaster had a fire crackling cheerfully in a fire pit, and was inspecting his sword.

"Well, the horses are pretty well settled in," Kevon reported. "Any sign of Waine?"

A triumphant shout rang out from just inside the tree line. Kevon heard a thump and a loud cracking noise directly behind him. A fat partridge lay at an odd angle, skewered by the splintered remains of a flight arrow. The feathered end of the shaft lay a few feet away on the other side of the rock that the arrow must have splintered on when it fell.

Waine leapt from the cover of the trees, holding up a length of rope with half-a-dozen more birds tied by the feet. The Seeker stalked back into camp with a wide grin. He flopped the bird-laden rope down on the rock by the last one he'd shot. "I killed 'em. Someone else gets to cook 'em," he announced.

Kevon and Carlo looked at each other questioningly as Bertus moved to pick up the rope, and lifted the other bird by the arrow-shaft. Both made half-hearted efforts to help, but the boy shook his head. "Most likely I'm the best cook, anyhow," he taunted, retreating to a corner of camp to begin preparing the birds for dinner.

Carlo watched for a while as the boy sat down and began plucking the birds. Nodding approval, he turned back to Kevon and Waine. "Get your swords."

Waine unstrung his bow and exchanged it for his long-sword. Kevon braced himself for the jolt of touching his new saber, and pulled it free from its scabbard. He turned to join the others, but Carlo called, instructing him to bring the other sword instead. Puzzled, Kevon replaced the saber and took up the fallen Warrior's heavier sword.

By the time Kevon got over to them, Carlo was already showing Waine the proper balance for the slant-bladed stance that Kevon had used in his Trial. Kevon watched, following along with his own sword for a few minutes. Soon, Carlo decided Waine had a solid grasp of the stance, and ended that part of the lesson.

Carlo spaced his students out a few sword-lengths away from each other and went through basic sword swings. He had them do half a dozen of each, starting from different positions and slashing at different angles every six strokes. When Kevon didn't perform a technique correctly, they did six more.

Within minutes, Kevon's arm was aching and starting to go numb. Just before he was afraid he would drop the sword on his next set of swings, Carlo had them switch hands and practice a few more times this way. After just four variations, only one of which they had to repeat, Carlo had the younger Warriors switch to two-handed grips and showed them a few technique combinations that they repeated several times each. These proved to be awkward for Kevon. The sword that he was using would have been a fine two-handed weapon for someone with smaller hands. As it was, he had to grip the hilt just short of the crosspiece with his right hand, and his left fist was barely wrapped around the iron sphere on the end. His sweaty hands did not grip as well on the iron as they did on the leather wrapping, and he found himself having to constantly shift his grip and wipe his hands dry on his tunic.

Kevon was nearing his limits. Sweat poured off his brow into his eyes. His breath burned in his lungs, and his legs began to ache from the low crouching positions and steps he'd been taking while performing the two-handed techniques.

Carlo called a halt, and reminded Kevon to care for his blade.

Kevon searched through the saddlebags until he found the cloth, oil, and whetstone. He made a mental note to repack them in the saddlebags he kept on the stallion. He sat down on a large rock outcropping near the fire where Bertus was spitting plucked partridges. He noticed that Waine had checked his sword and was already tinkering with his arrows. Kevon sized up the blade and began scraping away at it with a whetstone.

Carlo, sitting nearby, made a distressed noise and sheathed his own blade to rest it against the rock he'd been sitting on. He rushed over to see what Kevon was doing. Carlo took the blade and looked it over; finding only one spot that even remotely needed sharpened out, and showed Kevon the proper way to go about it.

When he was finished, Kevon switched the larger blade out for the lighter saber, and found a few places that he dealt with fairly easily. Watching from his new seat next to Kevon, Carlo nodded his approval as Kevon re-sheathed the saber.

Wanting the practice, Kevon drew out his knife and looked it over.

"That's quite the pigsticker," Waine commented from across the fire, where he was now helping Bertus roast the birds.

"It looks very much like…"

"The sword. Yes," Kevon said, interrupting Carlo. "That's why I bought it. The shopkeeper said the Warrior that sold it to him came from the Southern Frontier."

"So if we don't find anything out in the Inner Cities, we'll head for the Frontier?" Carlo asked.

"I might need to take care of that *other thing* in the west, first…" Kevon responded, wincing.

"Yes," Carlo agreed. "And you might want to let these two in on it if you plan on having them around for any length of time."

Waine and Bertus looked at Kevon and Carlo in turn.

"Well…" Kevon hesitated.

"C'mon, tell us!" Bertus urged.

"It's just that…" Kevon started, "Knowing this could be dangerous for you, and speaking of it around others could endanger us all."

"Not a whole lot that I'm afraid of," Waine answered. "Dragons, probably, but I've never seen any of those."

Kevon looked at Bertus.

"I've just barely got my freedom…" Bertus said thoughtfully. "And you ask me if I want to spend it on a dangerous adventure with three Warriors I've only just met?"

Kevon sighed and nodded.

"Just try and stop me!" Bertus laughed. "I'm gonna be in storybooks!"

Kevon smiled, knowing how it would have felt to have been offered the same chance when he was Bertus' age. "All right. Where should I start?" Kevon sheathed the knife and began talking. He told them of the encounter with the Warrior and the bear. He told them of the Wizard he had known and trusted. About Holten paying him to return a book to a Wizard friend. He mentioned his meeting Carlo, Rhulcan, and Marelle, and finally the misunderstanding that had revealed Holten's true intentions. His story concluded as they were almost done eating.

"Well," Waine said, tossing the gnawed bone he'd been working on into the fire and licking his lips. "You can add evil Magi to the list of things that make me nervous."

"Me too," Bertus agreed. "But, they're evil, and they're up to something." He frowned. "Probably something big." He peered at Kevon. "And… we might be the only ones that know about it at all?"

Kevon nodded.

"Well, we've got to stop them," Bertus stated flatly. "We'll ask around about your dead friend with the sword, then head on over and kill that Gurlin guy."

The Warriors turned as one to look at Bertus.

He's right, Kevon thought. I'd been considering it to keep myself safe, alive. But I need to do it because it needs to be done.

"By the gods!" Waine chuckled. "If this boy has the stones for the job, I'm with him."

Carlo nodded, the hint of a smile touching his face.

The four finished eating, bantering between nervous silences. As the evening deepened, the Warriors worked out a watch rotation and settled in for the night.

CHAPTER 21

The days passed swiftly, a blur of travel, training, and planning. They had been traveling through the woods for nearly two weeks. The trip was progressing nicely, the only time they had stopped for more than one night was when Waine had taken a small deer instead of game birds. They spent the afternoon butchering the animal. The entire next day was devoted to curing the meat that they would not eat right away.

Bertus did most of the cooking. The horses, even Carlo's stallion, seemed offended if anyone besides the young man tried to care for them. The Warriors split watches at night, and trained unrelentingly at every opportunity. The arrangement seemed to please everyone.

In the evenings before combat practice, Kevon would sometimes read some of the book that Holten had given him. One night, Bertus asked him why he would study such a thing. Kevon answered that reading it could give some insight into the author's personality. He reminded the boy that Gurlin had written the book, and was their intended target. That had satisfied Bertus's curiosity.

That was only part of the truth, however. In the quiet times of his watch, Kevon sometimes toyed with the bits of knowledge extracted from his reading. By visualizing the Enhancement rune alongside the Movement rune he was already getting very accustomed to using, his magic seemed to be more potent. It also seemed not to drain as much power from Kevon's reserves as it would normally.

Kevon also experimented more with his magical reserves

and steel. After testing himself several nights in a row, he discovered he could use the Enhance/Movement rune combination soon after touching a sword. His magic was good for only small bursts, but the finding cheered Kevon. He wondered if there would ever be a point where his spellcasting with certain runes would be so effortless that he could use magic immediately after releasing a sword-hilt.

His joy at learning new things about magic was soured by his need to keep them secret. He had grown to trust his companions with every other aspect of his quest, his life. But talk around the campfires at night always seemed to turn to stories of evil sorcerers, and the heroes that slew them, or more often died trying. A Magi who could only attack an armored foe indirectly, and who died at the first sword-stroke was deadly enough. One that could use magic and a sword, even if not at the same time, would be unacceptable.

So, Kevon made the best of the situation. He trained hard with the sword, not once using magic to help himself when sparring with the wooden blades. When not sparring, Kevon used the heavier blade almost exclusively, and soon he could swing it quite easily in the two-handed grip. The sword was still heavier than Kevon would like to use one-handed for any length of time.

Carlo also devoted a small portion of Kevon's training to the knife. He wanted Kevon to be able to do something with his off-hand, and lacking a shield, the knife paired well with the lighter saber.

Travel through the woods varied from day to day. The main track was always wide enough for a wagon, easily wide enough for three to ride abreast. Lesser tracks occasionally intersected or crossed the main path, but the party did not stray from the road.

The trees grew close in some spots and opened up in others to give an unobstructed view of the sky. Twice already, the group had ridden through tracts of burnt land. Both times, they had seen signs of life returning to the forest, new growth and smaller animals, but there was no game and they were grateful for the stores they carried with them.

One afternoon, just before the midday break, the four rode leisurely along when the horses began sidestepping and snorting uneasily. This had happened several times before, when downwind of some of the forest's more pungent inhabitants, or when they were near one of the burnt swaths.

Carlo pushed the stallion ahead, but the rest of the horses kept acting too spooked, and refused to follow. The Blademaster limbered his sword and scanned the surrounding area.

Before Kevon had thought about taking any action, Waine's bow was strung and the Seeker was fastening his quiver to his leg.

Wanting to help in any way he could, Kevon focused and paired an Enhancement and a Control rune and reached out to touch the minds of each of the four horses that were becoming increasingly difficult to manage. He slowly calmed them down with a light touch on their minds, and they stood still, but remained alert. Maintaining his focus on the first spell, he spun an enhanced sound-muffling illusion much like the one he'd used while rescuing Carlo from the bandits, making sure to allow sound in, but not out.

If not for the flash of motion, Kevon might not have heard the muted *twang* of Waine's bowstring, but he could not have missed the results the arrow produced.

A strained squeal and a raspy gurgle accompanied the thrashing as a dark, misshapen figure stumbled from behind the bush where it had been hiding, clutching the feathered shaft buried in its throat.

Startled, Kevon lost his concentration and heard the second shot thrum louder as another bush rustled and Waine sank an arrow into the back of another one of the creatures who was just attempting to flee.

As Kevon's Control spell dissolved, the horses began to react to the commotion. It was all Bertus could do to stay in his saddle with his horse and Kevon's mare trying to go in two different directions.

"Whoa!" Bertus called, and Kevon seized the opportunity to reform his runes and pour energy into them. The horses quieted almost at once. "There," Bertus smiled. "That's better."

"Orc scouting party," Carlo said, spitting.

"Thought so." Waine nocked another arrow. "I thought they were tougher to kill, though."

Carlo grunted in amusement. "Believe me, they usually are."

Kevon eased back on the magic. "Scouting party?" he asked. "There's more then?"

"Twenty or thirty at least," Carlo nodded. "Otherwise they would all stay together. Half an hour or so at most before these two are missed." The mercenary peered through the trees and looked up and down the road. "My guess is they're coming from the south and haven't reached the road yet. We'd likely be able to outrun them either way we want to go."

Kevon nodded. "Isn't it unusual for them to be this far north?" he asked.

Carlo nodded again. "It's rare for more than one or two to slip past the frontier." He paused. "I think I'll go have a look. You should be all right here with Waine. If there's trouble, keep on going, I'll catch up."

The remaining three nodded in acknowledgement as Carlo urged his stallion off the track in the direction the orcs had been coming from.

A few minutes later, Bertus piped up and broke the strained silence. "So… do we get to loot the bodies?"

Waine was able to stifle only part of his laugh. "I don't think *you* should go anywhere near them. Personally, I feel safer up here with arrows at the ready."

Kevon agreed, and after a moment noticed that both of his companions were looking at him expectantly. "Ohhhh…" he said slowly.

"I won't pull rank and make you do it…" Waine began, "But if you want to…"

Kevon tossed his reins to Bertus and slowly released the runes that he had let dull to a slight shimmer in his mind. Satisfied that the horses were calm enough, he dismounted and drew his saber before edging cautiously toward the first fallen orc.

"Don't touch their weapons!" Waine called after him. "No telling what's on them."

Kevon reached the orc and prodded the prone form with the tip of his sword. He found it difficult to tell what was orc and what was armor. Patches of what he thought must be skin poked out from place to place from under what could have been three layers of tattered leather. Dust and grime made the differences in texture hard to discern. The rivulets of blood that had flowed away from the body were now dried into the dust and seemed to have a greenish-black cast to them.

Assured that the orc was dead, Kevon kicked it over onto its back, getting a good look at its face for the first time. Aside from the greenish-gray cast of its skin and the large, misshapen teeth in its mouth, the fallen orc could have been a human child. The body proportions were off somewhat, but the slackened features were smooth, a far cry from the leathery hulks orcs were portrayed as in stories.

"A... child?" Kevon asked, stumbling back a few steps.

"Orc scouts are usually between two and three years old," Waine called softly from behind him. "Old enough to know what to do, small enough to sneak around."

"Three years old?" Kevon stared at the corpse in disbelief.

"They rarely live past ten," Waine explained, guiding his horse closer to get a better look himself. "They don't stop growing until they die. But, the older ones usually kill each other fighting over food. That, or the rest of the clan will turn on them when they start eating the younger ones."

Shuddering, Kevon returned to the body and began pulling pouches free from the rope the orc had been using for a belt. The first two pouches held rancid chunks of meat, and Kevon threw them into the bushes as soon as he opened them. The last pouch held bits of stone, wood, string, and twisted scraps of metal, among other things. Kevon sifted through the rubbish, not expecting to find anything really worthwhile. A smooth chunk of white material that he had passed over a few times already caught his eye as it fell to a new position in the pile. It appeared to be a small section of bone, half an inch thick and a little over an inch wide at its widest points. The carved faces were polished smooth, evidently both by design and from wear. The thing that caught Kevon's eye, however, was the symbol carved on the now-upturned face. It was not a symbol he knew, but he did not doubt that *something* would happen if he ran some magic through it.

Kevon shuddered once again. He was not sure what made him more uneasy about the runed bone, the fact that it was carved in bone, that he had found it in the possession of an orc, or the appearance of the rune itself. Not only were the lines composing the symbol twisted and severe, but the etched grooves appeared to be filled with dried blood of some kind.

Kevon pushed aside the rest of the junk and carefully picked up the carved bone. "What do you make of this?" he asked, walking over to where Waine sat scanning the surrounding forest.

Waine sniffed. "I don't know if it's an orc toy or something he picked up somewhere else." He shook his head. "It's garbage. Go check the other one."

Kevon walked over to where the second orc had fallen. This one seemed a bit larger, and had luckily fallen on its side, leaving its pouches easily accessible. Kevon poked them carefully and threw the squishy ones into the bushes without opening them.

The two pouches Kevon was brave enough to open held refuse similar to that he'd found in the other pouch. This orc had better taste or judgment; Kevon found several coppers and a silver amidst the rest of the junk. Nothing else unusual caught Kevon's eye, and he felt a strange mix of relief and disappointment. Gathering the small handful of coins together, he abandoned his searching and returned to the others to offer the money to Waine.

Seeing only the single glint of silver, Waine made a face and shook his head dismissively. "Let the boy have it," he said, glancing to the side for a second to check on Bertus. "He's more than earned it, putting up with us."

Bertus quietly accepted the coins, quickly putting them in a pouch and back in his pocket, still watching the forest intently.

Several more minutes passed uneventfully. The boredom grew palpable and Waine slackened his grip on his bow. The three companions talked amongst themselves, pointedly avoiding the question that they all wanted to ask.

Where is Carlo? Kevon wondered, grinning dutifully as Waine told of a hunt for cougars on Mount Elenna.

Twigs snapped in the undergrowth in the direction Carlo had gone, and Waine was instantly at a full draw, searching for a target to go with the sound. Several runic images formed in Kevon's mind, and he tried to estimate how much power he had regained since touching his sword last.

"Easy!" Carlo called. "It's just me, so far." The Blademaster rode into sight and approached the others.

"So far?" Waine asked, lowering his bow.

Carlo reined his stallion in as he reached the others. "There's a sizeable force of them heading north just about half a mile from here. I saw about a hundred in the main group, and no other scouting parties that I could see." He hesitated. "There were at least three bulls."

"Headed for Eastport," Waine said softly.

"We have to warn them!" Bertus cried.

"Yes," Carlo agreed. "*We* do."

If there are orcs here, this far north... Kevon thought, *Could there be more to the east?* His heart pounded as fear for Marelle's safety threatened to turn to panic.

Kevon looked at Carlo, and the Blademaster continued. "We know the road behind is clear. We're about halfway to East Thaddington, and the road ahead is not as known to us. Going back, we can stay ahead of the orcs easily if we push the horses, and be in Eastport inside of three weeks. That would give us two, maybe three days to raise the militia." Carlo looked at Kevon. "Can you afford this delay?"

Kevon sighed. "I don't know how much time I have. The sooner I deal with my problems, the better. And if we happen to find out more about the orcs breaking through the southern defenses, it could set my mind to ease."

Carlo nodded. "I think the boy will be safer going back with me. Find out what you can in East Thaddington, and then head to the Warrior's Guild in Navlia. If we don't meet you there in twelve weeks, go on without us." The Blademaster turned to the Seeker. "Waine?" he asked.

"I'll go with Kevon." Waine chuckled. "He'll be safer with me."

"All right, then. We'd better get moving!" Carlo announced.

Bertus tossed the mare's reins to Kevon. "Can't have your nag slowing us up," he giggled, smiling. His look grew more serious. "Be careful."

"Good luck to all of us," Kevon said. "See you in Navlia."

Carlo and Bertus took off at a gallop in the direction they had come from.

As the Blademaster and his charge rounded the corner and disappeared from sight, Waine spoke.

"They're going for speed, to put as much distance between themselves and the orcs as possible," the Seeker began. "We've got to be a little more cautious."

Kevon nodded in agreement.

Waine waited a moment, and then continued. "If we run into any more orcs, hopefully I can deal with them as easily as I did this time. If not..."

"...I could help out." Kevon began hesitantly.

Waine sighed. "We don't have time to make you a bow and teach you how to use it."

Kevon smiled. "That's not what I meant, but we'll have to

do that soon, too."

"You're not really up to fighting them close-in either," Waine advised. "Even ones this young are sneaky little bastards. *All* orcs do is fight."

Kevon bit his lip in concentration. "That's not what I meant, either." He waited a moment longer as Waine's expression turned to one of interest. "How much do you trust me?" he asked, finally.

The Seeker took a minute to answer. "With my woman, but..." he paused, "Only because you'd just turn red, like now."

Kevon sighed. "I'm serious, Waine. This is *important.*"

"With my life." Waine answered without hesitation. "We're guild-brothers."

Kevon fidgeted tensely. "You know I wouldn't lie to you, right?" he asked, "Because... I haven't told any of you... everything."

Waine's look of puzzled amusement hardened into a suspicious glare. "What... have you done?"

Kevon shook his head. "It's not really what I've done, and it's not like I've lied about it..."

"Well, then, just say it and be done with it." Waine said, shrugging.

"I'm a Journeyman Mage." Kevon said, watching the Seeker for a reaction.

Waine laughed and reined his horse around to begin heading on to East Thaddington. "We don't have time for jokes, Kevon. Let's just get going."

Kevon clucked and wheeled his stallion about, the pack mare in tow. "I'm serious, Waine," he said, pulling up beside him.

"Magi can't handle iron or steel," Waine snapped. "Or didn't you learn that when you were an *Apprentice*?"

"*I can.*" Kevon hissed back at him. "I don't know if I'm different or if I just figured out the trick to it, or what... but I can!"

Waine jerked back on his reins and his horse nearly skidded to a stop. Kevon had to ease back a little more slowly to prevent the mare from plowing into his mount.

"Show me, then." Waine demanded. "Do some magic."

"I will in a few minutes," Kevon stammered. "Using swords and stuff keeps me from casting spells for a little while, and..."

Waine snorted derisively. "Whatever."

Kevon rolled his eyes. He formed an Enhancement rune and an Illusion rune. He pulsed what little magic he had accumulated in the last few minutes through them, and for a little more than a second a ball of blue flame burned in his upturned palm. It sputtered out almost immediately, leaving only afterimage and a hint of mage-smoke hanging in the air.

Waine's eyes widened. "Was that?"

"Just an illusion," Kevon explained. "That's what I'm best at, so far." Kevon lowered his gaze sheepishly. "I've also used it once or twice when sparring with wooden swords..."

Waine's jaw dropped. "I knew it!" he yelled, forgetting the orc situation for the moment. "I knew there had to be something going on in the Trial, especially since sparring with you afterward. Your Trial was the best I've seen you do..." he paused and peered closer at Kevon. "You haven't been using magic to spar with since then, have you?"

"No, I wanted to learn how to do it right." Kevon said. "The Trial was different. There was no way I would have passed without it."

Waine furrowed his brow thoughtfully. "Not against me, but I'd have bet on you against any of the Novices in that hall." The Seeker slugged Kevon in the arm. "Anyway, I don't see anything wrong with using an advantage if you have it. You should try it more during practice to help me train."

"So... it doesn't disturb you that I can..." Kevon trailed off.

"Like you said, if I didn't know you, then yes, it would." Waine said after a moment. "But since I do..." he shook his head and laughed. "I can see you having a lot of potential, and I know I can't possibly see it all. You'll be very interesting to be around."

Kevon breathed a sigh of relief. "You're the only one that

knows. I've been too afraid to tell anyone else."

Waine nodded slowly. "It's probably a good thing. You never..."

There was a rustling in the undergrowth and Waine whipped around, training a freshly nocked arrow. A raccoon poked its head out of a bush to look at them, and the Warriors both laughed.

"We'd better get down the road," Waine decided. "I know it'll make me feel better."

Kevon agreed, and as they set off down the road again as quickly as they dared, Kevon could not help but feel renewed hope. Though he had lost, hopefully for just a short while, Carlo's guidance and Bertus' cooking skills, he felt better. In Waine, Kevon had found an ally he could depend on. If the road ahead proved to be clear, as the Blademaster suspected, Kevon and Waine would be able to continue their weapons training. And now that Waine knew Kevon's secret, Kevon could begin testing the limits of his magical skills once again.

With any luck, Kevon could have Gurlin dealt with before two seasons passed. After that, only one more obstacle stood between Kevon and the life he wanted to lead.

Holten.

CHAPTER 22

Kevon yelled and launched into a flurry of slashing attacks intended to throw his opponent off balance. His arms were beginning to burn with exertion, but his full-force strikes, strengthened and steadied by his Art, took their toll on Waine.

The Seeker parried the first strike, dodged under and around the next two, stepping aside for a better attack angle. By the time Waine managed to swing his practice blade to attack, Kevon had already wheeled around on one foot and his sword was interposed between them. Waine swung twice more, and each time was parried easily.

Kevon put his other foot down and settled into a lower, more conventional stance. The focus he had shifted to keeping his balance was redirected back to his arms and sword, and the attack began anew. He slammed his sword into Waine's with resounding force, causing the Seeker to take a half-step to his right. Kevon followed the motion around to his left. He turned, crouched, and whipped his sword over his head to block the answering stroke from Waine. Meanwhile, he kicked out his left leg to sweep around and hook the Seeker's feet out from under him.

Waine saw the attack coming at the last second and jumped over most of it, landing a bit off balance but recovering in time to block yet another follow-through attack from Kevon.

The two clashed another half-dozen times before Kevon felt the sweat starting to slide down into his eyes. Modifying his Movement spell, he swept the sweat away, hurling it as an afterthought at Waine's face.

The surprise of the droplets splashing into the Seeker's face and eyes gave Kevon the opening he needed, and he slid through Waine's defenses to stab him with the blunted end of the wooden sword, square in the gut.

Waine 'oofed' and dropped his sword, spreading his hands outward, palms facing Kevon in a gesture of surrender. As soon as Kevon nodded acknowledgement, Waine made a face and began rubbing his eyes. "Kevon?" he asked.

"Mmm?"

"It wouldn't hurt my feelings if that *never* happened again."

Kevon snickered. "Sorry, it was kind of a reflex." He reached into a pack and drew out a rag to toss to Waine. "Besides, you told me not to hold *anything* back this time. Be glad it wasn't fire."

Waine finished wiping his face and tossed the rag back to Kevon. "Yeah, it's probably best if you keep the fire in the middle of camp. We're still deep enough in the forest I'd hate to see it get away from you."

Kevon shuddered at the thought of the forest burning around them. It had been two weeks since they had parted company with Carlo and Bertus, so they were still a week or two of steady travel from the forest's edge. Once they left the woods, it would be another week's travel to East Thaddington.

The exhausted Warriors sat about for a while, as was their custom, enjoying the cool of the evening while the horses fed. Not much in the way of game had presented itself that day, so they would make do with cold rations.

"You know what the best way to kill your old Master's evil Wizard friend is, don't you?" Waine asked, seemingly at random.

Kevon sighed. He hadn't really wanted to think about it. He was *almost* content living, traveling, and training. "How do you think that is?" He asked.

"Well, Carlo had the first part of it right, carving that signet stamp," Waine said, thoughtfully. "And you have the book to deliver."

Kevon gave him a look of mild annoyance. This was nothing he'd not already considered.

"Wait a minute..." Waine protested. "Hear me out. You go in with a good enough letter, all cloaked up Mage-style, with that knife of yours, and just stab the guy."

"They'd know I wasn't a Mage, then, because I wouldn't be one the instant I touched the knife." Kevon groaned, rolling his eyes.

"Just wait!" Waine persisted. "Wear the knife under your cloak. I can rig your sheath somewhere that won't be obvious, upside down on the back of your leg, maybe? You could draw it through a slit in a pocket. You would have to be careful when you sat, maybe fake a limp, but..."

The simplicity of the plan struck Kevon like a hammer. If he did it right, he could get more information about what Gurlin and Holten were conspiring to do. In any case, he could surely get close enough to Gurlin to strike a killing blow.

"Do you think we could get to Gurlin's tower and back to Navlia before Carlo and Bertus arrive?" Kevon asked quietly.

"It's in the Western Ranges, right? We'll have to feed the horses more to push them any harder, but I think so. I've made the trip faster, riding alone." Waine answered. "We'll turn west when we hit the open, avoid East Thaddington altogether. A quick stop in Navlia for supplies and your... costume. If everything goes well," Waine laughed, "We'll have a week or two to train at the Guild in Navlia so that you can challenge for Seeker when Carlo arrives."

"And after that we could go to East Thaddington to find out about the sword," Kevon finished. "And no one else would have to find out about me."

As they ate, they fleshed out some of the particulars of the plan. Kevon began thinking again about how to revise the letter; what would be best to get him into Gurlin's confidence.

Kevon's mind reeled with schemes late into his first part of the watch. When he finally roused Waine for his half, Kevon easily drifted off to sleep.

For the first time in weeks, his dreams were untroubled.

CHAPTER 23

Kevon had never been so happy to see the sky. The strangled ribbon of blue that hovered over the road, punctuated rarely by small clearings, had begun to depress him. Kevon had grown used to seeing perhaps one star at night through the dark forest canopy. He marveled at the half-dozen that still glimmered in the slowly brightening morning as they rode clear of the trees.

The two Warriors made better time since their decision to bypass East Thaddington. Instead of training every evening, they opted for extra travel time every other night.

Kevon insisted, and Waine agreed, that for each training session until they met Gurlin, he would use no magic. He either used the knife, or one of the practice knives that Waine whittled out of broken branches, touching something metal before the sparring began. Kevon was fairly certain that offensive magic against a Wizard that outclassed him so completely would be largely useless. Metal in his blade would be proof against most magical assaults, and deadly offense as well. He wanted to be sure he was in top condition when the time came to use it.

Two days after exiting the forest, the track the Warriors were following ran through some fields. They spotted the first farmhouse and the first people they had seen since they had left Carlo and Bertus. Waine nodded amiably at the couple sitting by the front of the farmhouse, but pressed on ahead as Kevon was just about to ask about lodging for the night.

"We didn't want to stay there," Waine said after they were half a mile past the house.

"Did you know them?" Kevon asked.

"Didn't have to," Waine answered. "Did you notice how many repairs that place needed? Or the weeds in the fields?"

"Not really," Kevon admitted. "But why?"

"Any decent farmer would be out tending his fields if they looked like that, or fixing his house." Waine looked at Kevon soberly. "If you ever need to stay at a place like that, sleep sitting up with your back in a corner, and your sword drawn."

Further down the road, they rode through some fields that were far better kept, and saw a farmhouse that was much nicer looking, with several outbuildings. As they neared the house, Waine pulled his amulet out of his tunic and straightened it on his chest. Kevon noticed and followed suit.

Waine began speaking in a low voice even though no one was visible and the house was still a few hundred yards away. "It's customary for folks to lodge Warriors for free. It's also common practice to overpay for traveling supplies when you leave, if at all possible." Waine continued to explain. "Money here's not as scarce as it is in Laston, I'd imagine, but it's still a fair distance they'd have to go to spend it."

Kevon nodded in agreement. In Laston, money was something nice to dream about having. You couldn't eat it, ride it, or any number of other things that you could do with hard goods.

The two Warriors slowed to allow the farmer, who they spotted returning from a field, to reach the house first. When they arrived at the main house, all five family members were outside, waiting. The farmer, his wife, two boys perhaps nine and ten, and a little girl that half-hid behind the family dog that bristled slightly at the newcomers.

"We require lodging for the night, and could use some supplies, if you can spare them." Waine said, dismounting and extending a hand to the farmer in greeting.

The older man clasped Waine's arm in greeting, smiling warmly. "You're welcome to it. It's not much, but please, make yourselves at home."

The boys helped Kevon lead the horses to the barn and showed him where he could unload the gear. They chattered and bickered as they brushed and grained the animals, then turned them out into the fenced pasture with their own horses. Then they raced each other back to the house, a grinning Kevon following closely behind.

As he entered the building, Kevon smelled something delightful, and followed it to a stew bubbling in a copper cauldron over a brick oven. The farmer's wife stopped stirring long enough to shoo the Novice into the other room where Waine and her husband were sitting in chairs at the large table. The boys had flopped down on the floor and were listening to one of Waine's many hunting adventures.

"The boys want to be Warriors when they grow up," the farmer said after Waine's story concluded. "We had a Warrior stay here about a year ago. He needed supplies, but didn't have any money. He stayed on here for a few weeks building the sheds, helping out wherever it was needed. The boys loved watching him practice the sword."

Waine glanced over at Kevon. "We didn't train last night. Supper's not quite ready..."

The boys nearly tied themselves in a knot in their mad scramble to be the first out the door. Kevon walked out to the barn and retrieved the practice blades.

"Let's give them a show, shall we?" Waine said with a wink as Kevon handed him his wooden sword.

Kevon smiled and dropped back into a defensive posture. He blinked slowly, and when he reopened his eyes the runes for Enhancement and Movement already glowed faintly in his mind. He wrapped the spell around himself using a bare minimum of power, not wanting to waste good magic on the opening moves of the demonstration.

Waine began as usual, darting in and out with quick single strikes or two-hit combinations that Kevon no longer needed magic to parry easily. He quickly stepped up the attacks to longer strings of strikes, faking one direction before shifting his grip or balance to make the practice sword whip around at Kevon from a completely different direction.

Things were quickly reaching the point where Kevon could not defend much longer. He released more power into the already glowing runes, and they flared more brightly in his mind's eye. Kevon felt the magic solidify around him, guiding and speeding his limbs in turning the tide of the match. He allowed the symbols to burn more brightly than ever before. The rush of magic gave him speed and control in quantities he'd never before experienced, and he had to hold back to keep from completely overwhelming Waine. Kevon found that the edges of his runes were beginning to frazzle, and he felt his magical energy bleeding out far faster than normal. He slowed as he clamped back down on his reserves to focus on re-visualizing the spell symbols.

The moment of hesitation was all that Waine needed to penetrate Kevon's defenses. The Seeker pushed hard into a parry, levered Kevon's blade downward with his own, and brought the upswing crashing into the side of Kevon's head.

Kevon had recovered control of the Movement spell too late to defend against the strike, but had time to shift his focus to Waine's sword. Figuring the Seeker had not really planned for his blow to land, Kevon assumed that Waine was not holding back. The Movement rune flared brightly as the blade *thwacked* into Kevon's cheek, the magic checking most of the force almost as completely as if it had been parried by another blade.

Kevon made a point of whipping his head away from the impact to make it seem more painful and dramatic. The boys both gasped in shock, and their father winced. Kevon and Waine both took a step back to face each other, and raised their wooden swords in a military salute. Waine handed Kevon his practice sword so the Novice could put it away.

When Kevon returned to the house, the boys were jabbering away, telling two different accounts of the match to their mother simultaneously. The farmer's wife said nothing, nodding and smiling as she crowded the table with four place settings and prepared to dish up bowls of soup.

"That was quite the display," the farmer said as Kevon approached. "Are you sure you two are a Seeker and a Novice?"

Waine chuckled. "We've been training endlessly under a Blademaster. We'll both advance before the season is out," he assured the man.

"This is the best meal we've had in weeks." Waine said, smoothly changing the subject after sipping some of the steaming broth. "What do you use to flavor it?" The Seeker was his usual charismatic self, slipping from conversation to conversation. Whenever circumstance allowed, he told a bit of one hunting adventure or another.

Kevon ate in silence. He wasn't sure if it was his imagination, or if the farmer was studying him more intently than he was comfortable with.

I shouldn't have used magic, Kevon thought to himself. Waine was a capable fighter, and it was evident in the way he carried himself. Though Kevon had begun to notice a bit more grace in his actions from time to time, he was clearly not the Warrior that Waine was. Kevon did not know if the unwanted attention was real or not, but he swore inwardly never to use his magic for show again.

After dinner and a few hours of storytelling, the Warriors retired to the barn to bed down.

"So what happened during the match this afternoon?" Waine asked. "I know I started off faster than usual, but you were keeping up fine. Better than usual, if you ask me. But then..."

"I slipped up." Kevon sighed, causing dust motes to swirl through the shafts of moonlight that pierced the barn. "I kept using more and more power, and it got away from me. I couldn't control it, couldn't keep my spell together."

Waine let out a low whistle. "That's what you need to practice, then. Burn through your magic while you have it. There's always your sword to fall back on."

Kevon laughed, amazed that the Seeker, who knew little or nothing about the Arts, had once again shown keen insight in how Kevon might best use them. "Yes, I think I should. He pulled his blanket up about his shoulders and settled in. "Good night, Waine."

CHAPTER 24

The journey to Navlia wound up taking the Warriors nine more days. Kevon and Waine met up with a three-wagon caravan led by a Merchant on the second day, and advised them of the danger on the road to Eastport. The Merchant immediately reversed course, and hired Kevon and Waine on as extra protection on their return to Navlia. The caravan already had two veteran Warriors; tired looking Adepts older than Carlo. Kevon and Waine refused payment for the job, accepting only meals with the rest of the group; the caravan's cook was almost as good as Bertus.

Since they were not pushing the horses later into the night every other day, the younger Warriors resumed their evening practices, without magic. The Adepts seemed never to take any time to train, and Kevon saw only one of the men's swords cleaned at all.

Evenings were the worst for Kevon. Listening to the Merchant's tales of trade runs, the Novice was sure he would be a better businessman. *Rhulcan would never have made that mistake*, he found himself thinking. The Merchant had several bad trades to his name, resulting in losses that were covered by his father. *Marelle would be too proud to accept that, let alone admit to it.* His mind sought out her memories often in the evenings.

Kevon and Waine's fourth day with the caravan, the Adepts seemed to liven up somewhat. The extra sleep gained from splitting watches with the younger Warriors seemed to have refreshed them. The more capable looking of the two sat near, watching Kevon and Waine as they sparred. After a while, the older man pointed out some minor things, shifts in stance, weight distribution, and sword position that he said would help. The younger men made the adjustments and worked on their sword form for a while before returning to sparring. The changes felt a little strange, but Kevon thought that they would make them more effective fighters in the long run.

At the gates of Navlia, Kevon and Waine rode on through, leaving behind the caravan and its hired escorts.

Kevon likened Navlia to Eastport, but on a grander scale. Where Eastport bordered the sea, Navlia was a city that sat atop a sea of hills. The colors and shapes of the buildings were a very different scheme, less functional and more ornate. Where Eastport had been built up around trade and hard work, Navlia had not. The nobility that had been in power before the current prince, Waine explained, had taxed the people harshly and built lavishly without much thought. The basic city structure had luckily been built long ago. The hot springs that flowed from the upper side of the city were channeled cleverly through shaded cisterns that cooled to provide warm and cold water at many fountains, and carved stone canals carried waste away from the city.

Kevon and Waine slowed as they approached the gates, making sure their medallions were visible as they entered town. They rode past the line of wagons that curved around from the southern road waiting for inspections. Curt nods were exchanged between guards and Warriors, and they crossed the bridge into the business district.

Stables, smithies, and a tannery were among the things that Kevon noticed as soon as they crossed the bridge. Muted clanging from the north underscored the underlying tang of forged metal and horse manure. Waine explained that the louder and more foul-smelling industries were confined to the lower end of the city, as far away from the upper-class section on the south end of town as possible.

Kevon noticed that nearly all of the buildings were made from stone or brick. He asked Waine why there was so little wood despite the nearness of the forest. Waine told him that the area beyond the castle at the south end of town had been the rock quarry the stone for the castle had been mined from. As the castle was being built, they decided a cliff would be easier to defend than a wall. The stone was used for the castle, the canal ways, and the walls on the northern end of town. To make the castle even safer, the whole hillside on the south end of town was leveled, the excess stone used to build within town.

Kevon and Waine stopped at the first inn they found, not wanting to stay at the Warrior's Guild on this short trip through. Kevon gave Waine money for the stables and extra fodder for the road ahead. Then, after stowing their gear, he went to find a tailor.

Kevon had no trouble getting a tailor to start work on his two sets of robes right away. Posing as guardian to a Mage that was about the same size as himself, *"Maybe a little fatter,"* he whispered to the tailor with a sidelong glance, he ordered and paid for them, making arrangements for pick-up the next morning.

Kevon returned to the inn and had the innkeeper handle the arrangements for reprovisioning by morning. He did not relish the thought of wandering and haggling as he had done in Eastport. He wanted to relax and study in peace.

As an afterthought, Kevon wandered briefly until he found a place he could purchase inks and parchments. He bought a box full of different colors of ink in small ceramic jars, a small case of quills, and a bundle of parchments.

Upon returning to the inn, Kevon re-read some passages in the book of Gurlin's that dealt with the similarities of Enhancement and Enchantment, specifically the scribing of scrolls. Not having dealt with the written side of magic before, Kevon was surprised to learn that scroll making was not so very different from Alchemy. Focus on the desired effect, large detailed drawings of the runes to be used, and time, were basically all it took. The process of writing the scroll gathered power onto the parchment to be released when used for casting that particular spell. Depending on what scroll was scribed, the scroll, or part of it at the very least, would be rendered useless. Some parchments could hold several spells of certain types safely. Others could not. Fire scrolls burned to ash when cast, or worse, could explode if another Fire spell was scribed on it. Water scrolls got soggy, Wind scrolls tore themselves to shreds, and Earth scrolls turned to dust.

The book did not go into much more detail than that, but Kevon was eager to get some scrolls scribed to see if he could possibly cast spells off them after handling metal. He began with his favorite rune, choosing a light blue ink that came closest to how magic looked in his mind. He took great care in outlining the large symbol in the center of the page, taking nearly half an hour. Once the outline was complete, he began inking in the insides, holding the runic image in his mind all the while, brow furrowed in concentration. Kevon focused his entire being into every brush stroke, losing track of time and stopping only to light a candle when it grew too dark to see.

As he filled in the last little bit of the rune on the parchment, Kevon returned to his senses, felt how tired and hungry he was. He left the parchment unrolled on the table to finish drying and left for the kitchen to see what he could get for a late supper.

CHAPTER 25

Waine was up and pounding on Kevon's door before dawn the next morning. Kevon answered the door with a handful of silver and told the Seeker to go buy them breakfast. Blinking his heavy-lidded eyes several times, Kevon surveyed the mess he'd made of his room, and closed the door.

Two more scrolls were laid spread out to dry. Kevon had decided to make a scroll of Light, and had broken down and scribed a Fire scroll before falling asleep. His ink bottles were scattered about, and one of his quills had dried stuck in his bottle of red ink, both ruined. Kevon estimated he'd gotten a little less sleep than a regular night when sharing watch on the road. He hoped the softness of the bunk made up the difference. He began picking up his supplies, replacing his inks in their case, rolling his completed scrolls up separately and stowing everything in saddlebags. He sat on the edge of the bed after he finished dressing, yawning for several minutes. As his head cleared and the sense of urgency about the mission returned, he shouldered his gear and left to find Waine and breakfast.

The Warriors ate in silence, not wanting anyone to know their business or identities. Planning to murder a Wizard was not something you discussed in a town where the Arts were so highly regarded.

When they had finished their meal, Waine took all but one of the saddlebags and headed for the stable to ready the horses. Kevon hurried to the tailor with the remaining set of pouches to pick up the robes. Disappointed that the Mage himself had not shown up to see if the garments fit properly, the tailor insisted on bundling the robes in coarse cloth bags before he let Kevon put them in the saddlebags.

Kevon made his way over to the stable through the rapidly filling streets. After making wide circles around loud vendors that claimed to have anything that you could ever want, he rounded a corner, and saw *them*.

Kevon had not yet seen any Magi in Navlia, just as he had not seen any in Eastport. He had assumed that coach travel would be safest for Magi in crowds where anyone might be armed, and no matter the intent, a brush with steel could mean death.

This group was not concerned by that in the least. Two men in hoodless black robes were followed closely by three green-robed and hooded figures. The crowd parted quickly around the group, which strode rapidly down the center of the road. Not wanting to stand out, Kevon sidled over to the edge of the building he had just rounded and watched them out of the corner of his eye.

The first thing Kevon noticed was their walk. Where Carlo and Waine stalked along out of habit after years of training and high levels of physical prowess, these Magi all but swaggered. Their exaggerated movements and condescending glares were practically daring anyone to come too close.

As the group passed by, Kevon got the impression of gathered energies ready to be unleashed. Murky images of rune fragments poked at the corners of Kevon's mind, vanishing too quickly for Kevon to even attempt to identify. A faint Fire rune floated across Kevon's inner vision, snapping taut as Kevon noticed a tongue of flame lick up from one of the Mages' upturned palms. The Master closest to him shot the casting Mage an icy look over his shoulder, and the flame wisped out as the shadowy symbol did the same in Kevon's mind.

Kevon tried to not think of any runic symbols, so of course the rune for Illusion sprang instantly to mind. The Master who had glared at his subordinate moments before now turned to look in Kevon's direction.

Coolly, Kevon brushed his arm on the hilt of his sword, grounding away all of his magic. The remaining four Magi turned to look his way. Kevon feigned a yawn and kept walking toward the stables. Behind him, the knot of people that he'd been standing by fidgeted uncomfortably under the scrutiny of the five Magi, who had stopped in their tracks.

Great, Kevon thought. He'd spent so much time visualizing runes that he always had one or two dancing around in his head, needing only the spark of will to begin working. Now he would need to practice not visualizing *anything*. If he was presenting himself as a Warrior, he needed to be more careful about when he grounded out his magic, or find a way to keep grounded at all times.

Waine was waiting impatiently at the stable when Kevon arrived. Kevon hurriedly fastened his last few items on his mare, and swung up into the stallion's saddle after double-checking the straps.

"Ready?" Kevon asked, then grinned at Waine's mutterings.

The Warriors rode, as swiftly through town as they dared, needing to hurry, but avoiding unwanted attention. They slowed as they passed the central fountain, which threw water hundreds of feet into the air to splash down before running off into different underground channels. At Waine's urging, they resumed best possible speed and reached the west gates of Navlia by noon.

Once outside of the city, they pushed the horses for a good two hours before stopping to eat.

"You look worn out," Waine observed as Kevon's head nodded into his biscuit and the Novice startled himself back to alertness. "What were you doing all night?" he asked, eyebrow raised, a grin spreading across his face.

Kevon ate his last bite and washed it down with a swig of water. "This," he said, pulling the scrolls from their pouch and handing them to Waine.

The Seeker unrolled one and looked at it. He rotated it upside down, looked again, and re-rolled it to hand back to Kevon. Not recognizing the symbol on the second scroll, he handed it back almost immediately. When he opened the third, he held it closer, then further away. "What's this supposed to be, *Fire?*"

As he said the word, the scroll erupted.

Kevon, back turned to replace the other scrolls in their pouch, felt the release of magic almost as acutely as he felt the wash of heat on the back of his neck. He whirled around to see what had happened.

Waine stood, frozen in shock, holding the crumbling ends of the charred scroll. "I can't see!" he screamed, releasing the scroll at the same instant it reduced itself to soot in midair.

Kevon rushed over to steady the Seeker as Waine waved his arms about, trying to feel his surroundings for a safe place to sit down.

"Here, I've got you," Kevon reassured his friend, helping him down. From what he could tell on first examination, Waine was not too damaged. Aside from the blindness that he hoped was temporary, most of the hair on Waine's arms was missing, and his mustache still smoldered. There did not seem to be any burns.

The scroll, which Kevon had wanted to produce a focused stream of flames, had not worked as intended. Evidently, the release of the magic by an unfocused mind had expended it all at once in no particular direction.

But how? Kevon's mind raced frantically as he tried to calm Waine down. *I've never heard of anyone using a scroll but a Mage!* Kevon sighed. *I've never heard of a Mage using a sword before, either. Maybe Waine has some potential he's never developed.*

Waine calmed as his vision started to return. The Seeker chuckled nervously. "I always thought that magic was complicated," he joked. "If a knucklehead like me can do it…"

"That scroll took me about three hours to prepare." Kevon sighed. He struggled to find a way to explain it so Waine could understand. "I… bent the bow. You just shot the arrow." He snorted softly. "Into your foot."

"It was the strangest feeling..." Waine said, eyes distant. "I could see..."

"I saw it too," Kevon interjected. "It's what *we* see when we do magic. The True Runes. The clearer we can picture them, carve them, paint them... the more powerful we become."

"It was... fantastic... and terrible at the same time," Waine said. "It's not something I think I'd like to do again."

Kevon nodded. Inwardly, he was relieved. Part of him wanted someone else to be like him, to be able to understand him. Another part was proud of his uniqueness, elated to be the first and only to walk the two paths at once.

"We'd better get going again," Kevon said, making sure his belongings were snugged back into place. "Are you all right to ride?"

Waine scoffed at the question, and after checking the straps on his saddle, swung up and was ready to go.

Kevon was only moments behind Waine, and as he settled into his saddle and nodded, the Warriors flicked their reins and pointed their steeds back down the road.

CHAPTER 26

Travel resumed its now familiar rhythm. Evenings were far more interesting, however, as Kevon stepped up his training on all fronts. After dinner, while Waine cared for the horses, Kevon would practice controlling large releases of various types of magic, and then start scribing a scroll. When Waine was ready, Kevon would ground himself to iron before a vigorous sparring match. Afterward, Kevon would finish his scroll while Waine saw to the repairs and modifications of their equipment.

The Warriors left the hills surrounding Navlia and were in sight of the Western Ranges in less than two weeks. According to Holten's directions, Gurlin's tower was near. Waine completed Kevon's dagger-rig, and Kevon was traveling for the first time as a Mage. After so long on the road in lighter clothing, the red robes seemed constrictive. After only two days, he felt comfortable with his false limp. Instead of practicing swordplay, he learned how to use a staff for defense in combat. One set of saddlebags bulged with completed scrolls. Kevon had scribed three more each of Illusion and Light, emptying the jars of blue and gold ink in the process. He had taken three nights to complete a Movement scroll, taking extra time and scribing the Enhancement rune alongside it.

In the calm after sparring one night before he began scribing another scroll, Kevon sat talking with Waine.

"We're getting close to the tower," Kevon mused aloud.

Waine nodded. "You should start taking a shorter evening watch. I'll take a long night watch, and nap while you cook breakfast." Noticing Kevon's puzzled look, the Seeker explained further. "You're going to be doing most of the work when we get to the tower. You need to be completely rested."

Kevon nodded thoughtfully, and continued readying his scrollwork supplies. *I'd better rewrite the letter,* he thought, and began searching for the notes he'd written weeks ago while traveling with Carlo, Rhulcan, and Marelle. His eyes glazed over as he remembered the events around the time of the revelation of Holten's betrayal, and he rubbed the scars on his left arm. The scars made him think of Marelle. Thinking of Marelle made him think of *Marelle.*

"You okay?" Waine asked, tossing Kevon an apple as soon as the Mage looked up.

"Yeah..." Kevon sighed.

"You look like you were somewhere else," Waine commented. "That's not normal. You're always so focused on whatever you're doing."

"Well, I..."

"She must be something." The Seeker smiled and crunched into an apple of his own.

Kevon swallowed hard and nodded. A cascade of memories flooded over him, memories that could be put off only so long by focusing on everything else. Heartsick, Kevon sought the comfort of his Art, forming an Illusion rune. He formed a second rune alongside it, the rune of Enhancement, and flooded them both with power.

Kevon's illusion glowed into being so swiftly and completely that the realism startled him. The image wavered slightly as he refocused. This was Marelle as he remembered her, her bright green ribbon above a light green dress, coy smile in between.

"Wow," Waine said, peering at the image. "Hey, wait." The Seeker glanced from the illusion to Kevon and back again. "Is this what she really looks like, or just what you want her to look like?"

Kevon split his concentration enough to fling a nearby pebble with a hastily imagined Movement rune, sending it caroming off Waine's shoulder.

"Okay." Waine chuckled, raising his hands in surrender. "Just asking." He turned to admire the image for the remaining seconds Kevon held it together. After the illusion dissipated, he turned back to Kevon. "It's nice to see how strong your motivation is. I think we're gonna be all right." He finished the apple he was eating and tossed the core to where his stallion was tethered. "Wake me at full dark," he said, flopping down into his bedroll and drawing a fold of it over himself.

Kevon nodded and returned to his writing.

Brother Gurlin,

Here is the book I borrowed some time ago. My student, Kalron, is instructed to repay the money I owe you as well.

I've not yet had time to introduce him to our cause. Due to urgent business, I shall not. Kalron is bright, his ambition and thirst for knowledge should serve us well.

Until we meet again,

-Holten

Kevon inspected the letter half a dozen times, making sure everything was perfect. He could think of nothing in it that would give him away. He called up a small flame to melt some of the red wax onto the scroll, and pressed into it with the carved stamp that Carlo had given him. He packed the wax and the stamp away deep in one of the saddlebags, and waited for the seal to set.

Unwilling to devote his attention to scribing while on watch, Kevon surveyed the surrounding landscape as the evening deepened. The sun had set behind the mountains that Kevon and Waine were headed for in the west. The light reflected from some of the higher clouds and the hills to the east would keep the area illuminated for some time yet.

Kevon gathered his notes and some nearby branches to

start a fire. He smiled as the papers burned, feeling that things might finally start to work out. He sat and watched, relaxed, nearly forgetting to wake Waine at full dark.

When he finally rose to wake Waine, the Seeker spoke before Kevon had a chance.

"Someone's out there," Waine murmured softly, opening his eyes to narrow slits. "Horseback, headed this way."

"Call me Kalron," Kevon whispered, straightening his robe sleeves.

Waine nodded and sat up as Kevon crouched by the fire to warm his hands, symbols dancing in his mind, ready to cast at a moment's notice.

"Ho, there!" Waine called as the hoof-beats drew near. They slowed and quieted as a red-cloaked rider entered the flickering firelight.

"Good evening!" a cheery voice called.

"Identify yourself!" Waine challenged.

"Pholos Magus," the rider answered, pushing back his hood to reveal short blonde hair and features that put him at Kevon's age, or younger. He saw Kevon and corrected himself. "Pholos 'ap Tarska, to be exact."

Kevon stood. "Kalron 'ap Holten," he announced. "And my escort, Willem." Kevon ignored Waine's upraised eyebrow and continued. "What brings you down the road at this hour?"

"Overconfidence," the Mage called. "I pushed for a place I know to spend the night, and it's still miles distant. May I share your fire?"

"Willem?" Kevon asked.

"It's your choice, *Kalron*," Waine replied, a hint of sarcasm creeping into his voice.

Kevon shot him a reproachful glance and the Seeker nodded.

"Of course, join us," Kevon answered. "Willem, will you take his horse and put it with ours?"

"Certainly," Waine said with a half-bow, embracing the role. He took the offered reins as the Mage rode closer and dismounted.

Pholos approached the fire, ruffling his cloak and shuddering. He knelt and rubbed his hands together before spreading his palms out to catch the heat. The young Mage sighed in exasperation. "I really should have traveled farther tonight. I don't think I'll be able to make it back to the tower tomorrow, now."

"Tower?" Kevon remarked. "We're headed to a tower near here."

"You have business with Master Gurlin?" Pholos asked, peering at Kevon. "There are no other towers anywhere near here."

"Yes," Kevon answered. "I bear a message from..."

"*Holten!*" Pholos exclaimed. "I knew I recognized the name! Master Gurlin has mentioned him several times." The Mage's searching gaze turned to something more like admiration. "You apprenticed under Holten... Our meeting is fortunate, indeed. We'll be at the tower in a day and a half, at most."

"A day and a half?" Waine asked, returning from unloading the Mage's horse. "What's in a day and a half?"

"We'll all reach Gurlin's tower," Kevon answered quickly. "Pholos studies there, correct?"

"Yes," Pholos beamed. "I was fortunate enough to Apprentice under Tarska Magus in Navlia, and have been studying with Gurlin and the others for about a year."

Kevon saw Waine's eyes widen at the word 'others'. "I've only studied with Master Holten, as his only Apprentice," he began. "What's it like with... how many others are there?"

"Myself and four others," Pholos answered. "Two other Journeymen, and two full Mages, though Mirsa will test for Master very soon." The young Mage seemed aquiver with excitement. "Are you going to be staying to study?" he blurted.

"I think I would enjoy that, Pholos," Kevon answered, smiling. *I'd probably enjoy it more than killing you and your friends, but some things can't be helped.*

"You two had better get some sleep," Waine said. "This talking isn't getting us to that tower."

"Oh! ...Willem, is it?" Pholos asked. "You'll be able to sleep too. I can take care of the watch tonight, and tomorrow."

"How's that?" Waine asked cautiously.

"I'll show you," Pholos answered cheerfully. "Kalron, would you put the fire out?"

Kevon hesitated a moment, saw the half-shrug that Waine gave, and with a short burst of power snuffed the flames into muted embers.

After a moment, Kevon felt a deepening of the darkness. He could feel only faintly the workings of magic by Pholos, but what he did feel turned his stomach.

Gradually, a spot in midair between Kevon and Pholos began to darken even further. Kevon found he could not tear his eyes away from the darkness. It deepened farther than he thought possible, darker than nothingness. The patch of blackness continued to darken, becoming increasingly difficult to bear looking at, but impossible to ignore. The bad taste in Kevon's mouth became acrid, sulfurous. Just when he felt he could not take any more, unsure if he would scream in terror, or spit from revulsion, Pholos sprang forward, thrusting his arms into the nightmarish nothingness.

The young Mage lurched backwards, holding his prize at arm's length. Kevon heard hissing, screeching, and a wild flapping for the first few moments. Then, the unnatural darkness seemed to collapse in on itself before diffusing into the night. The oppressive feeling that had weighed down on Kevon lifted abruptly, and the commotion stopped.

"Kalron, the fire, please?" Pholos asked, voice strained.

Eager to banish the remaining darkness, Kevon brought the flames back to their previous levels instantly, causing an intense wash of heat and a loud 'woof'.

Waine reacted instantly, jumping back from the fire pit and drawing his sword. "Demon!" he cried, rushing toward Pholos.

"No!" shouted the young Mage, turning to shield the creature he'd pulled from the darkness.

"Willem!" Kevon barked, and the Seeker stopped short, but kept his blade at the ready, and started to circle Pholos.

As Pholos turned again to keep himself interposed between the creature and Waine, Kevon got his first good look at it.

Kevon could see right away why Waine had charged at the creature. If his disguise had not forbidden it, he would have drawn steel himself. Kevon wondered if the creature truly was a demon. It had a small, bulbous body and long spindly limbs. Its skin was dull black, leathery, and hung in folds on its body, but stretched taut over the arms and legs that seemed to have no defined muscles. The three claws on each limb were tipped with sickly looking yellow talons roughly twice as long as human fingernails. The creature's wings were at least as long as its arms, shaped somewhat like bat wings. In the firelight Kevon could see the orange tint in the dark translucent wing material, and red fingerlike veins spread through them.

"You're scaring him, Willem!" Pholos cried. "It's just an imp! Back off and let me work or I'll lose control of it!"

Kevon could see the Dark spell and his efforts at Control were wearing on Pholos. He made up his mind, waved Waine back, and formed the Aid rune in his mind.

As Kevon let the first bit of power flow through the symbol, Pholos relaxed visibly as he used the offered magic. The Mage put his summoned imp down on the ground, where it sat crouched, motionless as a statue. Pholos reached into a cloak pocket and drew out a coil of braided rope with a section on one end wrapped in leather. He wrapped the leathered end around the imp's leg near its foot, taking care not to touch the rope itself to the creature. He tied the other end firmly to a protruding loop of an exposed tree root, yanked on it hard a few times to test it. He then moved to the other side of the fire, well out of the rope's three foot length. After looking to see that Kevon and Waine were far enough away as well, he whispered. "Don't panic," and dropped the Control spell.

The imp launched itself forward at Pholos. For a split second, Kevon saw the fire reflected in its eyes, far too large for its face, looking for the world like two polished obsidian spheres. The creature reached the end of its rope and barely missed landing in the fire by contorting its body as it fell. It howled, turning to slash at the rope that bound it. The howl changed to a shriek as it contacted the rope. It drew its hand back and cradled it as if it had been burnt.

Pholos snapped his fingers and the imp's head whipped around to fix directly on him. The Mage raised his arms menacingly and the flames in the fire curved toward the imp. The imp cringed, hissing. Pholos lowered his arms and the fire resumed burning normally. He turned his back on the creature and sat down, making himself comfortable.

"You should both threaten it and then act bored," he commented. "It settles them down quicker."

"What is it doing in our camp?" Waine growled, keeping the Mage and his pet both squarely in view, still brandishing his sword.

"It's going to keep watch for us. Imps are quite good at it if you know how to handle them," Pholos remarked. "It's fascinating, really. The plane I Summoned it from? They're as common as birds, and flock like them, too. A single imp will attack if confused, but on the whole they're cowards and..."

"I don't like it." Waine leapt toward the creature and took a swing that would have connected if the imp hadn't jumped back. The Seeker snorted, stepped closer, and spat at the wide-eyed, hissing prisoner. He sheathed his sword and walked over to Kevon.

Despite his revulsion at the casting of the spell, and the considerable discomfort at having the creature nearby at all, Kevon couldn't help but wonder why the imp was held so easily by the rope. "When it tried the rope, it looked like the rope hurt it," Kevon observed. "How does that work?"

"Ahh..." Pholos sat up, eager to have another Mage to converse with. "The rope is enchanted with strength, normal rope could not hold up if it were only that thick. The other enchantment is Light. Since imps are from the Dark realm, they can't stand light. They see in the dark and have great hearing. It makes them ideal for this. He's afraid of us, but figures we're not interested in killing him. Anything else that could pose a threat would have to be pretty sneaky to even get within bowshot of us."

"I still don't like it," Waine grumbled, hand still on his sword hilt. "I don't know if I can sleep with it here."

"It'll be hours before I have the strength to send it back. Less if Kalron helps..." Pholos paused. "Maybe much less. You're the easiest Mage I've ever drawn aid from." He began to ramble on the tangent. "Borrowed power is always easier to use because the effort is shared, but you're either very practiced at aiding, or have a huge amount of raw magic."

Kevon shrugged. "The excitement, maybe. I'm not all that powerful. My best Art is Illusion."

Pholos frowned. "The way you handled the fire, I assumed you were a Pyromancer. *Illusion* is your primary Art? What can you do with it?"

Kevon had more than enough magical reserve left to pull off a decent illusion. Tonight had been the first time he'd made an illusion of a person, so he thought he'd expand on that. He formed the Illusion rune, and the Enhancement rune alongside it. He hoped the combination would sustain multiple manifestations of his spell. Concentrating deeply on the details, he let the power flow into the runes, and stepped off to the right. Twin images of himself stepped off to the left, and stood still. He made a show of looking around at both of the other images as he forced them to do the same.

"Who"

"Is"

"The"

"Real"

"Me?"

The voices came from his throat and the directions of the false images in turn.

"Amazing." Pholos grinned after looking from one to another for a few moments. "I can't tell."

"That one," Waine grumbled, pointing at Kevon. "Dust swirled when you stepped."

"I'll have to remember that for next time," Kevon said, dropping the spell and watching the Mage-smoke from the illusory copies disappear into the night. "Although that was difficult by itself. I don't know if I could do more than that."

"That was the first time you've ever done that?" Pholos asked, eyes wide.

Kevon nodded, and staggered, feigning weakness. He'd forgotten what effort it used to take to cast even simpler spells. He didn't want to raise suspicion now.

Waine stepped forward to steady Kevon, but was waved away.

"I'll be fine; I just need to get some rest." Kevon said, standing straighter and taking a deep breath. "You're sure that ... thing is safe?"

"Never had a problem with one," Pholos reassured Kevon. "They're better than roosters too, they start howling before first light. Afraid of the sun. Then..."

"The less I know about these demon-spawn, the better," Waine interrupted. "You two get some sleep. I'm going to stay up a while."

"Demons, hmph." Pholos muttered under his breath.

Kevon and Pholos arranged bedrolls in comfortable spots near the fire, across from the imp. Both were soon sleeping soundly.

Waine sat some distance away, watching the surrounding area. After two hours of watching its all black, lidless eyes flicker over the camp, to the horses, then to him, and watching the imp's head whirl around at the slightest natural noise Waine would simply ignore, he gave up.

Waine shrugged down into his blanket. "Demons..." The Seeker sighed and shook his head, then relaxed and drifted off to sleep.

CHAPTER 27

The imp's frantic howling woke them as the first hint of light became visible over the mountains to the east. Pholos was the first up, having slept more soundly due to his complete confidence in the captive imp. Kevon rose slower, pretending pain and stiffness in his right leg to legitimize the limp he needed to conceal the knife.

"Are you all right?" Pholos asked, genuinely concerned. "There are plenty of potions at the tower that would heal that, I'm sure."

"It's an old wound, beyond healing," Kevon reassured him. "It helps me focus on the magical, rather than the physical, and reminds me what carelessness can cost." He felt a wave of revulsion towards himself when he saw the spark of admiration in the young Mage's eyes. *I sincerely hope I don't have to kill you, Pholos.* Kevon sighed. "Should we dismiss our guardian?"

Pholos nodded. "How is your Control?" he asked. "If you can Control the imp to stillness, I can unbind it and open the portal. But the Control is essential… they're poisonous."

"Not so good," Kevon admitted.

"I can do it myself if I hurry before the sun comes up any further," the young Mage explained. "The darker it is, the easier it is to open a portal to *there*." He paused for a moment. "It would be easier with help."

"I could help." Waine half-drew his sword.

"That, *Warrior*, would be like me striking your horse down with a bolt of lightning," Pholos said, voice hard, glaring at Waine. "I brought it here against its will, it served its purpose, and I will send it back, unharmed."

"Get on with it then, before it panics the horses." Waine growled and stalked away from camp.

Pholos glared until Waine disappeared from sight in the distance. "Shall we begin?" he asked, turning to Kevon.

Kevon nodded and formed the Aid rune in his mind. He felt Pholos take control of the power, and saw the Control rune the younger Mage was using. With that image in his mind to guide him, Kevon superimposed his own Control rune over Pholos's, and let the power flow.

Pholos approached the immobilized imp and untied it, leaving the rope lying on the ground, and backed away.

Kevon saw another rune form alongside the Control rune, and felt the extra drain on his reserves as the air near the imp became noticeably darker. The feeling of *wrongness* that he'd gotten from watching the spell the night before returned tenfold now that he was assisting in the casting.

The opening portal wrenched at his senses, contrasting more than it had last night now in the pre-dawn light. Kevon knew he could not bear to form the Dark rune to help steady the spell; he struggled to keep himself from vomiting as he felt his reserves flowing into it.

The Control rune shattered and Kevon felt Pholos refocusing the energy to the Dark magic. A chill ran down Kevon's spine as the imp shrieked in triumph and launched itself into the blackness and vanished.

As one, the Mages released the magic. The darkness turned in on itself and collapsed with a soft *thump*.

Pholos wiped his brow with a cloth fished out from one of his robe pockets, and took a swig of water from a skin only to spit it out after a few moments. "It gets easier, with practice," he told Kevon. "Not many have the stomach to wield such power."

Kevon shuddered and nodded. "I'd rather keep watch, myself."

Pholos snickered. "You'll learn. The Dark rune is the first that all of Gurlin's students are required to master."

Kevon nodded mechanically, mind racing. A Master Wizard, two full Wizards, one nearly a Master herself, and three Journeymen, all of whom were trained to use this vile rune. Kevon wondered what they were like, how using magic that even *tasted* evil for so long had changed them. Kevon wondered if the teaching of the Dark rune was a focal point of the plan Gurlin and Holten were a part of, something larger that required Dark magic. Something sinister enough that it would merit killing someone just because they might not be interested in helping.

The guilt that had been nagging at Kevon over the possibility of the use of deadly force to deal with the threat that Gurlin represented suddenly vanished. The steely glare that Waine gave him as Kevon glanced at the Warrior almost made him smile. Kevon knew that if there was any way that Waine could get in on the impending action at the tower, he would be sure to make it happen. Even though his friend had not felt the taint of the magic himself, Kevon sensed that Waine *knew* it was wrong beyond any explanation.

Heartened by his rediscovered sense of justice, Kevon fetched something to eat, and began bantering in earnest with Pholos. Pretending eagerness to begin studies, he tried to dig subtly for clues about connections between the two Master Wizards, and anything else that would give him more information or an edge in the coming battle.

Kevon inquired what the schedule was like, a typical day in the life of a student Journeyman. He was somewhat disappointed to learn that Mirsa, Gurlin's top student, was housed in a distant part of the tower's structure. All of her training was now private, and she rarely consorted with the others.

Kevon had hoped to catch them all together, killing Gurlin first, and then the best-trained student next, while he still had the element of surprise. He figured panicked Journeymen of lesser abilities would be easy enough to deal with as needed. In close quarters his knife would be both deadly offense and effective magical defense. *As long as Gurlin is the first to go,* Kevon thought somberly.

Pholos chattered on amiably whenever travel slowed or they stopped to rest and water the horses. Kevon made mental notes and reformulated attack strategies at least a dozen times before they even stopped for the evening. After a light meal and even more talk, Kevon decided that no amount of planning would take all of the possibilities into account. As long as Gurlin was the first to fall, Kevon hoped he would be able to figure out what to do as events unfolded.

The travelers sat talking over a small fire until late in the evening. Waine did not tell a single story, and responded to direct questions with one and two word answers. As full dark neared, the Seeker excused himself, grabbed some gear, and headed out into the night. Shortly thereafter, Kevon once again aided Pholos in Summoning an imp and binding it. After the imp calmed, the Mages conversed quietly until the creature panicked at Waine's return.

Waine stalked into camp, spat contemptuously on the tethered imp, and lay down to sleep in his already arranged blanket.

Kevon and Pholos both laughed at the imp's puzzled silence briefly before following Waine into slumber.

CHAPTER 28

Kevon woke before the imp panicked at dawn's approach. His stomach felt knotted up, he'd slept badly, having several nightmares. Time was growing short until he would have to confront and kill the evil Magi. Although Kevon had seen death, and felt partly responsible for the bandit's death on the road to Eastport, he'd never killed before.

They're just a half a dozen problems, Kevon thought, eyes closed tightly, hand moving unconsciously to the hidden sheath on the back of his right leg. *And I've got a handful of solutions.*

Kevon forced himself to rest, knowing how important every ounce of strength would be later.

Soon enough, the imp began squealing in terror. The Mages rose quickly, and Kevon could see that Waine had already left camp.

Without preamble, Pholos began untying the already immobilized imp. Kevon formed the Aid rune and matched the Control rune that materialized in his mind. Pholos backed safely away and formed the Dark rune, pumping power into it almost recklessly. The rapid power drain alone did not faze Kevon, but added to the sheer vulgarity of the spell, it made Kevon stagger a few steps before he caught himself.

As soon as the imp entered the portal to escape to its own plane, Pholos released the spell.

Kevon thought the rift closed a little slower, the mind-warping edges of the tear in space wobbling like a drunkard's smacking lips. The sound it made as it collapsed in on itself this time was more of a *squish* than a *thump*. Somehow, Kevon felt less drained, but more violated. He placed a cupped hand to his mouth and breathed for a few moments before Pholos commented.

"It's easier to do it before it gets any lighter, isn't it?" he asked Kevon. "Most things are like that, easier to cast if they're already present around you. Fire when it's hot, Water when it's raining. It's rarely useful."

Kevon nodded numbly, recalling conversations in his studies with Master Holten about elemental affinities. The stress he'd felt before, the taint of the Dark magic, and the thought of his former mentor weighed heavily on Kevon. Sighing, he shuffled over to his pile of saddlebags and pulled out some bread and jerky.

"Put that away," Waine called as he strolled back into camp with two skinned rabbits slung over one arm and a handful of empty snare lines in the other hand.

Pholos whispered something, pointing to a nearby deadfall, and a small round snapped off and rolled lurchingly into camp to tumble into the used fire pit.

Kevon took over, bringing the wood to a full blaze in under half a minute. By the time he'd gotten it going well enough to release his spell, Kevon noticed Pholos was sitting by the fire, shaking almost convulsively. *After casting the Dark portal, he would have been better off gathering wood by hand,* Kevon thought. *It was more impressive his way, though.*

Waine had the rabbits spitted and cooking over the fire in no time. When they were done, the Seeker took the smaller and let the Mages split the larger of the rabbits.

Kevon knew that half a rabbit wouldn't satisfy him, but remembered how little he used to eat while he'd been apprenticing with Holten. The work of a scholar did not require the same meals as a Warrior. Kevon made a point to not even finish his half, though he did eat more than Pholos.

"That was very good, Willem," Pholos commented. "Don't you think so, Kalron?"

"Willem is a fine cook, when the mood strikes him," Kevon agreed.

"I don't suppose you'd consider wielding copper instead of steel," the younger Mage joked.

"I rather enjoy being in a kitchen," Waine responded.

"Oh?"

"When I'm looking for a wench to tumble."

Kevon laughed, half at the joke, and half at Pholos's gaping expression.

Pholos's look of shock slowly lifted into a grin. "Fair enough," he conceded.

After the three of them were done and had disposed of their scraps in the fire, the Mages repacked their belongings and Waine saddled the horses.

Once the three were back on the road, talk was sparse. Kevon could not think of anything else he really needed to know, and had no desire to get to know Pholos any better. After a few attempts on Pholos's part to strike up a conversation, Kevon told the Mage that he was road-weary, and looking forward to a real night's rest.

Shortly after the midday break, they spotted the tower in the distance. As they drew nearer Kevon could see that it was easily eight to ten times wider than any he had ever seen before. It was also taller than it looked at first glance, easily twice the height of some of the palatial towers Kevon had seen in Navlia. The sheer magnitude of the building was intimidating on a level Kevon had not been prepared for.

The group followed the streamside track up to the tower. Pholos briefly explained how the moat surrounding the tower was fed from a magically forced spring, much like the canalways and fountains of Navlia. Pholos's spirits seemed to lift the nearer they got, in spite of his companions' lack of enthusiasm.

The group topped a small ridge, and outbuildings came into view. One was clearly a stable; the other could have been a large farmhouse.

"You'll have to stay there, Willem," Pholos said, gesturing

toward the building. "It's rare that anyone but Mages gain admittance to the tower, and Warriors, never."

"I've no problem with that," Waine countered. "I daresay I could use some time away from magic."

The three continued, passing through an apple orchard, a hay field, and finally close by a flock of sheep tended by a young boy. Upon seeing the travelers, the shepherd walked closer until he recognized Pholos, then stopped to wave as the three rode past.

"Master Gurlin has a hand in everything that goes on in sight of his tower," Pholos commented. "His protection is repaid in gifts and service from all the nearby families."

"Protection?" Kevon asked, throwing a sideways glance at Waine. "Protection from what?"

"Whatever people need protecting from, I suppose," Pholos answered. "Years ago, when Master Gurlin first arrived, he rid the area of orcs that had been marauding around the valley. The locals banded together to help construct the tower, and have traded service for security ever since."

"So..." Waine began slowly, "Your boss is rather well liked around here?"

"Children of the families in the valley squabble over which one of them gets to serve in the tower. Master Gurlin will only allow one per family, so that the households remain intact," Pholos answered. "Right now, the tower outbuildings house around two dozen, half of which spend the day inside the tower walls, but leave at night."

Waine spat into his hand and ran his fingers through his hair to slick it back. "I'd better make myself presentable if I'm to meet all these new people," he grunted.

Pholos looked away, disgusted, but Kevon saw how the Seeker's free hand moved to rest on his sword hilt. Kevon knew now that he would be on his own once inside the tower, but there might be danger outside once the locals knew of the attack. Waine would have to be the one that made good on their escape once Kevon had seen justice done. Kevon decided to trust Waine's judgment in this matter.

They arrived at the stable and dismounted. Pholos introduced the two hostlers to Kalron and Willem. The young Mage took only one saddlebag, leaving the rest of his tack and supplies for the servants of the tower to deal with.

Kevon said a hasty goodbye to Waine as he shouldered his Mage-appropriate saddlebags and followed Pholos to the tower. His skin crawled as he set foot on the drawbridge that was the only entrance to the gigantic stone structure. Without trying, he could feel the enchantments that protected the bridge from the weathering of the elements, and strengthened it to withstand nearly any kind of attack.

Pholos looked back at Kevon and smiled as if recalling the first time he had crossed the bridge. "Follow me to the kitchen. After we have a hot meal, we'll find Master Gurlin, and arrange your quarters."

The two Mages continued on across the bridge, nearing the stone archway that led into the tower, and Kevon got his first glimpse of the inside. What he'd thought was an inner stone wall was really a central tower within free-standing outer walls. The central tower took up perhaps a third of the area inside the outer enclosure, and rose almost to the top of the outside walls. Kevon saw three rope bridges with wooden slats spanning the distance from the top of the inner tower to the flared balcony battlements that curved inward near the top of the outer wall. Noting that the three he saw were in roughly cardinal directions, Kevon assumed there was a fourth bridge on the other side of the inner tower.

Pholos led Kevon through the large archway, and veered off to the right as soon as they were clear of the entrance, headed toward a squat, boxy structure with smoke coming from a chimney. Other multi-story buildings of various shapes and sizes seemed to grow out of the walls of the outer enclosure.

Before the two Mages reached the building, Kevon could smell bread baking. A young girl sitting by the door to the kitchen rose as she heard the outer door opening, starting across the room toward them. Pholos held up two fingers. The girl smiled, turned on her heel, and darted back through the kitchen door.

Shortly after they had dropped their gear, washed up, and seated themselves, the girl reappeared. She carried plates with bread, corn, and thick slabs of roasted pork. She struggled a bit, and almost dropped Kevon's plate on him. Red-faced, she managed to save it at the last second, and hurried away as soon as she set the plate down.

As they ate, Pholos described various parts of the compound. Most interesting to Kevon was the layout of the central tower. The first floor was a large meeting hall and several small storerooms. Half of the next floor was housing for students, the rest divided between several small libraries and laboratories. The third floor was a library reserved for full Mages. Above that, only Gurlin and visiting Masters were allowed.

Pholos chattered on between bites of food, and Kevon nodded along absently, paying little attention. His mind wandered to the possibilities that lay above the third floor of the tower. He wondered if the answers he was looking for were there, waiting for him.

Sensing Kevon's lack of interest, Pholos quieted and ate rapidly, finishing about the same time as Kevon did. The younger Mage stood, dusted crumbs from his cloak, and motioned for Kevon to follow. Kevon stood, stretched, and shouldered his bags once more. The pair ventured outside into the heat of the afternoon.

Kevon followed Pholos to the entrance of the inner tower, and into the building. They passed without pause through a small ceremonial antechamber, down a short hallway that opened into the formal greeting hall. As they moved through the hall, Kevon could see openings along the sides of the chamber that opened to hallways running parallel to the length of the larger room. The hallways were bricked to blend with the room from several angles, and a casual observer might miss them completely. Kevon smiled and walked faster to catch back up with Pholos.

A similarly concealed hallway at the far end of the greeting hall led to twin staircases that curved up and back along the outer wall of the tower. Pholos turned to the right and began ascending the steps quickly, Kevon close behind.

The pair had advanced less than twenty steps up the shallow stairwell when they met another robed figure descending.

"Who is this?!" the newcomer snapped, stepping to the side to get a better look at Kevon. The short, harsh echoes of the stone passage seemed to fit the woman's voice to her appearance. She was no taller than Kevon's sister, but that was where the resemblance ended. Her startling red hair was pulled back in a braid that whipped around to the side as her head twisted to fix on Kevon. Cold blue eyes were framed in her severe, pinched face.

"What a surprise!" Pholos cried, almost masking the sarcastic overtones in his voice. "Mirsa 'ap Briltor, this is Kalron 'ap Holten." The Mage paused for a moment as the woman's eyes widened. "He's come to study with us," he added happily.

Mirsa refocused her gaze on Kevon. "Master Gurlin is in his study, and will not be disturbed. What were you planning on doing with *him*?" she sniffed.

"I'm going to show him to his room, Mirsa," Pholos chided. "The Master would expect no less for a student of his friend."

"We shall see." Mirsa ruffled her cloak dramatically and swept down past Pholos and Kevon, huffing slightly.

Kevon looked questioningly at Pholos.

"She sees you as competition," Pholos explained. "Not just you, all Magi. And if you're not a Mage, you're nothing. It's sad, really." He flashed Kevon a smile and started back up the stairs.

Kevon followed Pholos to the top of the stairway. Another narrow hallway doubled back along the stairwell before turning to head back in the direction of the tower's entrance. They passed two doorways in the first section of hallway, rounded the corner, and passed two more before Pholos stopped at the next door.

"This is the best room we have open now. It's not the biggest, but it's halfway between the entrance and the laboratories," Pholos explained. "There's library access on the other end of this floor, through the workshops, but it's easier to take the left staircase from the main floor."

Pholos turned to go. "I don't know that I'd wander around just yet. Mirsa's the only other one here that knows you, and she'd forget if it suited her. Get settled in your room and come to the dining hall for dinner later. Master Gurlin usually takes his evening meal there with us."

"Thank you, Pholos," Kevon answered. "You've been a great help, I won't forget it."

Pholos waved and disappeared around the corner.

Kevon opened the door to the room and went in. He quickly closed it, pausing only to light the torch with a quick burst of magic. He set his baggage down and took a look around.

Evil has its advantages, Kevon thought grimly as he studied the furnishings. Any of the items arranged around the small room would have been out of place in even the nicest inn Kevon had stayed at during his travels. The wooden chairs and table were smooth and polished, not with age, but by artisans with tools and oils. The bedposts and accompanying tables were made of a dark wood that Kevon had not seen before. Wherever there was a flat surface, it seemed as if he could see inches into the grain of the wood, even though it was perfectly ordinary to the touch. The blankets on the bed looked newly made, stitched with a decorative pattern around the edges. The pitcher and washbasin on the table next to the door were bone-white porcelain.

Kevon sat down on the bed, wondering what to do next. He didn't particularly want to be seen snooping about before the other Magi knew about him. The only thought that crossed Kevon's mind was that if he was meeting Gurlin for the evening meal, there might be a chance the Wizard would be tired from the day's work.

Any advantage I can get, Kevon thought. He reached back to adjust the hidden knife so that it would be a bit more comfortable, slumped over to the side, and closed his eyes to take a nap.

CHAPTER 29

K evon startled awake at the light knocking on his door.

"Kalron?" Pholos's voice strained through the thick door. "Are you still in there?"

Kevon rose, yawning and stretching as he went to open the door.

"Ahh. You are still here." Pholos smiled happily. "I thought I would stop by on my way from the library to take you to meet Master Gurlin."

Kevon nodded. "I just need to collect a few things." He quickly located the book and the letter, pocketing them both carefully before returning to his waiting escort. "Lead the way."

The small dining hall was as crowded as a busy inn. Three other Magi were already seated at two of the smaller tables, and it looked like the tower's support staff were just finishing up their evening meal before the Mages were expected. The gathering seemed to be missing only Gurlin and Mirsa.

The three other Mages did not seem surprised at Kevon's presence, and Pholos introduced him to each in turn before they sat at another table.

The first was an older, somewhat overweight fellow, sitting reading a text, oblivious to what went on around him. Pholos had to wave his hand in front of the book before the Mage took any notice of them.

"Shofud 'ap Geppe," Pholos said as the seated Mage lowered his book, "This is Kalron 'ap Holten."

"... Pleasure." Shofud grudgingly released his book with one hand to shake Kevon's hand. He gave a halfhearted smile, and seemed annoyed until Pholos moved on.

"Rettun and Pætub 'ap Liffid. Brothers, as you might guess," Pholos continued, gesturing to the other two Magi.

The brothers sat silently at their table, looking at a small game board. The lone piece in the center of the elongated board was quivering, seemingly at random. As Kevon approached the table, he could feel the separate Movement runes each pushing against each other.

Pholos stood by quietly until the game piece flew suddenly toward the end of the board nearest the larger brother, caroming off the raised edge. Huffing, the defeated brother snatched the piece out of the air as it flew by.

The younger brother laughed. "Keep trying, Pæt."

Pætub glared and placed the piece in the center of the board before folding it up and latching it closed. Pholos continued the introduction, but Kevon's attention was focused on how dangerous these two would be when the time came to deal with Gurlin. Kevon did note, however, that even the sulking Pætub was more interested in meeting him than Shofud had been.

Kevon quietly processed all the information he was gathering, constantly revising his plans for the coming attack. The brothers were dangerous, in some ways more dangerous than a skilled Elementalist. Attacks with the more volatile elements, Fire and Wind, were easily disrupted by iron and steel. Water and Earth were not usually effective or practical for a quick assault. Normal objects propelled by magic, however, did not dissipate when intercepted by the forbidden metals; momentum was momentum. Rettun and Pætub had most likely been practicing against each other for years. Perhaps they played their game often and Kevon could time his attack to take advantage of the brief period when they would be weakened.

Kevon hoped the opportunity presented itself quickly. The longer he stayed here, the greater the chance that he would slip up and give himself away. Worse, if Holten happened to show up. Kevon would be as good as dead.

Kevon and Pholos had just seated themselves when everyone else in the room stood. Looking toward the door, Pholos retook his feet as well, and Kevon followed.

"Good evening," the stooped figure at the door rasped.

"Good evening," murmured the crowded servants and Magi.

The tap-tapping of the old man's cane against the hardwood floor, loud in the hushed room, ended abruptly as his gaze fixed on Kevon.

"Who is *he*?" Gurlin hissed.

"A student of your longtime friend," Pholos said, stepping forward. "A friend who sends his greetings. This is Kalron 'ap Holten."

"My Master has often spoken highly of you," Kevon offered quickly. "I look forward to hearing your side of some of the... adventures... you had as Apprentices."

Gurlin chuckled, a hoarse gurgle that led into a short fit of coughing. "Spoken often of me, eh? Did he ever mention the money he owes me?"

"He did. And your book, as well." Kevon nodded, and pulled both the book and the letter from his pockets.

A tug of Movement followed by a gust of Wind tore the parchment from Kevon's grasp, carrying it across the room to Gurlin. The Master's bony hand shot out to snatch the letter as it reached him.

Still clutching his cane in one hand, the old man held the edge of the scroll in the other. The wax of the seal writhed for a moment like a living thing before dropping to the ground, motionless. The letter uncurled, flattening out as Gurlin looked it over. After a few moments, the Mage flicked it casually aside as it flared to a blinding brilliance and was reduced to powder-fine ash in an instant.

Each display of magical prowess made Kevon's stomach twist uneasily. Kevon had known coming here would be dangerous, but this Wizard was effortlessly performing feats of combat-oriented magic without pause for concentration. How was Kevon supposed to get the advantage of surprise he'd been counting on when Gurlin could set him ablaze the moment he touched the knife hidden under his cloak? There was no way anyone would miss the discharge of magic when Kevon pulled the blade.

"I trust Brother Holten sent all twenty gold with you," Gurlin half-asked, eyes gleaming.

"No," Kevon answered, shaking his head. "Master Holten bade me give you thirty, for your time, and your trouble." He paused. "Would you like it now?"

"Now is not the time for business long overdue," Gurlin said, lips curled back in a disturbing grin. "Now is a time for celebration, as we prepare for the advancement of one student, and the brotherhood of another!"

As Gurlin's voice rose and began cracking toward the end of his last sentence, the servants who were not already moving to finish preparations for the meal sprang into action. It took only moments for the clutter on the smaller tables to be trundled into the kitchen. No sooner had the last servant entered the kitchen than they began pouring out again. Loaded serving platters and brimming pitchers of drink soon filled the center of the long table in the middle of the room. Gurlin shuffled to the head of the table, and addressed the staff, who stood in a semi-circle at the opposite end of the table.

"Thank you, my friends. This looks wonderful," he began. "Tomorrow is a different matter. We shall have three visiting Masters to attend Mirsa's promotion test." He looked over the lineup of servants for a few more moments. "Spare no expense. Refuse no request. There will be additional Magi accompanying them, along with some of their servants. If we treat them well, they may decide to study here, and in doing so, ensure the continued safety of this valley."

The servants stood silently until Gurlin dismissed them with a smile and a nod. They filed out through the front door without so much as a word.

"Kalron?" Gurlin asked as the last serving maid exited the

building.

"Yes, Master?" Kevon answered, smiling and fighting the disgust that made the corner of his mouth twitch ever so slightly.

"Would you do me the honor of sitting at my right hand?" Gurlin rasped.

"Of course," Kevon responded, walking over and around behind the old man to his appointed place. His hand flexed involuntarily as he passed behind the Wizard, it was all he could do to keep from reaching through the slit in his robe pocket for the knife in at his back.

Pholos followed Kevon around and sat to his right. Shofud sat at Gurlin's left, across from Kevon, and the brothers filled in the two remaining chairs on that side.

As soon as everyone was seated, platters and plates began making their way around the table, everyone helping to serve each other. Kevon thought it reminded him of an evening meal at any farmhouse he'd ever visited. The evil seething under the surface that had been so apparent only minutes before was now nowhere to be seen.

Pholos chattered all throughout the meal about the other Magi that would be attending the Test tomorrow. Kevon began to feel sorry for the young Mage as he saw the rolled eyes and knowing glances the other Magi exchanged when Pholos was not looking.

Kevon silently decided that if there was any way he could spare Pholos, convince the young Mage that Gurlin was evil, he would make every effort. Since he dared not try anything with additional Magi around, there would be time to see if he could open Pholos's eyes and turn the young Mage to his cause.

The meal drew to a close, and Gurlin began asking questions about Holten, and about how Kevon's former Master had been doing. Kevon saw no reason to lie about anything other than the letter, or his true intentions here, and so spoke openly about his training. Gurlin frowned when Kevon mentioned illusion, but Pholos broke in, telling of the spell Kevon had worked the first night they'd met.

Gurlin listened quietly, and after Pholos had finished the tale, spoke softly. "You may be closer to attaining full Mage status than you know, Kalron. I'll not try you for promotion tomorrow, having only heard of your skills. You've been Journeyman for less than two seasons, and full Mages are rarely promoted as soon as two years." He laughed with a rasping cough. "Holten always did push his students harder than anyone else, though. The brothers should be ready to Test in two seasons. Perhaps you will be, too."

The news earned Kevon a beaming smile from Pholos, and silent stares from the rest of the table.

"Wouldn't that be wonderful?" Gurlin continued. "A Journeyman student of mine, advancing to Full Mage in less than a year?"

Dull murmurs of affirmation from the other side of the table contrasted with Pholos's enthusiastic shaking of Kevon's left shoulder. Kevon was unsure if Gurlin had intended the friction from the comments he'd just made. Competition and pride about the strength of one's Arts, or different learning speeds had never been mentioned. Competition and animosity could be the tools of a teacher trying to get the best from his students, but Kevon chose to believe the old man was just being cruel.

Hoping to draw even more anger from the other students, Kevon's lips twisted into a grin that mirrored Pholos's. "Nothing would please me more, Master," he said, inclining his head toward Gurlin.

Pholos continued picking at his food and talking. A few minutes later, he leaned back in his chair and set his utensils down. The other three Magi appeared relieved as Gurlin told them they were dismissed.

"Kalron, please stay a while," Gurlin rasped as Kevon stood to leave with the others.

Kevon nodded and sat back down.

After the others had left, Gurlin spoke again. "Shofud did not seem as upset as the brothers at my evaluation of your potential... Any other time and I would have said that Mirsa would be the one to be... concerned about."

Kevon nodded. "Pholos briefed me on her temperament after we met her on the way in."

"Pholos... has a degree of potential." Gurlin shook his head sadly. "It is possible his best use is as a pawn, rather than one of us. If he were made an example of by you..."

"The others would fear me properly?" Kevon asked. "This is the first time I've studied with more than one other Apprentice, and that one, sadly, had an accident when he asked Master Holten too many questions." Kevon tilted his head and smiled. "When shall our naïve friend have an accident?"

"Sometime after tomorrow," Gurlin said, gesturing for Kevon to be patient. "Even amongst sympathetic Masters, such things are... unpleasant to explain. Pholos's patron, Tarska, is one of the Masters that is attending tomorrow. He would ask too many questions, and that could destroy all we have worked to achieve."

Kevon's heart leapt. Pholos's previous Master was not in league with Gurlin and Holten! Maybe there was a way...

Kevon's thoughts hardened. He had no proof. If Tarska confronted Gurlin, the tower grounds could erupt into a battlefield, and Kevon would most likely lose a potentially powerful ally. His best option was still to get Pholos to realize how the others saw him, treated him. If he could get Pholos to see that power need not be painful, but joyful to use instead, he might turn him back to the right path, away from the evil he was unwittingly doing. That possibility could save a friend, begin his revenge, and open the door to the aid of Pholos's patron, Tarska.

Kevon shrugged. "Whenever you think is best."

Gurlin grinned widely. "I think Shofud has the most to fear from you. I had thought to make him my successor, he seemed the most driven. But his is a thirst for knowledge, where yours is a hunger for power."

Kevon leaned in closer to the old Wizard. "I'll only take as much as I deserve."

Gurlin's laughter started a coughing fit worse than any Kevon had yet seen. After a minute, the Master calmed enough to take a few swigs of some kind of potion that seemed to ease his discomfort. "Enjoy the festivities tomorrow," Gurlin said, finally. "Your training begins the day after."

"Thank you, Master. Is there anything you need before I retire?" Kevon asked.

Gurlin shook his head. "Rest up for tomorrow," he suggested. "Sometimes the festivities can be... taxing."

Kevon rose and excused himself. He exited the dining hall and walked across the torch-lit compound to the central tower building, all the way to the back staircases. Instead of turning to go to the rooms, he took the other stairwell and headed up to the library side of the second floor.

The first room he passed was a laboratory. He only glanced long enough to know there were potions in progress; he did not want to tamper with potions he was not familiar with. He continued on past another laboratory room which did not appear to be in use. Kevon wandered through it, marveling at the variety of herbs, at least five times as many as Holten had accumulated with Kevon's help. Deciding to wait until later to inspect the laboratories, Kevon moved on.

At last Kevon found a library room. With a gentle flick of power, he lit an ensconced torch and began reading book titles. The first that caught his attention was a small black leather volume simply titled 'Enchantment'. He pocketed the book and moved on.

Many of the volumes appeared to be studies of specific things that Kevon had no time at present to be interested in. He kept looking until he spotted a faded, tattered book lying on top of one of the bookcases. The words 'Advanced Elemental Combat' were barely legible on the binding. Kevon smiled and pocketed that book as well.

Done looking for books, Kevon looked around at the other things in the library. Several wooden staves were set on holding pegs in one case. Kevon felt the magic as he neared the case, not as strongly as he had felt the spell on the street in Navlia, but similar. He reached out to take the top staff, noticing that one end of it was much darker than the rest of the wood. Touching the staff brought instant awareness. The symbol for Fire formed in his head and would not go away, though it did not fill with power. Kevon examined the darkened end, and saw the rune carved in the end of the staff. *A staff enchanted for focusing Fire magic?* Kevon wondered to himself as he placed it back on the pegs.

Leaving the other staves on their pegs, Kevon picked up a small wooden sphere that was lying on a shelf. The symbol for Light entered his mind, and Kevon found it drawn on the flat bottom of the almost spherical object. As soon as he saw the rune, the sphere flared brilliantly, not even the surprise of the sudden light caused the symbol to waver for a moment. Wary of the excess light, Kevon put the sphere back on its shelf and moved on.

The next shelf held bottles of ink. Kevon looked at all of the colors, took two of the three bottles of red ink, and shuffled the other colors around so that the red would not be missed.

Satisfied with his newly acquired supplies, Kevon extinguished the torch on his way out of the library. He hurriedly retraced his steps back down the hallway, and went down the rounded stairway to the first floor. After listening for a few seconds and hearing nothing, Kevon walked quietly up the stairs and down the hallway to his room.

CHAPTER 30

K evon startled awake in the complete darkness of his room. He reflexively brought his illusion of light into being, throwing sharp shadows against the stone walls. Nothing appeared out of place, and after a few seconds of silence, Kevon released his illusion in favor of the torch he lit on the wall.

The three Fire scrolls he'd hastily scribed before going to sleep were dried on the desk near the bed. Kevon grimaced as he re-checked the imperfectly drawn runes. He'd hoped they would turn out better, but as long as they worked half as well as the one he'd scribed before, they would suit his purposes. He turned to walk to the washbasin, and took two steps before he realized that he could *feel* the scrolls.

Kevon stopped and turned back around. There was not as much detail in his mind as he'd seen when sensing magic being, or about to be cast. The scrolls were more of a flicker at the periphery of his mind's eye, but they were there. The other scrolls in his saddlebags were gently poking into his awareness, also.

Great, Kevon thought, as the ramifications of this new discovery bloomed in his mind, giving him an instant headache. *I've only been around scrolls and enchantments for a short while, and if I can sense them, I have to assume everyone else can.* He wondered what Pholos and Mirsa had been thinking about the scrolls he'd been packing around when he met them. *At least my first Fire scroll didn't make it this far, that could have wrecked everything,* he thought grimly.

Kevon spent the next few minutes using up the Fire scrolls. He picked up the first scroll, and the crudely drawn rune sprang instantly to mind. Kevon felt the power stored in the scroll, like a stoppered flask waiting to be opened. With just the slightest mental nudge, the scroll activated. Under the focused attention of a trained Mage, the magic released as intended, and a jet of flame lanced from Kevon's palm, playing harmlessly over the bare stone of the wall he had aimed at. The outline of the inked rune on the parchment glowed red, then the parchment puffed to ash in his fingers.

Curious, Kevon rolled the second scroll up as if for storage. The imperfect rune kept its shape in his mind's eye, and Kevon whirled around to point the scroll like a wand toward the same spot on the wall. The released jet of flame erupted from the end of the curled-up scroll, making a soft whooshing noise with its passage from the confined space. The rolled parchment turned to ashes in the same manner as the first.

Kevon rolled the last parchment up and sat for a minute, thinking. He stared at the space on the wall where his previous attacks had only smudged the stone faintly. Upset by the waste of time and magic invested in the now-useless scrolls, Kevon hurled the scroll at the wall, activating it just before he released it.

The scroll sailed toward the wall, flames licking out both ends of the roll, curling around to lap hungrily at the unlit outside surface. When the scroll impacted the wall, the rune inside fractured prematurely, releasing the rest of its stored energy at once. The remainder of the magic erupted with a loud bang, amplified by the bare stone that comprised most of the room. Several rock chips skittered across the floor, blasted from a small indentation where the scroll hit. The porcelain pitcher by the washbasin rocked back and forth, kept upright only by the water still left in the bottom half of the vessel.

I'll have to make more of those, Kevon thought absently as he slumped back onto the bed, still not fully awake. Sighing, he sat back up and shook his head furiously to try and clear the cobwebs from his foggy mind. Several splashes of cold water from the washbasin helped, but Kevon still yawned as he emerged from his room dressed and ready for the day.

As Kevon exited the central tower, he saw the kitchen staff milling in across the drawbridge. When one of them waved at him, Kevon was shocked to see Waine, in unfamiliar garb, and weaponless, among them.

"How are you this morning, Willem?" Kevon asked, walking parallel to the stream of workers heading toward the dining hall.

"Just fine, Kalron," Waine answered, sidling to the outside. "They needed some extra help in the kitchen today, so I volunteered. Maybe we can talk later." Waine was swept into the building with the rest of the crew, leaving Kevon standing by the doors watching the rest of the locals filter in after.

When the last of the workers had made it into the mess hall and the door closed, Kevon was left alone in the courtyard. The sky was beginning to brighten, but no light yet shone even on the upper battlements. He stood a few minutes, thinking about breakfast that would not be ready for some time, and wondering what the other Magi were doing.

Yawning again, Kevon walked back to the central tower.

"Kalron! Come in!" Pholos exclaimed as he spotted Kevon looking into the laboratory. "I'm almost finished here, but I do need to go down to one of the storerooms afterward for some fennel. You'll need to know where everything is soon, so..."

"Sure," answered Kevon. "I'll go with you." He walked in to watch Pholos finish tending potions much like he had done for Holten, though none of them looked or smelled familiar. "What are you brewing?"

Pholos rolled his eyes. "These are mostly antidotes for livestock. There's a poisonous weed in the valley that herders can't get rid of. The cows and goats like to eat it, and die in a few hours without this stuff." He wrinkled his nose. "Sometimes I wonder if it's worth all the trouble."

Kevon smiled.

"It's going to be so great that you're studying here," Pholos commented, stirring the next potion in line absently.

"When the brothers aren't bickering or competing, they're always off somewhere planning something. Mirsa is always grumpy, and Shofud is always reading. It seems like we two have more in common than anyone else here."

"More than you know," Kevon mumbled, nodding.

"Hmmm?" Pholos looked over at Kevon quizzically.

Kevon smiled again. "I'll tell you later. Is there anything I can help with?"

"Nah," Pholos answered, shaking his head. "This is the last one." The younger Mage finished stirring the unpleasant looking brown fluid in the flask before him, and carefully wiped the stirring stick clean on a cloth before setting both to the side. "Done," he announced cheerily. "Let's go find that fennel."

Kevon followed Pholos out and down the stairs. They walked through the great hall to one side and entered one of the concealed hallways. As they entered the storeroom, Kevon could not stifle the gasp that escaped his lips.

"Nice, isn't it?" asked Pholos, smiling.

Kevon nodded, speechless. The laboratory upstairs was designed much like the one in Holten's home, on a larger scale. The shelves were larger and better stocked, and Kevon had noticed there were no drying racks or other places to handle unprepared herbs. Now he saw why.

The walls of the storeroom were lined with deep shelves and bins filled with every manner of herbal ingredient that Kevon had ever used, and many he could not identify at first glance. Drying racks were built around every support beam in the surprisingly large room, and there were two small tables where other equipment for processing and storing herbs were arranged.

"There's enough here for..." Kevon trailed off.

"Years?" Pholos finished. "Mostly. There are some things that we can't get here, though. Wolfsbane, for example. It doesn't grow here at all. That's why I was in Navlia, buying odd herbs that we were running low on."

"But why so much?" Kevon asked.

"We have four potion labs on the second floor alone," Pholos answered. "We rarely use more than two at a time, but I have had to tend all four a few times. Plus, there's Master Gurlin's private laboratory. It must be at least twice the size of any of the others, considering the amount of herbs I've seen Mirsa carrying upstairs."

"Mirsa is allowed above the third floor?" Kevon asked, mildly interested.

"Yes, Master Gurlin, visiting Masters, and the top student are always allowed to go wherever they please in the tower." Pholos furrowed his brow thoughtfully. "That will be Shofud after tomorrow, and as soon as he tests for Master, it might be you!"

Kevon shrugged, grimacing. "I'm not sure I'm going to be here that long."

Pholos tied the drawstrings of the pouch he'd just filled from a bin. "Planning on leaving already? When?"

"Pholos," Kevon began, sitting on a stool near one of the preparation tables. "Do you trust me?"

"Of course," Pholos answered, sitting down on another stool. "What does that have to do with..."

"I've lied to you," Kevon admitted. "I'm going to tell you the truth now, but you have to promise to listen to the whole story before you do anything."

"Kalron, what is..."

"First of all, my name's Kevon, not Kalron. My friend is Waine, not Willem," Kevon began. "It's true that I was Holten's student, and that he sent me here, but that's where it ends."

Pholos sat, wide-eyed and unusually silent.

"My *Master*..." Kevon almost spat the word, his face twisted in disgust. "Holten... sent me here to be killed."

Pholos opened his mouth to speak, but Kevon interrupted him.

"The only reason I'm telling you this," Kevon continued, "Is that we have more in common that you know. Your *Master*... ordered me to kill you last night. He expects it to be done tomorrow."

The younger Mage shifted on his stool, as if to stand, but Kevon motioned for him to stop.

"If I had to kill you now, I would lose nothing but the ally you might have been," Kevon cautioned. "If anything it would make it easier for me to get within striking distance of Gurlin at will." Kevon steepled his fingers and stared at Pholos over them. "But I don't think either of us wants that."

Pholos's hands flexed on the table, and he shook his head in disbelief. "How dare you accuse my Master of this?" he asked, eyes quivering. "The others would..."

"The others are quite aware," Kevon interrupted. "I saw as much from one meal with them. It might seem that they treat you differently because you are the youngest, the least powerful. It's more than that. They're part of something you aren't, something you would not choose. They know it, and they amuse themselves at your expense."

Pholos sat, stern faced, a small twitch in one corner of his mouth, the only visible movement. Watching the younger Mage's eyes dart back and forth, focusing on things that were not there, Kevon imagined he had looked much the same after reading the letter Holten had sent with him.

"Wh... What are they a part of?" Pholos asked, looking to Kevon as if his answers could piece back together the fragments of his shattered reality.

"Something larger than this place, but beyond that, I know nothing," Kevon admitted. "I've been wondering the same thing myself for more than a season now, and I'm honor-bound to the myrnar to find out on their behalf."

Pholos's eyes widened at the mention of the sea-people, but Kevon continued.

"We don't have time to talk about it. I have to know if I can count on you to keep this to yourself, even from Master Tarska." Kevon answered Pholos's questioning look as soon as it crossed his face. "If they would kill us for no reason at all, I doubt they would hesitate to kill even a Master who asked too many questions."

Kevon saw the realization washing over Pholos as concern for others brushed aside his fear for himself.

"What do you need me to do?" he asked.

After confirming with Pholos that the best way to find out the secrets the other Magi were keeping would be to kill them, and look around afterwards, they devised a quick plan. Mirsa was likely to leave with the departing group of Magi in the morning, and would thus be one less danger to face immediately. Kevon was adamant that Pholos not do any of the killing himself, but instead provide a distraction or cover from attacks by the brothers, if needed. Pholos had no objections, and mentioned a few items in one of the libraries that might help him do just that.

Deciding they had taken enough time, Kevon reassured Pholos that they were going to be all right, and left the younger Mage to continue his duties.

Playing the part of the eager student, Kevon headed back upstairs to explore the libraries. Not surprisingly, Kevon found Shofud poring over a large text in the back corner of the first library he happened to enter. The portly scholar nodded smugly at Kevon when he scuffed a boot too loudly over an uneven part in the floor, but otherwise continued his studies, oblivious.

Kevon worked his way around the room, skimming titles and flipping briefly through any books that caught his interest. He continued until he came to a shelf that contained mainly combat-oriented magic. Kevon slowed to pay more attention to the various subjects, and one of the books in particular caught his eye. It was titled 'Counters and Concealment."

Kevon pulled the volume from the shelf and opened the cover.

Since the War of the Magi, magic users of all types have shunned the use of the Arts against one another. However, there are those who do not adhere to these conventions. Therefore, the knowledge of means to stop them, and take them by surprise if needed, must be preserved.

Kevon flipped past the rest of the introduction to the notes and diagrams. His heart skipped and thumped as he saw the level of detail and explanation of the runes and their uses. This book was more precise and organized than any he'd ever read before. Watching Shofud from the corner of his eye, Kevon formed a few of the runes in the Concealment section in his mind, still not daring to allow any power into them. The other student ignored him completely until Kevon formed a simple Illusion rune. Shofud looked up disapprovingly. Kevon grinned and forced the image from his mind. Shofud rolled his eyes and resumed reading his book.

Kevon noted the spot where he replaced the book. He would have to come back for it later. He browsed through some more books, but all he could think about was the one he'd put back. His stomach started grumbling, he was so hungry that he thought he could smell roasted chicken.

Kevon kept looking at book titles, but the smell seemed to be getting stronger. It got harder and harder for him to concentrate, so he closed his eyes and tried to force the phantom scent from his mind. Then he heard the rustling noise behind him.

Opening his eyes, Kevon turned to look over at Shofud's table. The Mage was almost shoulder-deep, reaching into the case on the table that Kevon had assumed held quills or ink. Shofud's arm was not visible under the table, so Kevon figured the case was somehow similar to Holten's Traveling Tome. Shofud grunted and half-stood before pulling a chicken leg out of the case and closing it. Kevon watched while the other Mage finished the meat and placed the bone in a small pile Kevon had not noticed before.

A traveling cold box? Kevon wondered. I know just where to put that in my saddlebags... He frowned a moment. Perhaps I shouldn't think too far ahead.

Kevon turned and left the library room to see if breakfast

was ready.

When he reached the dining hall, Pholos and the brothers were already eating, along with roughly half of the kitchen staff, and one other person Kevon did not recognize. Everyone seemed to be clustered near or around the newcomer. From the chatter that rattled around the room, Kevon gathered that this was a messenger from the party of Magi that were to arrive later in the day.

"Yes, midday, as I've said..." the man sighed as yet another servant asked him when the group was arriving. "There are twenty of us in all." He took one of the four mugs of cider that were offered to him, and carefully selected meats and cheeses from the platters that paraded in front of him.

Someone noticed Kevon and he was ushered to a seat near Pholos. He ate quietly, taking a little bit of everything, savoring each bite.

Convinced the man had no more information to give, the crowd surrounding him melted away, trickling back into the kitchen. The man breathed a sigh of relief, and began to enjoy his food in peace.

Not particularly concerned with the man, or the others that followed behind him, Kevon finished his meal and carried his own dishes back to the kitchen. He found Waine soaked to his elbows in dirty dishwater, scowling.

"I think we'll have to put off that ride we were going to take until *tomorrow*, Willem," Kevon said, stressing the word just enough to catch Waine's attention without raising undue suspicion. "You're far too busy today."

"Yes, they're expecting we'll be busy at this until at least mid-afternoon," Waine answered, eyeing Kevon briefly. "Allowing for that, tomorrow should be better."

Kevon nodded and turned to leave. He made a mental note to slip away and return here around mid-afternoon to see what Waine had to say then. With just over two hours until noon and the expected arrival of the visiting Magi, Kevon walked unhurriedly back to his room.

Time seemed to crawl. Kevon was frustrated that he was unable to scribe any scrolls that would be of use in the coming conflict. After about half an hour of pacing, he decided to return to the library to see if it was unoccupied. Finding no one else there, he walked directly to the shelf where he'd left the book he wanted, pulled it out, and dropped it into his pocket. After returning to his room, Kevon spent the next hour thumbing through the book, looking forward to having more time to study its contents at length.

Kevon left his room and started down the curved staircase at the end of the hallway. Before he had taken more than a few steps downward, the jumbled murmurs of many voices drifted up from the Great Hall. When he reached the end of the stairs, Kevon peeked around the corner to see that the expected party of Magi and attendants had arrived, and were now assembling.

He slipped around the corner and into the crowd, feeling more than a bit uneasy around so many other robed Magi. He accepted the glass goblet of wine he was offered by one of the several kitchen servants milling through, but declined food from the trays that were circulating around the hall.

The bulk of the activity in the room was focused on the three black-robed figures that were spaced a good deal apart from each other. Each Master had in attendance a green robed Mage, a Journeyman, and three brown robed Apprentices. The groups seemed to keep to themselves for the most part. After a minute of observation, Kevon could also match some of the attending servants to their respective Masters by the hems of their tunics. There were well over twenty visitors; Kevon imagined that the herald that arrived earlier had not counted the others, merely himself and the Magi.

The crowd quieted as Gurlin tapped into the room with his staff. Mirsa followed closely behind him, an intriguing expression of anticipation and superiority on her face.

Gurlin coughed twice and cleared his throat. "For the public half of this Test, Mirsa will perform a demonstration of the Elements in the courtyard."

He turned to the side as Mirsa stepped in beside him, and both gestured to the open entry door.

Murmurs of approval rustled through the crowd, and they began moving outside. The group clustered outside the door, and when Gurlin and Mirsa exited, Mirsa headed toward the outer northwestern section of the courtyard, the sector least crowded with buildings.

As the Mage approached the outer wall, she stopped and turned to face her audience. She stretched her hands out forward, a look of supreme concentration on her face. The snippets of conversation that had been continuing from inside wound down to silence as Mirsa closed her eyes and dropped her hands down to her sides.

From his place near the center of the crowd, Kevon watched, curious to see how powerful Mirsa really was. At this distance, he could feel her spell beginning as a mere twitch in his mind's eye.

Mirsa's palms turned upward and she began raising them slowly.

Kevon could feel the ground shudder as the earth beneath Mirsa parted, and she was lifted by a shaft of stone that rumbled upward beneath her feet.

By the time her upturned palms were raised to shoulder level, the stone pillar Mirsa stood on was already taller than she was. It ground to a halt, and Kevon could feel the magic waver and change as her arms continued to rise. Mirsa's elbows bent slightly as she turned her palms outward as she lifted them further skyward. For moments nothing happened, but Kevon felt the twinge of release an instant before twin gouts of flame erupted from the performing Mage's hands, shooting high into the air above the assembly.

Gasps broke the silence, but hushed as Mirsa drew her hands back down to her chest, clasping them in concentration. Kevon felt the breeze stirring, and saw Mirsa's cloak and loose strands of hair ruffle and whip about unnaturally. The wind

Chris Hollaway

swirling around Mirsa began whistling from the force. Kevon could see the dust in the air outlining the funnel that stretched from the base of the pillar to the top of the outer wall.

Smiling, Mirsa stepped off the pillar and extended her arms, buoyed by the whirlwind. She completed a perfect rotation and landed gently, having to bend her knees only ever so slightly. The breeze died down and Mirsa ran her fingers over her ears, straightening her windblown hair before continuing the demonstration. Closing her eyes once more and steepling her hands in front of her, Mirsa began another spell.

Kevon felt the magic begin, more strongly because Mirsa had drifted closer since dropping off the pillar. He also noticed that he'd moved closer without meaning to. Kevon watched Mirsa's face relax into a genuine smile, her head tilting back slowly as the power built. The realization struck Kevon as the rune became visible in his mind; Water was Mirsa's Art. Just as Illusion was Kevon's, Mirsa loved Water. The fact that there were no visible effects to so powerful a spell made Kevon a touch nauseous.

Kevon focused on Mirsa, watched the color drain from her face as her back arched with the effort for the spell. Just as Mirsa began trembling, Kevon spotted the effect her efforts were producing.

Three pillars of water loomed over the outer wall behind Mirsa. They snaked up and over, then began weaving in and out, around each other in a giant braid that extended nearly to the inner tower, above the crowd.

Mirsa let out a soft cry as she convulsed and dropped to her knees. The water formations exploded into a heavy mist that rained down, and one Mage yelped as a stray fish fell onto him.

Gurlin, now standing at the front of the crowd in the center of the only dry spot in the area, turned to address the assembly. "Does anyone here object to the elevation of Mirsa 'ap Briltor to Master status?"

After a moment of silence, Gurlin hobbled over and

offered Mirsa a hand in getting up. "Masters, if you would accompany us inside for the conclusion of the testing; the rest of you are dismissed."

The group of onlookers parted as Gurlin led a wobbly Mirsa back into the central tower. The three attending Masters fell into line behind her.

When the last Master disappeared into the tower, the group that remained outside began drifting toward the dining hall. Kevon followed slowly, and soon found Pholos shuffling along at his side.

"Mirsa's always been good with the elements," the young Journeyman commented. "But that's the first time I've seen her go all out like that." They walked in silence a bit further. "I wonder what Gurlin could do if he really wanted to," he said, concern showing in his voice.

Kevon shuddered inwardly. He paused as he and Pholos entered the dining hall; the festivities were already in full swing. The large center table was filled with platters of food, servants wove in and out of the crowd carrying drinks, and most eyes were on the performance near one of the fireplaces.

Waine wobbled back and forth clumsily, managing to juggle four empty plates in a wide pattern. His drunken staggering was obviously for show; each time a plate fell too far it was expertly caught and launched back toward the ceiling in a flash. He griped loudly at all those nearby, and threatened to add another plate to his collection.

Kevon moved through the crowd, exchanging nods and handshakes with several Magi. He nibbled at the table for a minute, finished off a mug of cider, and drifted back toward the door.

Before Kevon reached the entrance to the central tower, Pholos caught up to him.

"What now?" the younger Journeyman asked.

"I figure I'll go try and find anything that will give us an advantage tomorrow," Kevon answered. "Any ideas?"

Pholos nodded slowly.

The younger Mage led Kevon into the building and up the stairs to the library side. They cautiously entered the first room. Finding it empty, Pholos led Kevon to a darkened back corner and walked into a solid stone wall, disappearing from sight.

Kevon followed hesitantly, passing through the illusion, feeling nothing magical or physical.

The storeroom he walked into was unlike anything he'd seen before. Staves and rods lined two walls, resting on pegs or stacked like kindling. Another wall held shelves full to brimming of potions and flasks of things Kevon could only guess at. The wall behind that Kevon had just entered through held another set of shelves with loosely stacked scrolls and the occasional book.

Kevon stood for a few moments, taking it all in before he realized that he could not feel any of the enchantments that surrounded him. He wondered if any of these were even enchanted at all. Curious, he reached out and grasped a nearby staff that was hanging on the wall.

As soon as he touched the polished surface of the staff, he could feel the enchantment, a Concealed Fire rune he recognized from the book in his pocket. The symbol burned brightly in his mind, and it took some effort to keep power from spilling out. Kevon could feel the layers upon layers of destructive force piled upon one another within the staff, and gasped as he let it go.

"The rods aren't as scary as the staves," Pholos offered, giving Kevon a knowing look.

Kevon hesitated before picking up one of the stubby short-staves from its place on the shelf. Again, the Concealed Fire rune sprang to mind, but there was no thrumming urgency, no sense of power barely contained. The symbol was merely there, crisp, clean, and effortless.

These must be focal enchantments, Kevon thought. The staves are more like scrolls, filled to bursting.

Kevon held the rod he'd picked up for a moment before

stuffing it into an inner pocket of his cloak. He rummaged through the shelves, touching the enchanted rods briefly until their magic revealed itself to him before moving on. He passed up several more of Fire, two that seemed to be Water, and a rod of Light before switching to the shelf that held the rods enchanted with Darkness.

Kevon staggered backward as the twisted image of the Dark rune formed itself in his mind. He shook his head and shuddered involuntarily before skipping over the rest of that shelf to the next one.

The very next rod that Kevon tried was a Movement one, or something very similar. He liked the way the symbol felt in his head, and he pocketed that rod.

Kevon turned to find Pholos carefully stuffing a satchel with scrolls, muttering softly because he could not fit as many as he wanted to in the small bag.

"How long before we're missed?" Kevon asked quietly.

"Hours, normally," Pholos answered hesitantly. "Today, though…"

Kevon nodded his understanding. "We don't want to chance Gurlin getting suspicious. We'd better hurry and leave."

Kevon watched out of the corner of his eye as Pholos stuffed half a dozen rods at random into different concealed pockets before straightening up and smoothing his robes out.

"I'm done!" the younger Mage announced, slipping the strap of his scroll-laden satchel over his head. Pholos contorted his arm out and back into his robe-sleeve and slung his bag snugly under his arm, patting it gently, the bulge barely noticeable under his cloak.

Kevon followed Pholos back out the enchanted doorway to the library.

"What about potions?" Pholos asked as they stepped into the empty corridor. "Will we need any?"

Kevon shook his head. "If we need to rely on potions, we're not ready. They're too slow. We might pick some up afterward if you think we could use them."

"It might be better if we weren't seen together," Pholos commented.

Kevon nodded, and started back down the way they had entered, as Pholos continued through the library side past the laboratories. Kevon went down and up the stairwells, doubling around and down the hallway to his room. Once inside, he swiftly packed his pilfered items out of sight underneath his other belongings.

As he found himself doing more and more often lately, Kevon went over his mental list of the weapons he had at his disposal. His knife and the two rods were all he really had left; he could not readily trust in scrolls as Pholos appeared to be doing.

The rods, the dagger, and the element of surprise... Kevon thought grimly. And Pholos... The afterthought came haltingly to mind, but Kevon latched onto it fiercely. He's a good kid. He'll do whatever he can.

"I've just got to do as much of it as I can myself," Kevon muttered, "so he won't have to."

Kevon paced back and forth around the front of the bed for a few minutes, finally stopping in front of the linen chest placed there. He rummaged through it and found an older sheet that was starting to wear thin. Straining, he tore several strips from it, which he folded lengthwise, making thin, flat cords. Kevon removed his cloak and pushed back his tunic sleeves. He took the Movement rod and tucked it under the bunched cloth of his tunic by his shoulder. After thinking about it for a moment, he shifted the length of wood downward to rest under his arm just far enough away that it wouldn't poke him in the armpit. He took one of the lengths of torn and folded linen and tied it around his arm gently. He then secured the other end of the rod just above his elbow, turning the tied ends of both cords down. Kevon straightened his tunic sleeve out, and it just covered the end of the anchored rod; someone looking for it might see it, but it would not be noticed by a casual observer.

Kevon secured the Fire rod on his other arm in the same manner, straightened his tunic, and put his robes back on over the whole thing. He walked around for a while, and after several adjustments found the right tension where the rods would not slip, and his arms would not go numb.

The symbols projected into his mind by the rods would take some getting used to. Kevon closed his eyes and rubbed at his temples for a few minutes. He adjusted the knife at his back carefully, using folds of his robes, then left the room for a trial run with his arsenal.

Kevon wandered from library to library until he found the one that Shofud was now studying in. He strolled through, browsing through book titles, working his way closer to the portly Mage, keeping watch out of the corner of his eye for any reaction. After circling around Shofud twice, and getting nothing more than the usual looks of mild irritation, Kevon concluded that his setup was as safe as it could possibly be. He met Shofud's next scowl with a smile and a shrug, and excused himself.

Kevon threaded his way back down the hallways and out-side to head back to the dining hall. He spotted Waine immediately upon entering. The Warrior was carrying a large tray, and was laughingly refusing to perform another juggling routine, to continuous noises of disappointment.

Waine saw Kevon as soon as the crowd thinned for a moment. He worked his way over, and addressed Kevon quietly.

"When were you wanting to take that ride tomorrow?" he growled under his breath. "I need some time away from here already."

"An hour or two after our guests leave, I should imagine," Kevon answered, just as softly. "Pholos is coming, too," he added.

Waine raised an eyebrow. "I've seen him ride," the War-rior commented, "but can he *ride*?"

Kevon kept his voice flat. "He knows how we ride. He'll keep up."

"Tomorrow, then." Waine whirled about and wove back into the crowd with his platter held high above his head.

The noise of the crowd lulled for a moment before erupting into cheers and applause. Kevon turned to the entrance just in time to see Mirsa sweep back the hood of her new black cloak and beam a rather genuine looking smile around the room. The rest of the Masters, followed by Master Gurlin, filtered in the door around and behind Mirsa.

Waine pushed through the crowd and gave Mirsa a brimming mug and a wink, eliciting an even wider grin from her usually pinched features. The party started back up again, less rowdy, but just as noisy as it had been before the last arrivals.

The celebration wore on, and Kevon found himself enjoying it despite his apprehension about the coming confrontation. He wandered through the crowd, witnessing displays of magical prowess that were just as impressive as Mirsa's had been, if on a smaller scale. Masters Conjured things from thin air, Transformed elements from one to another, and levitated with Movement. As soon as some of the older Masters excused themselves for the evening, Kevon began yawning in preparation for his own early exit. Scanning the room, he spied Waine and Mirsa off in a corner, and after watching for a moment, gave up trying to decide who had cornered whom.

Kevon sighed loudly and shook his head. He refused the next mug of cider that was offered him, and apologized to the group he'd been conversing with as he began heading for the door.

"Leaving so soon?" Gurlin rasped, catching Kevon by the arm, less than an inch from the concealed rod.

"Yes," Kevon answered, half-turning toward the older Mage, not meeting his eyes. "Important day, tomorrow."

"That it is," Gurlin agreed, releasing a relieved Kevon's arm. "Don't lose your nerve. Everything depends on it."

"Yes, sir. I know." Kevon answered, turning to meet Gurlin's gaze. "I promise I won't fail." Without waiting for Gurlin's smile of approval, Kevon continued out the door and over to the central tower.

Partway through the great hall, Kevon thought he saw a

figure lingering at the entrance to one of the side rooms. The torches on the pillars that flanked the main path through the hall did not provide enough light to see clearly, so Kevon concentrated and formed a Light rune, pushing a glowing sphere ahead of him as he walked toward the side room.

"Hello?" he called, slowing as he neared the hall junction, circling wide to get the best view of the entryway possible. Hearing no response, Kevon crept slowly into the room, his rod's Concealed Fire rune at the ready.

The storeroom looked as if it hadn't been used for ages. Dust covered shelves and crates, and barrels were stacked in pathways. The floor seemed to be the only clean part of the room. Kevon walked down the clearest path between shelves, shifting his Light spell to look around. The route dead-ended at a blank stone wall.

Recalling the armory upstairs, Kevon approached the wall and reached out touch it.

Solid... he thought, frowning. He looked around for other signs of recent activity, but found none. *I'm sure I saw someone.*

Kevon retraced his steps out of the storeroom, extinguished his light, and returned to his room for the night.

Mirsa waited behind the hidden door for several minutes before leaving the passageway back into the unused storeroom. The dim reflected light from the great hall was more than enough to see her through the familiar twists of the room, even through eyes narrowed in displeasure.

"Pity I'm leaving tomorrow..." the newly promoted Master growled through her teeth. "Your education might have been... interesting."

CHAPTER 31

After a fitful night of tossing and turning, Kevon woke midmorning, well after he'd intended. By the time Kevon secured his gear and made his way outside the tower, Mirsa and the other Magi were already departing. He followed the procession out of the tower walls and across the drawbridge, standing quietly amidst the crowd of waving and cheering servants and Magi.

The departing caravan pulled out of earshot, and the servants began to straggle back into the tower. Kevon spotted Waine near the stable. The Seeker nodded casually and walked inside the outbuilding.

Kevon turned and followed the last few servants across the bridge. He wandered through the second floor hallways of the central tower for a while, finally returning to the library where he'd spotted Shofud earlier.

"Is Master Gurlin about?" Kevon asked.

"I haven't seen him," Shofud answered irritably. "If he has need of you, he'll find you after he takes his lunch."

Armed with a better estimate of the timing of his confrontation, Kevon marched down to the dining hall to get himself breakfast. Entering, he spotted Pholos and the brothers seated at different tables. Not wanting to rouse undue suspicion, Kevon sat at a separate table and waited for someone to bring him food.

Pholos picked half-heartedly at his plate, staring off at nothing in between bites.

Is he all right? Kevon wondered. *Should I have trusted him with my secret... with anything?* He tried to push it out of his mind, but was unable to eat much more than his young friend.

Kevon sat sipping a mug of cider after sending his unfinished breakfast to be discarded. He kept losing himself in the swirls of spices that churned across the top of his drink as he blew on it gently to hasten its cooling.

Kevon sat upright suddenly as the wooden fork and spoon he'd been using stood on their own and began attacking each other fiercely. Feeling the two Movement runes pulsating individually, he glanced over to where the brothers sat watching his table intently.

"Ha!" the younger brother cried as the spoon swung its stem in shallow, sweeping attack that sent the fork clattering to the table.

Kevon shrugged and leaned back into his mug.

"Master Gurlin is waiting by the tower for you," the older brother grumbled.

Kevon took one last drink, nodded, and stood to leave.

Gurlin stood near the central tower, directly across from the entrance to the dining hall. The aged Wizard was leaning on his staff with both hands, eyes closed, face turned full into the late morning sun.

"Well, then," Gurlin said, turning to face Kevon as he drew near. "Are you ready to begin the next stage of your training?"

Kevon stopped and inclined his head slightly. "I am, Master," he answered.

Gurlin nodded, smiling. "Then show me what my friend Holten has taught you so far, this skill in Illusion."

Kevon nodded, inwardly relieved. This was what he'd been counting on. If he could completely drain his magical reserves, there would be no discharge of magic when he grasped the knife to kill the Wizard. Kevon had even given the illusion he was about to work quite a bit of thought since yesterday.

Kevon stilled his mind and formed the rune, paying much more attention than usual to every nuance of the symbol in his head. He evened his breathing and spread his arms away from his body, palms upward.

Kevon fed energy into the rune and began superimposing his illusion over himself. The sounds of a heavy breeze whipped up as the illusion started with false debris skittering across the grounds and funneling upward around Kevon. The illusion settled over Kevon and his hair appeared to whip about and upward, as did the corners of his cloak.

Kevon fed more power into the spell. He projected his illusory self upward, lifted by the false winds, while concealing his true self where he stood. When his false self was no more than a few feet off the ground, Kevon shifted part of his focus to the next phase of the performance. He mimicked the rumbling and shuddering of the ground as the illusion of the stone shaft that Mirsa had raised yesterday erupted from the ground to cover Kevon from view and 'support' his false image,

Kevon marshaled his magical reserves carefully as he continued the illusion. He formed the images of half-a-dozen geysers spaced evenly a few paces away from him, weaving illusory water jets in a spiral above him to collect in a growing globe suspended meters above even his false self.

Feeling his reserves nearing their end, Kevon slowly knelt to the ground, but caused the image above him to raise its arms triumphantly. Phantom flames burst from his double's hands to spray through the globe of water. As he shifted focus to the cloud of steam he was now projecting, complete with loud hissing, Kevon dropped the geyser illusions and flashed the trailing tendrils of water to steam.

Kevon caused the false image to take an elaborate bow before shrouding the figure in steam, and dropping the steam cloud down to cover what remained of the rest of the illusion. He maintained it for a few seconds more, pouring all he had into the spell. The Illusion rune went dull in his mind, and the glamour surrounding him abruptly vanished, silenced.

Kevon forced himself to breathe deeply, clutched at his chest for an instant, and reached into his robe pocket through the slit to finger the hilt of his knife.

The only reaction was applause and cheers from *behind*

him. Kevon turned his head to see Pholos and the brothers standing in the entrance to the dining hall.

Kevon slowly took his feet, wobbling slightly to maintain the appearance that the spell had drained him physically. He walked unsteadily toward Gurlin and the door to the central tower.

Gurlin turned to walk to the tower entrance himself.

Kevon stepped in behind Gurlin, the knife already pulled through the slit, waiting in hand in the deep robe pocket.

"That was very impressive..." Gurlin began, slowing his pace just a bit as he began speaking. "To fool a Mage with such things, you will need to master Concealment and...

The slight slowing was all Kevon needed. He closed half a step to his effective range. With a swift motion, he drew the knife from his pocket, whirled it into a better grip, and plunged it into the Wizard's back.

Even shielded by his grasp on the knife, Kevon staggered at the mental *whump* as Gurlin's magic was instantly nullified. Kevon wrenched the knife deeper, hoping that Gurlin had died the instant the blade pierced his skin, but wanting to be sure.

Gurlin let out a soft gasp and fell bonelessly forward. Kevon clutched at the knife-hilt and barely managed to free it before the dead Mage's momentum tore it from his grasp.

Kevon turned to face the dining hall.

Pholos and the two brothers stood, seemingly frozen with shock and fear.

Behind him, Kevon felt and heard the foundations of the tower begin to rumble.

Neither Rettun nor Pætub took any great action, but both seemed to tense in concentration simultaneously.

Kevon advanced toward the three Magi, blood-slicked knife held in front of him, concentrating on the danger he knew.

"Master!" Pholos's bloodcurdling scream from two paces behind the brothers appeared to break their concentration; they both turned to look at the younger Mage.

Pholos stood defiantly, aiming one of his filched rods at

Kevon.

No... Above me... Kevon thought after a moment of panic.

The rumbling and cracking sounds coming from the tower intensified, and Kevon ventured a look back over his shoulder.

A large slab of mortared stone loosened by the buckling and swaying of the tower slid free from the second-story wall. Defying gravity, it tumbled forward, spinning as it arced back up and toward Kevon. As the chunk of stone spun, books flew out at crazy angles, hurled from the bookcase that was still affixed to the section of wall.

Kevon threw himself to the ground and the stone slab whirled madly past him. The bookshelf tore from its mounts with a terrible shriek, and the thick oak shelf spun away from the stone, each hurtling slightly to either side of Pholos.

The brothers did not stand a chance. The whirling section of wall clapped the younger brother against the outer wall of the dining hall before crashing through and breaking into several pieces. The splintered oak shelves hit the older brother in the knees, chest, and head in rapid succession. The Mage convulsed once and lay still.

Pholos let out a great sob and fell forward, dropping the rod. Kevon scrambled over to make sure that he was all right.

Kevon reached Pholos as the younger Mage managed to pull himself into a sitting position.

"Are you all right?" Kevon asked.

Pholos's blank gaze betrayed no warning before the rod he'd picked back up flashed out to club Kevon alongside the head.

Pholos was no Warrior. The force behind the blow was considerably less than Kevon would expect in a practice session with Waine. It did, however, startle him enough to let Pholos get in a quick kick to the gut, which almost knocked the wind out of a still surprised Kevon.

In desperation, Kevon slapped Pholos with the flat of his knife, a sickening *smack* that splattered blood from Pholos's late

Master across his cheek and jaw.

Sanity returned to Pholos's eyes. "Shofud!" he screamed, pointing to the gaping hole in the central tower.

Kevon turned to see Shofud's look of frustration. No doubt he was wondering what had broken his spell controlling Pholos so easily.

Shofud unclenched his fist and gestured palm outward toward Kevon and Pholos.

Kevon flinched instantly at the heat he felt radiating upward from the ground beneath him. The grass in a large circle around the two of them was smoldering, turning brown as the heat increased. The ground Kevon was standing on buckled and started to give way, the sod layer tearing as it did. A jet of flame spewed from the tear. Kevon leapt sideways, but succeeded only in tearing another spot in the swiftly blackening grass as he landed. Kevon could hear Pholos screaming, but was too busy dodging the new geyser of flame that erupted near his feet to see what was going on.

Losing control, Kevon stumbled forward, and slammed onto the roiling surface of what had recently been solid ground. As he fell onto the increasingly hot surface, sure that he would break through and be consumed by the flames that lay only inches beneath him, Kevon stabbed his knife down through the charred turf.

He hit the ground, hard. The grass still smoked, was still hot to the touch, but the flames beneath had reverted to their natural form.

Pholos screamed again. Kevon turned to look. The younger Mage was sunk into the ground to his knees, spikes of stone and crumbling earth splaying upward and out from him, still smoking. Kevon smelled charred flesh. He turned and saw Shofud starting another spell.

Kevon yanked on the knife handle, but it would not budge. It was stuck in stone nearly to the hilt.

Pholos screamed again, but the cry seemed feral, angrier than it had moments ago.

Kevon turned in time to see the first bolt of flame shoot from the staff Pholos had pulled from inside his cloak.

Shofud hesitated and changed the hand motions he'd been using, swatting sharply to the side as the bolt neared him. The flames splashed into the shattered wall and fizzled harmlessly.

With a cry more animal than human, Pholos discharged a stream of flame from the staff that had to have been two feet in diameter.

Shofud strained against the pillar of flame, pushing to deflect it further away, barely able to keep it even an arm's length away from him. The stream of Fire snaked around him and further into the library.

Kevon wondered how long the two Mages could continue. Pholos was shaking uncontrollably, screaming rage in between ragged gasps for breath. After about ten seconds of deflecting the flames, Shofud staggered a few steps backward.

Pholos faltered. The staff clattered to the ground, and the young Mage collapsed forward at a grotesque angle, his legs locked upright by the earth.

Shofud shouted triumphantly as the last part of the flaming column slid past him, then staggered again.

Kevon's vision blurred, and his guts wrenched at something akin to the feeling he'd had when he'd stabbed Gurlin, but dozens of times worse.

Pholos laughed weakly as Kevon realized what was happening. Pholos had focused the flames into the armory they had plundered the day before.

The initial blast blew another chunk of library wall out to slam into the outer wall on the far side of the dining hall. Burning books and shattered shelves spewed from the first breach of the tower wall, carrying Shofud toward Kevon, depositing the lifeless Mage in a twisted heap at the edge of the blackened grass. The subsequent chain reaction worked its way upward through laboratories and libraries. Eruptions of flaming stone and other debris shot out in all directions. Kevon watched helplessly as a section of wall from an upper floor about the size of a wagon bounced twice before landing on top of where Pholos had passed out.

Kevon wrenched desperately on the knife handle one more time, and yanked the blade, still encased in stone, from the scorched earth. He stumbled toward the tower's entrance, vaguely aware of the fiery wreckage falling around him.

People from the outbuildings were beginning to crowd onto the lowered drawbridge. Seeing Kevon stagger alone through the continuing destruction, some began to shout questions, or accusations, Kevon could not be sure which. Between the rumbling devastation behind him, and the deaths of friend and foes alike, Kevon did not really care either way.

Waine galloped through the knot of locals clustered on the drawbridge, knocking several down, and one of the hostlers into the moat. The Seeker's horse reared up just after passing through the arched entrance, unwilling to go any further. Waine turned his mount to the side and cast an appraising glance at the destruction. He raised an eyebrow at Kevon, who was by now only ten feet away.

Kevon swung the stone encased knife at a nearby section of wall, and the stone cracked, letting the blade slide free. Kevon slipped it back through his pocket into its sheath, and looked Waine in the eye. "I didn't do it," he offered, shrugging.

Waine laughed and offered Kevon his hand, swinging the Mage up onto the back of his horse. He flicked the reins, and without further urging, the stallion barreled back across the drawbridge. One of the men on the bridge started to protest their exit, and found Waine's foot in his chest, and himself in the moat with his neighbor.

Kevon jumped down as they reached the stables and tossed the reins of Pholos's saddled horse to Waine.

"Where is…" Waine started.

Kevon shook his head, and then mounted his horse, almost getting tangled in his mare's lead rope that was tethered to his saddle. "Let's just go."

The angry cries of the locals began drawing near, but Kevon and Waine paid them little heed as they set off down the road at a medium pace. The farmers were no threat to the two Warriors, and Kevon did not want to catch up to the group that had left earlier.

They rode easily until late afternoon, then stopped and made camp at a spot above the road where they could see for a good distance either way. It would not do if someone from the tower rode ahead and alerted Mirsa and the other Magi.

They saw no one that night.

Kevon and Waine traveled at a leisurely pace, having plenty of time to reach the Guild ahead of Carlo and Bertus. Kevon began presenting himself as a Warrior again, his robes and magical supplies bundled neatly away. They left the main road in favor of a more direct route with fewer people to bother with their training and travel. The trip back to Navlia took ten days more than they had spent on the journey to Gurlin's tower.

When they reached the Capital, Kevon and Waine rode straight for the Warriors' Guildhall to avoid any chance encounters with any who had been present at Mirsa's test.

After a rowdy welcome, Kevon and Waine settled into a steady training routine, awaiting Blademaster Carlo's arrival.

EPILOGUE

Bertus rode uneasily between the two soldiers. Although there had been no signs of orcs since just before he and Carlo reached Eastport, he spent most of the day watching the tree line that they kept at least a quarter-mile clear of at all times.

The scar on his right leg ached again. It would be throbbing again by nightfall, of that he was certain. At least he'd been able to keep the leg. The herb witch in Eastport had stopped the festering in the cut from the orcish blade in less than a week.

The lead soldier called a halt at a small stream, and the horses drank briefly. When his horse had had enough, Bertus reined him up onto the bank, and then leaned forward to bury his face in the horse's mane, wrapping arms around its neck. The horse was the closest thing Bertus would have to a friend until he reached Navlia in about three more weeks.

Bertus's hand unconsciously moved to the pouch slung around his neck, as it often did these days. He wished the letter within did not exist, for it would mean that Carlo was still with him.

The Blademaster was needed elsewhere. He'd sent Bertus and two trusted men on the long route to Navlia, around the forests that were no longer considered safe.

Bertus glanced at the soldiers, standing together, talking in low voices so that he could not hear. Bertus did not dislike them, or even distrust them, but he did not feel as safe with them as he did with Carlo, Kevon, or even Waine. It did not help that these two men were following orders that they were not happy with, that they would rather be fighting with the rest of their respected units.

Three weeks, and he'd deliver the letter.
Three weeks, and he'd be with his friends again.
Three weeks.

Don't miss Volume II of The Blademage Saga, *Journeyman Warsmith!*

Kevon yelped and jumped back, left hand balled into a fist. The hammer tumbled to the dirt floor with a dull thud. Teeth clenched, the Seeker muttered under his breath. He heard a giggle from somewhere behind him, and the other boy in front of him looked about ready to burst from not laughing.

The Apprentice Blacksmith took a deep breath. "I'm going for a little walk... Why don't the two of you run and get yourselves a treat and nobody else hears about this?"

Grubby fingers snatched at the offered coppers, and the boys dashed out of the smithy, laughing and calling to each other. Kevon knew that before an hour passed, he would be teased about the incident, but he didn't mind. He pinched his thumb to make sure it wasn't broken, and walked outside.

The midday heat beating down on Kevon was a welcome break from the forge heat that had just been glaring up at him. The boys were already out of sight, on their way to the trading post in the center of the mining camp.

He faced into the slight breeze and closed his eyes. He took a deep breath that didn't smell of burnt iron, and smiled. Moments like these, Kevon could almost be happy. He could almost forget who he really was, what he'd done, what he was running from.

Almost.

Kevon heard a noise behind him, and whirled around to see what it was. He found himself staring at a surprised Marelle. She was taller, darker, and more pleasantly proportioned that he remembered, but was exactly as he'd imagined, it being over two years since they met last. She dropped the broken halves of the horseshoe she'd been carrying, and stepped closer.

"I came to buy a horseshoe," she began, her gaze drifting down to Kevon's bare chest. "I may need a few other things." She leaned in closer, and Kevon's already pounding heart leapt as she locked her deep green eyes onto his. Marelle's lips parted slightly, and Kevon's eyes closed in anticipation.

A crackling of thunder shattered the moment, and the Seeker turned toward the sound, Marelle slipping from the beginnings of his embrace.

The blazing rift in the sky spread like wildfire, painting the blue canvas of the heavens with a deep crimson stroke. Lightning danced between the new sky and the arid land below, the rumbling of its passage rolling over in waves.

"Anton," Marelle said, her voice cracking.

Kevon wondered absently how she knew the name he was using while staying here, his attention focused on the winged behemoth that flapped in the sky before him.

"Anton!" she said again, urgently, her voice distorting more.

He said nothing, gazing at the dragon, and the hooded figure he could barely see in the distance, standing tall in in the middle of the broken landscape.

The world shuddered as Kevon felt himself cuffed alongside the head.

"Wha-?" he mumbled, trying to re-open eyes that were unusually heavy-lidded.

"Wake up, Anton!" Nic whined plaintively, shaking Kevon. "It's late! Master Farren is looking for you!"

Kevon sat bolt upright. Even though he'd been apprenticing under Farren Smith for over a year now, the word '*Master*' still unsettled him.

He blinked several times and the mousy little junior Apprentice came into focus.

"Are you coming?" Nic squealed, eyes wide.

"Yes, calm down, Nic." Kevon reached down to the foot of the cot and picked up his arm braces. He squeezed his hands through and slid them to rest snugly on his forearms. The smooth steel strips woven into the inner padding felt cool and comforting against his skin. Kevon slipped the iron ring off his right hand and dropped it into a pouch that lay near where he'd picked up the bracers. He picked through the pile of clothing and found a light tunic that was not too soiled, pulled it on over his head, and stepped into his boots.

"Let's go."

Kevon led Nic through the main part of the barracks where the miners and garrison troops bunked.

"It's Anton and his pet rat!" someone called from the middle of the room, and chuckles roiled briefly. Kevon smiled, and Nic scowled and shook his fist in the direction the voice had come from.

They continued on through the hallway that led to the commissary. Kevon picked up a small, flat loaf of bread and two strips of jerky, holding them up until the record-keeper tallied them. Kevon handed one of the strips to Nic, and headed for the exit.

He walked unhurriedly as he ate his breakfast, finishing up as he reached the well near the north guard post. He hauled up the bucket and dipped ladles of water into the tin cups that Nic pulled off the hanging hooks at the side of the wall.

After the two had finished their drinks, Kevon set off for the smithy at a brisk pace, forcing Nic to run at times to keep up.

The sun was just starting to peek over the horizon, but glancing back to the east, Kevon could already see the wavy lines of distortion as the barrens to sunward began to bake. The junior Apprentice kicked Kevon in the shins.

"Go, already!" Nic yelled, scrunching his face up in an attempt to look intimidating.

Kevon smiled and resumed his faster pace.

They reached the smithy as the sun crept just above the horizon and other people started coming out into the street. Kevon noted that the woodpile was fully stocked, and as they neared the forge, he saw that the three quenching barrels were all filled correctly as well. The other junior Apprentice, Tom, sat on a stool, slumped over into a corner.

"You lout!" Tom jumped up and rushed toward Nic. "I had to fill all..."

Tom stopped, and hesitantly took the half piece of jerky that Nic held out to him. The junior Apprentices wandered toward the back of the smithy, Nic telling Tom about how he almost had to thrash a dozen miners, Tom nodding and gnawing.

Kevon pulled off his tunic and worked the bellows on the small forge to get the heat up to working temperature. Once it glowed brightly enough, he resumed the project he'd been working on the day before, a batch of hoof-picks.

His Warrior training served him well in the forge. His practiced manual dexterity and arm strength had been amplified over the last year, and he'd learned the slow, easy rhythm that raised a sweat without forcing him to gasp for air after a few minutes.

The tool quickly took shape, but started cooling before it was quite done. Kevon flipped the strip of iron back into the coals with his tongs and worked the bellows for a minute before retrieving it and resuming his work. He quickly made the last few adjustments, turning the tip and pounding it just so, making the slight hook that gave the tool yet another advantage over a knife when used properly.

Satisfied, Kevon dipped the still-glowing metal into the water barrel, swirling it in slow circles with the long-handled forge tongs. When he withdrew it and found it comfortable to the touch, Kevon scraped it thoroughly on the large whetstone that sat on a bench near the forge. Kevon finished smoothing the bumps off the business end of the tool as well as the stem for the handle. This would ensure there would be less chance of the tool's user scratching themselves accidentally. He tossed the finished product into the nearby pile.

Kevon walked over to the scrap bin and dug carefully through broken sword edges and other sharp objects that were not so readily identifiable. He quickly found a scrap that was about the right size, and returned to work.

He had just tossed the next finished pick into the pile when Master Farren arrived.

"Are you almost done with those?" the Master Smith

asked gruffly.

The Apprentice nodded. "All they need are handles. I can have then done..."

"No," Farren interrupted. "I'll have the other Apprentices split the batch, and see who can do the best job of putting handles on those picks." The smith spoke louder than needed to inform Kevon, but his words had their intended effect. Nic and Tom scurried in and began taking turns choosing hooked implements from the pile.

Kevon nodded to Farren, acknowledging the tactic. The boys always did better work when they were competing against each other.

"Besides, neither of them has the strength to work the bellows on the good forge," Master Farren commented.

"Awww..." Tom's outburst nearly drowned out Nic's sigh of disgust. The boys quickly finished sorting the pile and took their respective projects outside.

Kevon grimaced, but said nothing as he set about helping Farren prepare the forge for use. When Kevon finally got to working the bellows in earnest, Nic and Tom ventured in with their completed batches of tools for the Master Smith's inspection.

"Excellent work, boys," Farren said after making sure that every leather-wrapped wooden handle was snugly fastened so as not to slip during use. "I'm certain you both will be working the small forge by this time next year."

The Seeker nodded in agreement, in time with the rhythm of the bellows. He watched as the boys, obviously bothered by the heat of the larger forge, remained in the open-ended building. They roamed separately, well out of the way, each checking to make sure that tools and supplies were all in their proper places.

The Master Smith disappeared into the back of the building and returned quickly with a short steel bar in one hand, and his favorite hammer in the other. The Master Smith tossed the ingot into the glowing coals, leaned the hammer against the large anvil standing to the side of the forge, and walked over to sit beside Kevon.

"How is that helmet coming along?" Farren asked over the soft creaking and whooshing of the hide-covered blowing contraption.

"Not good." Kevon scowled. He paused for a moment. "I don't think it would even fit Waine's lumpy head." He pronounced the Adept Warrior's name like the locals here did, more like 'win' than 'wane".

"So you did see me," Waine chuckled from just inside the entrance to the building.

"The change in light reflected off the swords hanging on the side wall, a glance from Master Farren," Kevon commented blandly. "And you're not *that* quiet."

"Fair enough," Waine agreed. "I can see you're busy now, but we need to talk later." The Adept turned and left without another word.

Farren was already up, fishing the only slightly glowing ingot from the coals. He placed the block of metal on an anvil on an unused bench, and returned to drive Kevon from his spot at the bellows with a series of elbow pokes.

"Something tells me you'll want to finish your helmet today," the Master Smith said, grimacing.

Under the older smith's direction, Kevon finished the helmet to Farren's satisfaction in just a few hours. Nic and Tom sat on stools stitching the leather padding that was going in the helmet, gossiping like old women.

"That's it, then," Farren said, rapping an anvil lightly with his forge hammer. "You've done plenty of tools, several knives, and now armor." The gruff older man squinted and looked Kevon in the eye. "So now you're a Journeyman."

That last word made Kevon's blood run cold. It was not the first time he'd earned that title, though Waine was the only one here that even suspected.

Kevon was a Journeyman in the Mage's Guild, normally a feat that a Warrior or Blacksmith simply could not accomplish. Handling iron or steel was the touch of death for any accomplished magic-user, so the two worlds stayed well clear of each other.

It was only by accident that Kevon discovered he could survive the touch of steel the day before his mentor, the Magi Holten, had promoted him from Apprentice to Journeyman Mage. It was also by accident that weeks later, Kevon discovered his former Master was not as good a man as he pretended to be.

Kevon turned away from the forge, rubbed his eyes with the back of his forearm, and nodded to the waiting Smith.

Nic handed Kevon the completed helmet. Kevon ruffled the boy's hair, and earned a swift kick in the shin for his efforts.

The Journeyman inspected the headgear for a few moments, nodding appreciatively at the quality of the leatherwork. He handed the finished product to Farren, who handed him a hammer in exchange.

"Use it well," Farren sighed. "Return when you can."

The Journeyman nodded. He had picked up on the tension in Waine's voice earlier, and evidently Master Farren had, as well. He was not sure where he was headed, but was certain that in a few days' time he would be well away from this place he had called home for the last few seasons. He turned to say goodbye to the boys, but they were somewhere further back in the building. Kevon could hear their muted bickering over the low flames in the forge, and it brought a smile to his face.

"We'll..." Kevon began, choking on a bit of dust. "We'll see each other again."

Farren nodded once, and turned his back to Kevon. The Master Smith rattled around some of his tools until Kevon's footfalls faded into silence. After a minute of contemplation, Farren tossed the bar of sword-steel into the forge and shouted at the back of the building for his Apprentices.

Kevon hadn't been looking too long when he found Waine and Bertus at the armory. The Adept already had a small wooden case tucked snugly under his arm, and was helping their younger friend get the feel for a heavy crossbow.

"What are you going to be hunting now?" Kevon asked, jokingly.

"Orcs," Waine replied. "And Demons." The Adept waited for Kevon's surprised expression before continuing. "And you're coming with us."

ABOUT THE AUTHOR

Chris lives in a small town in Western Idaho, is a writer and Publishing Consultant by day, and is a were-cyborg by night. He is currently pursuing his goal of being able to write, spend time with his family, practice martial arts, and barbeque mercilessly.

Look for updates on future volumes of the Blade-mage Saga, and other projects on his writing blog at: sleepingdrake.blogspot.com